good for her

An Anthology of Women's Rage

sarah jules   **shauna mc eleney**

t c parker

To all those who paved the way, and those still fighting everyday

contents

introduction

Sonora Taylor

Horror is often described as a macabre mirror of society. This is true in the case of women, because in both our culture and in horror fiction, women are at their most valued when they are sacrificed. Think of a popular horror story, and you'll probably see a woman possessed, molested, raped, murdered, dismembered, beaten, or punished for refusing to be treated this way. Even the final girl, that venerated archetype of female resilience, has her well-being and peace of mind sacrificed in favor of a nameless killer who won't leave her alone and an audience who requires her suffering in order to feel hope.

No wonder women are so pissed off.

Good For Her sees women suffer, but they are not sacrifices. Instead, they're angry, and everyone who wronged them is sacrificed instead. There are a myriad of wrongs against women in the stories that follow, and a myriad of punishments exacted on those who wrong them - men, gods, creatures, and other women alike. From the mundane setting of the garden to the fantastic of a town controlled by a wayward pagan deity, from the workplace to the dinner table, the women in the stories bleed, gnash, weep, and get even - all of which women can do without losing themselves to a supposed greater good that wishes us dead.

The anthology showcases some of the best horror authors writing today. They are women from all over the world, all with different stories to tell, yet all rooted in feminine rage. It's a little sad that every woman is united in pain, but not when one considers that such a union creates an army - one ready to spill someone else's blood for a change and not feel sorry about it.

Good for them. Good for her. And good for you, the reader, about to embark on this journey through the sharper side of the feminine.

Have fun.

patient

. . .

M J Mars

2036

Elise Brennan shuffled the blank papers on her desk and beamed at the camera, waiting for her cue. When it came, she introduced herself, then let the smile fall to seriousness as she broke the first news item. "We are coming to you with some sensational news this morning. Vigilante women's rights group Pope Joan have released a statement suggesting that egg supplies have been tainted with a means to make men…well, pregnant."

Beside her, her co-anchor, Gav Moon, shook his head and let out a staged laugh. "It's preposterous, isn't it?"

"We certainly hope so!" Elise retorted. "We'll be hearing from two experts about this story, so stay tuned."

While Gav rounded up the lesser stories on the roster for the morning's show, Elise cast a sly glance at her co-host. He didn't look so hot. In fact, he hadn't looked good all week, something he'd put down to a questionable take-away on Sunday night. It was now Wednesday and when their researchers began to discuss Pope Joan's announcement in the early morning briefing, Elise had noticed Gav's eyes widen in slight panic.

Their first expert was a doctor who had an insight into the supposed technology used to introduce viable fetuses to men's bodies. When she'd first heard the announcement, Elise had thought it must be complete nonsense. But the more she learned of the science behind it, the more curious she became.

Dr Selena Hunt explained the technical aspect with a gentle voice, dumbing herself down for the audience. "In Pope Joan's full announcement, which hasn't been released to the public, they said that they had used malaria masking in order to design a fetus that could stay within the human body without being rejected."

"So, are you saying they aren't pregnant, just sick with malaria?"

The doctor shook her head. "Firstly, there is no 'just sick' with malaria. It is a complex disease made even more difficult to treat because of the way it shields itself from detection. This, coupled with the other techniques described by Pope Joan, have me convinced that this isn't just an elaborate stunt, and that we may really be about to see scores of pregnant men."

At that moment, Gav let out a strangled gagging sound and stumbled out of his stool. He clamped his hand over his mouth but didn't move fast enough to avoid the camera catching vomit spray out through his fingers, broadcast into countless homes over breakfast.

———

The bar was busy, and it seemed as though most people Elise passed were talking about the Pope Joan attack. As the presenter and her friend moved quickly through the Men's Area to the designated Women's Section of the establishment, the tone of the conversations around them shifted. While anger crackled around the tables for men, the women's room buzzed with joviality. Unlike the Men's Area, which women were not allowed to sit in, the Women's Section was usually plagued by one or two guys who liked to make themselves known. They always reminded Elise of lions, entering a watering hole and eyeing up potential prey. Since the rules of evening segregation for non-marrieds in public places had been brought into full effect, Elise had never felt more like a herd animal. Now, it seemed, the lions were under attack for once. And the watering hole was electrified with hope.

Elise's friend, Cleo, must have noticed it, too. As she slipped into her seat, she scanned the room. "We have half a chance of being left alone, tonight."

"This Pope Joan thing has really spooked them."

The divide the nightlife segregation rules had brought into play had driven more of a rift between sexes than ever. Elise visited her parents' house every few weeks, and she always liked to look through their old photo albums from the 2000s. The pages were crammed full of pictures of both of her parents at different ages, having a great time. The bars and clubs were mixed, and girls and boys posed with their arms around each other, their faces glowing with happiness. It made her sad for what society had lost in such a short space of time.

Cleo sipped her Martini, then fiddled with the cocktail stick garnish, an olive skewered on its sharp tip. "Remember Angela Horn from our drama class?"

"Of course." The girl had been the star of their group, bagging all the lead roles and sailing through countless auditions.

"She's dead now."

Elise nearly spat her mouthful of Sauvignon Blanc all over the table. "What?"

"Ectopic pregnancy. They wouldn't take it out, even though it had as much life in it as this fucking olive. So, they just let her die."

"Letting her die is pretty strong, Cleo," Elise corrected on autopilot, her presenter training instinctively causing her brain to play devil's advocate.

"Isn't that what you'd call it? I certainly do. They had the power to save her with a minimal procedure. Instead, they let her die in agony. It's practically murder."

Choked up at the thought of the loss of their vivacious classmate, Elise looked down at her lap. "I'm so sad she's dead."

"Really? Aren't you furious? You're in prime position to get this movement the traction it needs to make sure this doesn't happen to any other women. Doesn't that make you want to shout it from every platform you have?"

Frowning, Elise felt the weight of her journalistic power on her shoulders. What people failed to realize was that it *wasn't* power when it was constantly quashed from above, and she had learned that the hard way early on in her career. "It's not that simple. The bosses are coming down hard on us. Especially with Gav showing symptoms."

Cleo's eyes gleamed and she broke into an elated grin. "Are you kidding?"

"Oh, shit. Shh, I'm not supposed to have said anything."

"This is brilliant," Cleo said, excitedly.

After spending the last three days next to the man as he threw up and asked panicked questions about what might be going on inside him, and how in the hell he was going to get it out, Elise disagreed. "Tell that to Gav. Whatever it is they put in this Patient Griselda concoction, it's breaking him."

Cleo sat back, grinning. "Pope Joan and Patient Griselda? Brilliant."

The names were vaguely familiar to Elise, too, but she stared blankly at her friend.

"They're named after characters in *Top Girls*. The Caryl Churchill play. We tried to perform it that summer after Trump got back in, but we weren't allowed. They said it might *incite feminine rage*, or some such bullshit."

"Fuck. I didn't realize. I thought the 'patient' part of the name was in reference to them getting sick."

"Nope. Pope Joan, who they all thought was a man until she had a baby halfway through a religious procession, and Patient Griselda. Wait, I used to get Griselda and the concubine mixed up…she's the one whose husband said she had to agree to do whatever he said, and forced her to give up her children as a test. Right?"

The play came flooding back to Elise: a feminist powerhouse of dramaticism that won a host of awards in the early 1980s, but in the dire repression of the 2030s was no longer available.

She'd never been so certain that a group of women were behind the Pope Joan movement. And, with advanced science, access to the country's food supply, and goodness knew what else, she guessed it was a movement with hundreds of participants. She had to find out who was responsible and, once she did, she had to decide what she'd do with that information.

———

Clayton Carr sat in the boardroom and waited for Senior Judge Beardsley to begin. The Presidential Advisors had an important job to do, but it had to be done right. As a former professor of Reproduction and Early Development, this wasn't the first time Clayton had sat on a committee, but this was the first time he'd been involved in the aftermath of a perceived terrorist attack.

Beardsley was visibly trying to contain his anger as he pored over the existing legislation. "If it wasn't for this stupid wording here, we'd be able to nip this thing in the bud immediately. Why the hell isn't the law for termination gendered?"

Clayton knew exactly why. He'd been present for the crafting of the legislation back in 2028. Back then, Beardsley's predecessor - a man whose dogged allegiance lay to the far right reaches of the Republican mentality - had said: "We can't say, 'no women can have an abortion'. You know what those hippies in California are like. Trans men are legally women there. We'd better just say 'person' to avoid all that crap."

And so there it was, in black and white. No *person* could have an abortion under Federal Law.

And that meant the men who had been infected by Pope Joan were, at least for the time being, screwed.

———

Elise watched Gav trembling as the ultrasound clinician prepared the live scan. It had taken Gav a lot of convincing, but they were both journalists at heart, even when it came to personal discomfort. As she'd said to him in the dressing room before they came on set, he'd been on the frontline reporting the war of 2029. Bombs falling and bullets whizzing past hadn't stopped him from seeing his passion through.

Though there were private tests being undertaken on certain subjects who were pregnant with the Patient Griselda fetuses, this would be the first time the public would see what the fetus was like: its positioning inside the males, and its potential viability, if any. The viewing figures had skyrocketed that morning, as Ken had predicted. So had Gav's bank account, Elise guessed.

"Ready?" the clinician asked. As well as the ultrasound tech, a top obstetric surgeon, Dr. James Souk, stood by the monitor, practically frothing at the bit to see what was going on inside the patient.

Gav nodded and lifted his shirt, lying on his side. Early tests had discovered that the Patient Griselda fetuses latched on and grew near the prostate, using the nutrients created by the gland to feed and grow the cells. Although the baby was nearer the back of the body than with women, the growing mass forced their organs forward, giving them the rounded stomach of a standard pregnancy.

The tech squirted clear jelly onto Gav's lower back and pressed the gadget to his skin. A few moments later, strange smudges of light showed up on the screen.

The studio seemed to hold its breath.

The obstetric technician frowned a little as she roamed around with the tool, unsure of exactly where to go. This wasn't the same as scanning a woman, whose womb was unlikely to be anywhere but the usual spot. If the rumors were true, the fetus sacks all seemed to grow in the same area, but finding it was far trickier.

"There!" Dr. Souk said, lurching forward and pointing to the screen.

With his help, the tech guided the scope to the right spot on Gav's back. On the screen, a dark circle appeared, a small white form moving gently within.

Elise came to her senses and asked the doctor to explain what he saw.

"It's astonishing, really," the man gasped, staring from the screen to Gav's body as though he couldn't reconcile the two images. "There is a visible sac of amniotic fluid with a cord connecting the child to the host's prostate."

"You mean a placenta?" Elise prompted.

"Without further information about what it could be, yes. It appears to be a form of umbilical cord."

"The vigilante group claim they contaminated eggs with their technology in June. Does that match with the approximate age of this fetus?"

When she said the word "fetus", Gav scowled.

"By the size overall and the growth of limbs I'd say that matches perfectly." Dr. Souk cut his eyes to the obstetric tech, who nodded confirmation that was not required. The doctor nodded politely, anyway. "Incredible."

"And is there a heartbeat?" Elise asked, the atmosphere in the studio intensifying.

"Here we go..." the tech said, pressing a button on the monitor. A heartbeat sounded, thumping rapidly through the studio. Everyone gasped.

Someone whispered, "It's a miracle."

Gav kept his eyes on the ceiling, refusing to look at the monitor, his expression one of stony shock and anger.

———

Judge Beardsley was enraged. "These men have been violated! The pregnancy has come from a crime. They didn't even want it in the first place, so why should they be forced to continue with this nightmare?"

Clayton made ready with his pen. "So, within the legislation changes, should we decree that women who have been raped can have the fetus removed?"

"No, that's not what I said at all!" Beardsley's cheeks were purple. "This atrocity was put into the egg supply. This could have impacted children."

Calmly, Clayton tapped his pen against the legislation, appearing deep in thought. After a while, he said, "We could change it so that women and girls who have been raped—let's face it, any child who is pregnant *has* been raped, of course—can have their pregnancy terminated, in order to account for the Pope Joan attacks?"

Beardsley slammed a fist on the desk. "No! Not for women. This isn't about women. This is about men, damn it!"

———

The mother on the couch in front of Elise was small and fragile, but with the determined expression of someone who was ready to burn the place down if pushed. She held a photo in her lap, a young woman on her graduation day. Smiling and dimpled, the girl looked as though she was about to have the best years of her life. Less than a year after that photo was taken, the girl had thrown herself from the top level of a multistorey car park.

"She wasn't promiscuous. But to be honest, it wouldn't matter if she was. That's how I feel, now. I'm tired of women getting the blame for everything. She met a nice boy, and they dated for a while, then split up after simply realizing they weren't the ones for each other. They'd been careful the few times they had made out, but Missy discovered she was pregnant about a month after they broke up."

"That must have been extremely hard for you to hear," Elise prompted the bereaved mother.

"Well, sure it was. But right away, I was angry. When I was young, this was a mistake that wouldn't have ruined your life. There were clinics back then, places with qualified doctors and nurses who would take care of the women who couldn't bear to keep an unwanted pregnancy. Can you imagine that now? They even referred those women to mental health services, making sure they were okay after. Women didn't used to be treated like cattle or second-rate citizens."

"Steer her away from this," the voice in Elise's ear warned. She refrained from rolling her eyes on camera. Instead, she asked gently, "The pregnancy was unwanted. How did Missy deal with it?"

"Not well. Not well at all. She had suffered from anxiety and a few bouts of depression as a kid. She took things very literally, and so when she saw the perfect body on TV, she became certain that's what she needed. It brought on an eating disorder when she was fifteen, and she ended up hospitalized. It was a dreadful time for our family, but the treatment worked, and she went back to school. As you can see in this picture, she got her degree and was thriving. Getting pregnant ruined all the progress she made. My bubbly, bright little girl became a shell of herself again. She stopped eating because the fear of gaining weight returned with a vengeance."

"Did you seek treatment for her this time?"

The woman snorted. "With the waitlists for mental health services? You must be joking. They were backed up for years, mostly with referrals for girls who were forced to have babies, I'm betting."

Ken's voice in Elise's ear said sternly, "Fuck, we're going to get warnings after this. Move on!"

Annoyed at her dismissive boss, Elise thought of a report she'd been looking into. Missy's mother wasn't lying about the increase in pressure on an already floundering mental health service. The girls who got pregnant and didn't want a child suffered, then the children who were born into a household where they were unwanted suffered, and so on and so on. Suffering was on the rise. Sense was not.

Still, she didn't particularly want to get fired, so she said, "What happened to Missy, Anna?"

The woman's eyes went glazed and it seemed she was watching the day of her daughter's death unravel on a screen behind her gaze. "Missy was quiet at breakfast. She picked at the food I made her, but that wasn't too much of a surprise. Afterwards, she said she wanted to go for a walk, get some air. I was thrilled at the time. When she got up and out of the house, that had always been a sign she was starting to feel better. I feel so stupid about that now. Two hours later the police came to the door. She'd walked straight to the multistorey on Baker and jumped off the top, without any thought or hesitation."

"I'm so sorry," Elise whispered.

"She'd already received her death sentence, you see. That happened when the government decided women had to keep their babies, no matter what. There is blood on their hands, and they don't care because that blood belongs to women. Or did, until now." The grieving mother gave a triumphant grin at the camera and pumped a fist. "Viva Pope Joan! Bring on the revolution."

Hours later, the door to Elise's dressing room burst open and Ken stepped in, red-faced. "Jesus, Elise! Why did you let her say all that crap?"

"What crap?" Elise was gathering her things, ready to head home after the show and a brainstorming session in the conference room.

"The mother! I've just been on the phone to the senator's office for an hour. They are pissed. And who's getting it in the neck?"

"The countless people who are being forced to carry babies against their will?" Elise asked, sweetly.

"No. Me," Ken snarled.

Boo fucking hoo, Elise thought, biting her tongue.

He stared at her. "You're enjoying this."

"What? What are you talking about?"

"You like that Pope Joan has ruffled so many feathers. They're terrorists, Elise."

She shrugged. "It's not like they're planting bombs or posting anthrax, Ken."

"Just forcing men to be pregnant?"

She wiggled her eyebrows. "The government are forcing women to be pregnant every day. Are they terrorists?"

"That's different!"

"How?"

"It's natural! Men getting pregnant is the most fucking unnatural thing I've ever seen. Gav's in pieces. How can you support them?"

"Natural? Don't give me that. I know you're an atheist, Ken."

"So?"

"So, what does it matter whose fucking stomach the baby grows in?

You support test tube babies and IVF, but only if they're put into a woman? Don't you know how hypocritical that is when you think about it?"

"It isn't hypocrisy. It's just…normal."

Elise slung her bag over her shoulder. "Heaven forbid we do anything slightly abnormal."

"Elise," Ken warned, unwilling to discuss the matter.

She paused as she was passing him, ready to leave. "Wait, not 'heaven' forbid. You don't believe in that stuff, do you?"

Fucking hypocrite, she seethed internally, striding down the corridor.

———

Clayton sat in the conference room, quietly listening to the men debating around him. It wasn't a debate, not really. It was a raging argument with only one point. And that point was how to fairly make the ruling that men could have their fetuses removed without doctors going to jail and hospitals being sued into bankruptcy, while women of all ages and health conditions would be left with the same choice they had since the former ruling: None.

"There's going to be riots," Clayton warned.

"Let them riot! In fact, that's a great point, Clay. When we pass this bill, we need to be sure we put in some strict penalties for opposing actions." Beardsley made a few notes on his own pad, the loose skin under his chin swinging back and forth as he sketched out ways to punish his own citizens.

"There are some men who want these babies."

Around him, the room erupted into chuckles. "Well, they can't have them, plain and simple."

"Freaks," Trent Boon, the social strategy advisor, muttered.

For a moment, Clayton imagined what would have happened if the men surrounding him had eaten the contaminated eggs. If they were now sat with swollen bellies and life growing inside them, having to justify a blanket extermination to relatives who believed it wouldn't have happened had it not been God's will. It wouldn't be so easy, then, to make one decision for all.

"It's decided," Beardsley said, although Clayton didn't quite recall a unanimous vote being made. "We'll confirm the recommendation of Executive Order. These freak-show babies have got to go."

———

Elise smiled at the young men sitting on the interview couch, hoping they would refrain from swearing live on air. Although the studio knew the presenters weren't fully to blame when guests broke the rules, any misdemeanors resulted in a severe warning. The punk band sat waiting to be interviewed had hit the headlines over the last few months, since the lead singer/guitarist had been one of the men to ingest the tainted eggs. He sat in the middle of the couch, one hand resting under the swell of his bump, his thumb occasionally stroking up and down the side of his belly.

As well as the band's latest single skyrocketing up the charts due to their strange situation, the group was a prominent feature in the news because Chet Pearson was happy to be pregnant. It seemed the other band members felt the same, and they fussed around the singer with protective energy, offering him water and making sure he was comfortable.

Their fourth guest, Dex, was another man who was happy about his current situation. He and his wife welcomed the news, especially since she had been advised never to have children due to a serious heart condition.

Gav eased himself down onto the couch beside Elise with a grimace. He was persistently uncomfortable now the baby was well into the second trimester, and bouts of nausea had given way to searing pain in his hips, back, and belly. Elise was concerned it would be Gav who would forget the broadcast rules, so incensed was he at the idea that there were men out there celebrating their pregnancies. Whether it was hormones or futility at being in this situation without any way out at the current time, Gav was a ticking time bomb.

When the interview began, Elise took the reins, welcoming the guests and explaining to the viewers that the men were grateful Pope Joan had contaminated the egg supply.

The band was relaxed, and everyone seemed to be in great spirits, putting Elise in mind of an interview she had conducted a few years before when three members of the same movie cast had all happily had babies within a year of filming.

Chet grinned at Elise after she asked him if he was happy. "I don't think I've ever been this happy. It feels *right*, you know? Like, this should always have been my purpose."

Gav suddenly snapped. "Don't you see what you're doing? You're putting the guys like me at risk by supporting this abomination!"

"Our babies aren't abominations," Dex told him, splaying his fingers protectively over his bump. "Have you listened to its heartbeat? I have. We've already named him: Elliot. And my wife and I can't wait to meet him."

"Telling everyone you want to keep it is making the cause worse. I need to get it out of me," Gav exclaimed, tears filling his eyes.

The band's drummer sat forward, glaring. "If you think the rules should be changed, perhaps you should have fought harder when it only impacted women."

Ken's voice screamed in Elise's ear to take control of the situation.

Standing up awkwardly, groaning at the weight in his middle, Gav pointed a finger at the guests. "It's men like you who are making everything worse. We made the rules, we should be able to change them!"

"So, it's not about the babies themselves, it's about controlling women?" Chet's voice was calm, his face glowing almost angelic under the studio lights.

Elise was supposed to say something, to intervene and calm the situation. But there was something so striking about seeing a man with a baby bump himself shoot down the hypocrisy of the legislation against abortion. He was right. It wasn't about the right to life. It was about powerful men getting exactly what they want. At any cost.

Gav's tears flowed and Elise was aware that camera two had zoomed right in on his face. He shook his head in fury. "I shouldn't have to go through this. This was forced on me. It's…it's not right. And any of you who want this? You're a fucking joke."

The voices in her ear exploded as Gav rushed off the set. Elise looked at the camera. "We apologize for the language there, folks. As you can understand, this is a serious topic and emotions are running high…"

———

Clayton calmly read through the medical findings. It made for fascinating reading. Someone within the Pope Joan group was a biological genius, there was no doubt about that.

Beardsley called it "Frankenstein tech," but it was far more nuanced. This was the type of technology which, had it been allowed to be used for good, would have been revolutionary.

"Well?" Beardsley snarled. "Is there anything in there we can use?"

"Use?" Clayton asked, taking off his reading glasses and staring at the Judge.

"Anything dangerous that needs to be ripped out right away. If this comes to an Executive Order, if there's an element of danger to the men, we'll be able to justify it."

Clayton shrugged. "It doesn't appear to be any more dangerous to the host than a standard pregnancy."

That was not the right answer. Beardsley looked ready to flip the table. "How can that possibly be?"

"From what we've ascertained from the Pope Joan statement and scans of the males impacted, the Patient Griselda solution contains hydrogen sulfide, multiple human ova, endometrial nutrients, and a malaria enzyme."

"Malaria! Surely that's enough danger to use to our advantage in this case?"

"Not so. The malaria enzyme is used to mask the zygote, allowing it to latch onto the prostate without being rejected and absorbed as waste by the man's body. There is no active agent, no risk of the subject or baby contracting the disease." Clayton waited for the judge to counter-argue, but he stayed silent. "Somehow, Pope Joan managed to get this cocktail into our eggs, where the hydrogen sulfide bonded to the selenium in the egg."

The food standards official pre-empted Beardsley's question when the man swiveled in his chair and fixed him with a hawk-like stare. He spoke quickly, but kept his eyes lowered like a scolded child. "The source of the introduction is being investigated, and there doesn't appear to be one single production source for the contaminated eggs. Our theory is that Pope Joan agents may have injected the eggs in-store. It appears Pope Joan operates only in the US due to the anti-abortion laws, but it could also explain why there are zero cases in countries such as the UK, which keeps the hard cuticle of the eggshell intact prior to releasing them for public consumption."

Clayton nodded in agreement. "I think this seems like the most likely explanation. It's the one thing Pope Joan left out of their statements, too, as the contamination of the eggs is a crime."

Beardsley slammed his fist down. "This whole thing is a crime! I want to see the people behind this atrocity on Death Row before the end of the year. In the meantime, let's get this finalized so the Surgeon General can decide on how to take these fucking things out."

"Shall we make a recommendation about how the surgeries are conducted?" Clayton asked. "I have concerns that, depending on how the fetus is removed, it could be a traumatizing procedure which could even lead to infertility."

He'd seen it before; Republican states so focused on jumping to enforce a medical Executive Order, the patient's safety was an afterthought. As far as Clayton could tell, there would be two ways to remove the fetus from the host. The first was a longer, less invasive procedure that could be performed by carefully conducted abdominal surgery. The second, the fast and simple way that he knew the Surgeon General would approve simply to get this nightmare over and done with, involved fast access to the prostate through the perineum, with a high risk of damage to the vans deferens. If that was accidentally cut, the men would be rendered infertile.

The senior judge showed little interest in the men's health. "Well, they got themselves into this situation in the first place. They can reap the consequences."

It was fascinating to Clayton how quickly the judge flitted between outrage at the terrorist group and outrage at the men who had found themselves the victims. It was all just one big inconvenience to him.

They each signed the recommendation, eager to get out of the room and draw a line under the issue.

———

The young man on the television heaved devastated sobs, helped to the car by his wife, who looked just as bereft. He was ushered along by a legal team but, when one of the reporters shoved a microphone in his face and asked, "Do you have anything you'd like to say in regard to the Schlafly Executive Order ruling?" Dex stopped and found the camera lens, his eyes burning with anger and despair.

"I do. I have a lot to say. I didn't ask for this to happen. And I know that many other men in the same situation as me are nothing short of relieved today at being able to go on about their lives as though none of this ever happened. But in making a ruling that covers all opinions based on one, it isn't right. Pro-Choice campaigners tell the truth. It isn't about babies. If it was, I'd still have mine inside me. By making pregnancy and birth a black and white issue, you deny basic human rights to those of us who already live on this planet. Men and women, now."

"Do you wish Pope Joan had never created Patient Griselda?"

Clayton watched the young man contemplate the question, his expression flicking from hurt, to rage, to bleak acceptance. "No. I'm glad they did it. As much as it hurts to have Elliot taken away from me, I know this is how change is made. The people who created and infected the egg supply with Patient Griselda may be classed as criminals. But they shouldn't have been driven to do it in the first place. I hope that women aren't back to square one now. I hope that men have a better understanding of what it might mean to have to forcibly go through a pregnancy that you never wanted, or that might kill you to keep it. I hope the women and men of Pope Joan never get caught. And I hope they never stop fighting."

The man turned to climb into the car, blood already seeping out of the bulky pad that had been placed in his Y-fronts following the procedure. It stood out stark against his grey sweatpants, a blooming, dark red heart.

Clayton turned off the TV and rubbed his eyes, wearily. He'd done his best to advocate for fairer rules in the legislation, but he was only a small voice fighting against many far louder, far richer men. He had to be smart. Next time, he would push a little harder.

He picked up a photo frame that sat on his desk and gazed at the woman smiling back at him. It was in moments like this that it all came flooding back. Gloria so excited, holding out a pregnancy test, warning him not to grab it as it still had her pee on it. He'd ignored her, taking it and staring at the small plus sign before pulling her into his arms and swinging her around. Then the appointment, where they discovered the baby wasn't viable. Had already died as a barely formed humanoid.

He had asked the doctor when they would remove the dead fetus, and had been met with blank stares. "We can't do that, Sir," the doctor had replied, stupidly. "It's against the law."

Clayton knew—of course he knew. But some part of him hoped against hope that in those moments of cold, sterile loss in a hospital room, there would be some kind of workaround. A sly medicine given here. A quick, nondescript procedure there, for the right money of course. And he was a professor! He thought he had the right money.

But, it turned out, when hospitals were afraid of being sued and doctors were afraid to go to jail, women were left to die.

He'd taken her home, her grief soon turning to terror when she got sick. It began with fever and bleeding, her skin raging at the necrotized blob that was stuck inside her, festering and turning bad. He hated to think of his child in that way, but that was what it had been reduced to.

There was no humanity there. Because the people who had made the rules did not care.

So, alone and desperate, Clayton tried everything he could think of. He read online about an aromatherapy oil called Clary Sage that could cause miscarriage in the early stages and submerged Gloria in a bath of the strong-smelling oil. He guessed they were beyond that now, and that the dead lump inside her was more a tumor than something that could be shed with such ease.

One terrible morning, close to the end of a long, drawn-out week of Gloria screaming and pleading for mercy, he'd punched her in the gut. Her agony had cut him to the core, and it was the first and last time he would ever strike a woman. But in his despair, it was his last hope of causing this *thing* to dislodge from his dying wife's septic body.

He waited, fool's hope causing him to imagine blood and release between her legs. Instead, she heaved a wheezing, drawn-out death rattle just a few hours later.

A pointless death. An avoidable death.

One that so many other women had endured since the law had been changed.

And it wasn't just about that. It was the women whose mental health had been ripped to shreds having to carry a baby they did not want. Could not cope with. Those with body dysmorphia. Eating disorders. Genetic illness. Neurodivergence or clinical anxiety and depression. The women who already faced agonizing pain each day and would never have chosen to have a seven-pound baby stuffed into their already tortured bodies.

Then there were the women and children who were raped. The ones who had already been through torment and agony and violation, and risked looking into the face of their attackers each day as the child that shared a monster's genes grew into an adult.

For the children themselves, it was madness. Before the country changed the laws, child poverty and abuse had been at the highest level in years. Unwanted children were murdered each year. Many were sold. Others were pushed into the system to lead a life with little nurture and a pattern of disfunction that was surely an issue of greater importance than the tiny concern of women having control over their own bodies.

He trembled with anger at the injustice of it all. The system was broken. A system he was involved in creating but wasn't powerful enough to change.

Yet.

Clayton reached under a secret panel in his desk and pressed the button that popped out his concealed compartment. He reached inside and took out the burner phone, encrypted and connected to a VPN far across the world. He opened the Pope Joan group chat.

"Alright. Great job, everyone. Mission A successful. We will roll out Mission B as planned."

The chat erupted with comments. Clayton traced his fingers over his wife's image and smiled.

Lina, the scientist who had managed to adapt the Patient Griselda technology, added a new message to the chat, her code name hiding her identity. Clayton knew them all, however. Hell, he had started and funded this whole thing.

He typed in a number and sent out an invitation to the group, then returned to the chat. "Will you all please welcome our latest member, who will be a great help in handling the media exposure while we roll out Missions B and C. Code name, Axle."

Clayton slipped the phone into the compartment and sealed it up again. Satisfied, he folded his hands across his middle and leaned back, imagining his vigilante group setting the next part of the plan in action. All with a little help from a very successful TV news anchor.

"Welcome, Elise," he muttered.

Mission B was going to hit the government bodies who had made the laws exactly where it hurt them. Clayton couldn't wait to sit right next to them and watch. He just had to be patient.

babs

. . .

Anna Orridge

ROB HUGHES SUCKED HIS TEETH, staring at the bungalow.
Who the hell would adorn their front garden wall with *skulls*?

The skulls weren't real, of course – at least, not the human ones.
There were about a dozen of them, all the size of a fist. They had the
look of the Dia de Muertos sweets he'd once seen on a TV documen-
tary about Mexico. Their eye sockets were stuffed with fake plastic
jewels. They'd been embedded in the concrete of the new front wall,
like shells decorating a pretty little shingle house by the sea.

There had never been anything pretty about that bungalow, in all
honesty - a hunched red brick runt of a house. The farm was three
miles from the village, which in its turn was a good twenty miles from
Monmouth. The only way you could get anywhere without a car was
by river. Perhaps that was how the new owner intended to get around,
because he hadn't seen any vehicle other than the removal van that
had shifted its load of furniture a few days ago.

But a blue rowing boat had appeared yesterday, propped up on the
rickety little jetty at the back of the house.

Rob had been hoping for years that the biddy who used to live
there would have a fall, or perhaps a stroke or heart attack. He didn't
want her dead, mind; just something serious enough to get her

moved on to a nice, comfy retirement home. That way, he could buy that land up for a song, raze the bungalow and get something built there that would be a bit more appealing for the second home city sorts.

But the biddy ended up with a very aggressive form of cancer instead. It took her in a matter of months. And it seemed she'd left the house to someone with a heavy metal fetish.

Still, he hadn't given up hope yet. The inheritor, it seemed, was a young, hip sort. They probably thought that living somewhere like this would be a bit like camping at a festival. They might have romantic ideas about the Welsh countryside, but they'd be gone the second they got a whiff of heavy manure or realised there were no theatres or concert halls within pissing distance.

Then Rob would be ready with a smile and his cheque book.

He trudged closer to the wall. He was about to go and ring on the bell when he noticed more skulls perched on top of it. These were real ones, but clearly not human.

Rob picked up one and raised it up to his face height.

"Used to be a barn owl, that one." The voice behind him was deep and feminine – Welsh accent, but so soft he couldn't tell exactly where she was from. It had a rich timbre that, for some reason, put Rob in mind of the whorls of polished dark wood. "Be careful, or it might swivel 180 degrees in your hand, give you a nasty shock."

He turned to face the woman who had come out of the bungalow. She was leaning on one of the poles that held up the old porch. She looked almost as thin as the fucking pole, her blue velvet dungarees hanging off bony shoulders. Stretching long, tattoo-strewn arms above her head, she yawned and regarded him with laconic amusement.

"Help yourself. Feel free to pick another skull up. That's what they're there for."

She lowered her arms, smoothing down her spiky green hair. Then she came padding barefoot towards him. It was hard to tell how old she was – perhaps mid-sixties. She was certainly too old to be dressed like that, in Rob's view. Jesus.

He put the skull back on the wall hurriedly. She smiled and nodded at the skulls. "Good, aren't they? My own little memento mori chorus line. You often find the most innocuous little animals have the most terrifying, alien-looking skulls."

"How did you get hold of them then?" he asked gruffly.

"Some of them are roadkill. Others were once my friends and pets." She picked up one of the skulls and planted a kiss on the cranium. "This was my Patch – the cutest little guinea pig you ever saw." She laughed at Rob's look of revulsion. "It's just a souvenir, sweetie. Not much different from keeping a photo."

"How do you get them clean?"

"Oh, some I find already gnawed smooth by scavengers and bugs. Others I myself bury or put in an acid bath to clear away the rotting flesh and gristle."

Rob rocked back on his heel and blinked. "Fun hobby."

She flashed him a grin, and Rob noticed she had a couple of iron fillings – not at the back but the front. Did this woman think she was a rapper or Jaws from the old Bond film or something?

Those tattoos were bloody weird as well. He couldn't even make out pictures; they were just swirls, like fingerprints under a microscope, or a labyrinth.

He took a deep breath. "Well, I'm your new neighbour. Rob Hughes. I thought I'd better introduce myself. That's my farm over there." He turned and gestured at the fields, the corrugated roof of the barn gleaming under the sun.

"What are you keeping in there, then?"

"Chickens."

"Ah. Figures." She shut one eye so quickly, he couldn't tell whether it was some weird spasm or a wink.

He coughed. "I didn't catch your name."

"I didn't send it your way." There was a silence that was at least a couple of beats too long to be comfortable.

"I'm Babs," she said, before flicking him a little wave and heading back to the porch.

Babs. Barbara. That wasn't a name you saw on young girls any longer. He remembered, from some lesson long ago, that it meant 'barbarous woman'. He smirked.

The name fit her a lot better than those stupid dungarees.

———

After Babs had arranged the furniture to her liking, and got the beds in the gardens dug over and planted with the herbs she needed, she turned her attention to her rowing boat. It was time to get a sense for the waters here, find out what she could offer them.

She pulled the boat across the jetty, and lowered it down into the water. She closed her eyes as she put her feet in it – the feel of a river under old timber always sent a jolt through her. It was as if the wood was remembering the xylem veins that once shot through it, carrying water and nutrients.

It was much the same sensation as when she felt pelt peel away from bone when she was cleaning a skull. That...just-rightness.

She managed to sit down, and once she'd untied the boat from the jetty, she was swept downriver pretty quickly. For a while, she leaned back and let herself drift, until she came a little too near a bank.

The waters were lively, but as soon as she dipped the oar in, she knew all was not well.

She was miles from Monmouth, but the water was murky as French onion soup. Her own throat constricted as she sensed the presence of fish, far below the kayak. She felt their pain, the lesions in their scaly skin. Her eyes filled with tears.

Years before, when she had visited Alison here, she could only feel their freedom and ferocity, as the sunlight flashed on their silver bodies. Back then, all they had to fear were vigilant herons and the iridescent darts of kingfishers. But death from these predators would be a merciful release in comparison with the slow suffocation they would suffer now.

The water did not just look like soup, it was as near as dead as soup.

———

A few days after their first encounter, Rob was surprised to find Babs leaning on the side jamb of his barn door. No dungarees this time, but a floor-length sky-blue dress, fluttering in the breeze.

"All right there?" he asked, wiping his hands on his overalls.

"Yes, not bad. I wanted to talk to you about something, though. I notice you're keeping chickens near the banks of the river."

Rob nodded. "Aye. Free range. You look like the sort who'd be into that. Would you like me to deliver?"

"I'm vegan, as it happens. In fact, I was a vegan chef when I lived in Cardiff."

Rob tilted his head backwards in surprise. "Bit odd for someone who likes stripping skulls."

"Not at all. All those animals died before I skinned them. And none met their deaths at my hands."

Rob shrugged. He made his way over to his van. "Well, I'm going down there to feed the little buggers. You can come too if you fancy."

He started to haul bags of seed into the trunk. Once he'd finished, she wordlessly joined him in the passenger seat.

It was a bumpy ride down to the riverbank. Draping an arm over the lowered window, Babs asked him how many chickens he kept.

"Just over two hundred. As well-treated as you could please. They have the life of Riley. Out all day pecking at the ground, then tucked up nice and warm in the coop the rest of the time."

"You sound defensive."

"Got nothing to defend myself against."

He pulled up next to the field. It overlooked the riverbank, surrounded on all sides by high chicken wire. The ground was a mire of mud in front of a large coop. The chickens' squawks and clucks puckered the air, getting louder as Rob hauled one of the sacks of grain out of van.

He scattered one with a wave of his hand, and the birds instantly flocked around the arc, pecking furiously.

Babs stayed where she was, still leaning on the top of the van, her expression inscrutable. Rob made a gesture at the sack.

"You fancy feeding the buggers?"

She shook her head.

He emptied the sacks over the fence and came back towards the van, rubbing his hands on his overalls. "I've seen you on your boat, out on the river. You're pretty handy with it, I have to say. Wouldn't expect someone your age to be that agile. No offence, like."

"None taken. As I've been on the river, I've noticed that all is not well with the waters. There are algal blooms everywhere."

"Well, if there are blooms, it can't be dead, can it? Lots of biodiversity, exactly like your sort like."

"Biodiversity is life. But the algal blooms are choking the river. They're the result of excess phosphate. You know what's particularly high in phosphate, Rob? Chicken manure."

Babs spread her arms out, her many bangles jangling in the wind. She looked down pointedly. The ground around them both was covered in the distinctive murky green and white faeces of chickens.

Rob shrugged. "It's just as likely to be human shit. They're pouring it into the rivers all the time, aren't they? Blame the water companies. Blame the government."

"Oh, there's plenty of fault to be spread around. But why blame everyone but the farmer who's spreading chicken manure all over the fields next to the river? It's sacrilege, what you are doing. La agua es vida."

"Huh?"

"Water is life."

Rob warmed his hands on the cup before him and laughed. "It's the bloody Wye. Never been exactly a model of purity, but it's fine. Look, Babs. I'm sure you mean well, but a man needs to fertilise his fields, and what better than the shit I've already got right here? I'm not changing it for anybody. And, forgive me, I think a townie like you is a bit too, shall we say, 'chickenshit' to do anything about it. Catch me?"

"I catch you perfectly." Babs turned round and returned to the vehicle, primly gathering her skirt before she swung her legs in.

Once he'd finished feeding the chickens, Rob picked up a black plastic bin liner on the field. As soon as he'd got in the car, he popped it in her lap. "Look, sorry. I was a bit abrupt back there. I have a gift to make up for it. You'll appreciate this, I think."

Babs looked inside. To do her justice, she didn't flinch, only closed her eyes.

The dead chicken inside was already party rotten, its dirty feathers like wilted toilet paper clinging to a wet floor.

"I thought you'd appreciate it," he said. "I didn't kill it, in case you were worried. Got pecked to death by its friends. They're a very hierarchical lot, chickens. Anyway, I thought you might like to add it to your collection, once you've buried it or dissolved it or whatever it is you do."

"Thank you. Why don't you drive us back to my house? I'm planning on cooking a nice meal."

———

It was a fairly easy matter to strip the chicken's skull, since its decomposition was already quite advanced. Holding her breath to avoid smelling it, Babs carefully dropped one of its eyes in the mortar. She was surprised it was still intact, orange iris glowing with an oddly contained sort of light, like a candle viewed between the fingers of someone's cupped hand.

Babs added just a scrap of the flesh – it could not be more than that, or Rob would notice the flavour.

The beaker of river water was ready. Taking in a few drops with her pipette, she said the words.

"This eye has seen you, it has seen you,
Rob Hughes. But you have not seen it.
Now you will, whether you will it or not."

The uninitiated thought spells were something you got out of a book with dusty pages. But Babs knew you needed to coax the power from deep within yourself, like a childhood hymn once sung in assembly halls, now half-forgotten.

———

Bab's house was pretty much as bad as Rob thought it would be. All mirrors in driftwood frames and weird abstract pictures in psychedelic shades. It was like stepping into one of those New Age shops for the tourists in Monmouth. All it was missing was the damn fool keyrings with the meaning of your name in faux-Celtic lettering. It even had that clutching, stale stench of incense. She probably had all those weird little holders with it smoking all over the place, essential oils and all the rest of that crap. Doing the Upward-Facing Hyena or whatever it was on some grubby mat every morning.

He tried not to cough as Babs led him into the lounge. In all honesty, he was feeling bad about being rude to her earlier. They were never going to get on like a house on fire, but a neighbour was a neighbour.

They went through to the lounge and Rob blinked a few times. There was a massive indoor cage in front of the window. It was all hung with wooden ornaments carved in the shape of long apple peelings, twirling away like a barbershop blood and bandages.

In the middle of the cage was a table and two chairs. Rob hesitated before sitting down and she laughed.

"Sorry, a bit off-putting. I'm not going to lock you up. That's my old aviary. I gave away the last of my birds and cleaned it out before I moved here. I couldn't bear to get rid of it, though. Too many memories. So I turned it into a feature, as people like to say. Just give me a moment…"

She went into the kitchen and came back after a few minutes with two mugs, both steaming.

Rob looked down and sniffed. "Oh God. It's that green stuff, isn't it? I prefer Breakfast tea."

"I don't like tannins. Just try it. You might like it."

Rob shrugged and sipped from it. Not a bad brew, actually. There was a flavour to it he couldn't quite identify – somehow both sharp and earthy.

He put the cup down. "Aren't you going to join me?"

"In a moment. I'm just going to the kitchen to rustle up a treat for us both."

A few minutes later, Rob heard the hiss of frying. He got up and had a look out of the window. The garden was pretty overgrown. Rather than mowing and pruning, Babs adorned the crumbling rock garden with twirling wind chimes and chipped gnomes.

It wasn't long before she came out of the kitchen again with a plate full of what looked like fried chicken pieces with a side of barbecue sauce.

"I thought you were a vegan chef!"

"This is as vegan as it comes. Chicken of the woods – it's a fungus. I foraged it yesterday, lovely and young and tender."

Rob took a fork and skewered one of the pieces gingerly before putting it in his mouth.

She wasn't wrong, actually – in terms of texture, it was very similar. And it soaked up the flavour of the sauce well.

"Not bad, Babs, but I'm afraid you'll never wean me off my roast chicken. Speaking of which, going to have to love you and leave you. Need to get all the birds back in the coop before sunset."

She smiled. "Indeed. I would not want to distract you from your animal husbandry."

There was an edge to that. She probably thought he was too stupid to pick up on it.

At any rate, he tipped his cap to her before he left.

———

Babs was quite surprised by how gently the water received her rowing boat. She was expecting to have to wrestle with it, but the river was compliant, each stroke of the paddle a slight pull in their dance. She even closed her eyes as it bore her gently along.

The river wanted this as much as she did. It deserved it.

———

It was only once Rob had got the last chicken into the coop that he felt his bowels contract. It was way stronger than the usual stomach trouble – like some little wild beast fighting to get out of him. Fiddling with his belt, he was about to make a run for a clump of trees near the bank. Then he heard her voice.

"Bit squiffy, Rob?"

He gasped and swore.

Babs was at the door of the coop, her long blue skirt trailing over the entrance. She had that same, slightly detached amusement in her smile that had unsettled him when they first met. Something was clutched to her chest.

"What are you doing here?" he demanded. "And how did you get here so fast?"

She smiled. Bloody hell. He could have sworn she hadn't had as many metal fillings as that last time he looked. There was barely a white one in there.

"Sorry," he faltered. "Didn't mean to be rude. You just shocked me. Did you... leave something when we were out with the chickens?"

"I never forget anything, Rob. And neither does the river."

She closed her eyes, tilted her head back and started to sing. At least, singing was the only way he could think to describe that sound coming out of her. It was like that final glug you hear when the last bit of water's going down the drain – plump, wet and satisfied. She swayed from side to side.

Now he could see what she was holding – the cup she'd been drinking tea from in her house.

Realisation shuddered through Rob, as he felt yet another spasm in his gut.

"You old bitch!" he shouted, lifting a finger at her. "Those mushrooms you gave me were poisonous. Or you put something in that tea, didn't you? A laxative."

She blinked. "You say that the water in the river is fine, Rob. So why would it bother you to drink it, huh?"

"You put fucking river water in that tea?"

Babs smiled. "Not just river water, my pet."

She closed her eyes again. Her chest rose and fell slowly.

Rob's panic rose. But his unease was not just about this mad old biddy who clearly thought she was a witch. No.

Why was there silence? None of the usual clucking or scraping you'd get from chickens that had just been fed.

He turned round and round, in disbelief. All the chickens were facing him, motionless.

"What have you done to them? What have you done to my birds?" he murmured. He turned back round to Babs, but she was paying him no mind. Her lips moved silently, her eyes closed.

Rob was about to lunge for her, but then he saw something that almost whipped the air from his lungs. The lines of Bab's tattoos were twisting... warping. They made him think of a river's ripples in sunlight.

He shook his head. It had to be those whacky herbs or mushrooms giving him hallucinations.

"I'll get you for this," he growled. "Don't you think this is over. I'm not someone you mess with."

He was about to make a run for his car, but Babs' voice suddenly rose in volume, almost to the pitch of a scream, only musical in its undulations. The chickens, as if as one, began to screech and cluck along with her.

He smacked his hand on the nearest cage. "Shut the fuck up, make them shut the fuck up!"

The noise was unbearable. Rob covered his ears with his hands.

But Babs continued her chant.

"Stop," he begged, stumbling towards her. "I will take the chickens back, I will put them in another field, away from the river, I will..."

Suddenly, he felt something burst from his belly.

He yanked up his shirt and started trembling and gabbling. A bloom of overlapping bracket fungus was flowering from his belly button. But the caps weren't white or brown or orange; they were the moist deep red of a gleaming worm. From the time he had spent with butcher friends, he knew that was the colour of the small intestines.

Now, there was that similar feeling of bulging activity in his ears, his anus...

He clutched his face, weeping, but the chickens were clucking and shrieking again, drowning him out. They were rushing towards him. He covered his face, but multiple sharp beaks ripped at it, their wings flapping and claws scraping at him.

He stumbled out of the coop, the chickens in pursuit.

Babs' laughter reached his ears again.

"Who's chickenshit now, Rob?" she taunted.

"What are you doing to me?" he shouted, as he was driven down the muddy bank.

"I'm taking you to the river, Rob. Since you've said it's okay to pour excrement into the waters, I thought I'd throw the biggest shit of them all in there."

#

Babs sat down on the bank, her long skirt trailing in the water.

Rob lay face down just a few feet away, his broad back bobbing as the current carried him. That fungus protruding from his ears, a rather odd puffy white concoction, would certainly give the coroner something interesting to write about.

There was no more clucking of chickens to be heard. They had all retreated back to the coop.

She let her fingers drape along the river's surface. The great beast quivered and prickled in pleasure. The Waters of Life, ready to be revived. Lifting her head, she breathed out.

Most of her smiles were brief spasms.

This one she let unfurl slowly.

defensive architecture

. . .

TC Parker

IT WASN'T the first time that month Ally had been kicked awake, but it was the first she'd been woken by the taste of blood.

Even with the tip of a stranger's boot between her ribs, she was slow to open her eyes. The quarter-bottle of rum she'd liberated from the recycling bin of a Caribbean restaurant under the flyover - then drained before she'd fallen asleep - still circulated in her system, dulling her responses.

Not the pain, though. *That*, she felt.

"Lazy fucking bitch," someone spat from above her, delivering a follow-up kick to her stomach.

He was young, she saw as she looked up. Probably not that much older than her; nineteen or twenty. Nicely dressed, in a suit and loose-at-the-collar tie that suggested a special occasion, a wedding or an award show – the kind with an open bar. He was thin and white, his face blotched pink from the beer she could smell on him and the right-eous anger he'd worked himself into. One of his boots was spattered with red: a residue, she concluded, of his initial kick, the one that had caught her in the mouth, sliced open her lip and sent the blood cascading down her throat.

She curled herself into a ball, in anticipation of the kicks to come.

"Fucking piece of shit," the man said, catching his breath. "Can't even get up, can you? Pathetic."

Close by, another someone laughed. A girl, Ally thought. And not a kind one.

The man pulled back his leg, ready to strike out again.

"Don't," Ally whispered, feeling the blood trickle down from her split lip to her chin and into the fabric of her sleeping bag.

That same cruel laugh rang out from behind the man.

"Do her," said the unseen girl, alcohol and excitement slurring her words. "Fucking do her, Paul."

Ally covered her head with her arms, shielding her face – she hoped – from the worst of the impact.

The man drove a shin into the place her nose would have been but for the buffer of her forearms – the bone of his ankle making sharp, painful contact with her flesh.

She knew better than to cry out. The man, however, began to scream.

"Paul?" Ally heard the girl ask, a satisfying note of panic in her question. "Paul, what the fuck?"

"She stabbed me!" the man shouted back at her. "She fucking stabbed me!"

This was a lie, of course. Ally *had* a knife – a retractable box-cutter she'd taken from a hardware store a month or so back, on the advice of the same guy who'd given her the sleeping bag – but it was where she always kept it, under her pillow. Not in her hand, and certainly not anywhere near the man now screaming that Ally had cut him.

So what was he talking about?

She peered out from the crack between her elbows – taking care to keep her arms around her head, lest another flurry of kicks ensue.

The man was gone. Or at least, was no longer looming over her. He'd retreated instead to the bench directly opposite Ally's doorway, where he sat, and clutched his lower leg while the girl – a curvy blonde in a little black dress and heavy eye makeup running down her cheeks – crouched down beside him, apparently examining his shin.

And hard though it was to say for sure in the dark, with only an isolated pool of streetlight-yellow to see by... it did *look* like he might have been stabbed, after all.

There was a tear in his trousers: a long, ragged slash that could well have been made by a box-cutter, bisecting the fabric and exposing the bloody, shredded skin of his calf and a darker, deeper tissue visible below.

It was a new injury, one that hadn't been there even a minute before. But it hadn't come from Ally.

"What did you do to him?" The girl turned to face the doorway, apparently sensing Ally watching them. "What the fuck did you do to him, you fucking freak?"

Her ribs burning, Ally unzipped her sleeping bag and manoeuvred herself into a standing palms-raised crouch, bracing herself to say... what? Something; anything. Whatever it took to stop the girl throwing a punch, or the man *and* the girl pulling out their phones and calling the police on her.

The girl stared back at Ally, her teeth bared... then, her gaze alighting on a point just south of Ally's hands, froze.

"Paul," she called to the injured man, neither moving nor looking away from Ally, "we've got to go. Now."

The man looked up from the wound he was tending, confused. "I'm fucking bleeding here."

"I don't care. Get up. We're going."

The girl took one step backwards, then another, her eyes never leaving Ally – retreating and retreating, until the bare backs of her knees hit the bench where the man still sat. She reached down for him and, with a firmness of grip that seemed to surprise even her, grabbed him by the biceps and hauled him up to his feet.

"Look," she told him, pointing to Ally.

He looked. And whatever he saw, it made his wet mouth slacken and his eyebrows shoot up into his hairline.

"What the fuck is that?" he said, so quietly Ally barely heard him, even in the silence of the empty street.

The girl didn't answer him. Instead, she glanced away from Ally to the better-lit end of the road, like she was confirming it was still there, where it should be; then tugged again at his arm, and ran.

He hesitated, just for a second, and limped after her, trailing blood along the cobblestones as he fled.

It was only when he'd disappeared around the corner, and she was sure neither of them was coming back – for now, anyway – that Ally let herself slump back down to the ground, her sleeping bag and pillow cushioning the fall.

With the caution of a glazier assessing the damage to a cracked window, she ran her fingers along her jawline, feeling it begin to swell. She pressed the same fingers to her torso, her ribcage; breathed in, then out, and – on the basis of nothing more scientific than the amount of pain shooting through her with each breath – diagnosed the offending ribs as bruised, but not broken.

As an afterthought, she looked down at the arms she'd used to shield herself from the man's last kick – before he'd cut himself on whatever broken bottle or sliver of glass had sliced him open.

And saw what the man and the girl must have seen, before they'd run: twin rows of curved purple spikes, two inches long and drenched in blood, shooting up and out from the skin of her wrists.

———

There was no choice but to wait until morning to examine them more closely. When dawn rose and the early-shift workers began to bloom along the city pavements, she rolled the sleeping bag and pillow into her backpack, pulled the rolled-up sleeves of her hoodie down to her knuckles and walked five minutes to the Italian cafe by the cathedral, where the manager opened up at 6 AM and was happy enough for Ally to use the facilities without buying a coffee.

In the bathroom, with the door locked, she stripped off the hoodie, then the t-shirt under it, and studied the spikes.

And they *were* spikes, no question. Twelve of them altogether, running in vertical lines from the softest part of her wrists to the fleshier middle of each forearm. The skin around them was undamaged: not scabbed or healing, as it might around a jutting shard of displaced bone, but clear and unbroken, as if the spikes had always been there, an integral part of her anatomy.

She touched one, prodding at its curving edges with a fingertip, and regretted it immediately. A rivulet of new blood, her *own* blood, flowed into her palm. The spike had cut her, as it must have cut the man who'd kicked her, and it hurt like hell.

She ran the cold tap and let the water imperfectly sterilise her finger. Then, on impulse, thrust her forearm under the stream and watched the dried blood melt and peel away from her skin.

What *did* that? What made spikes, actual *spikes*, grow out of your body?

An infection, maybe? Something fungal, or worse? She'd seen something on Wikipedia once about a guy, somewhere in Indonesia, who'd developed warts so bad, so huge and hard and scaly, that his hands had ended up looking like gnarled tree bark. *The Tree Man*, people had called him, for reasons that became apparent the moment you looked at the twisted roots and branches growing where his thumbs and fingers should have been.

Was this... *that*, or something in the ballpark? Could she have picked up a virus, some mutant variant on HPV, or whatever caused verrucas, just from touching the pavement or rooting through a wheelie bin?

It wasn't out of the question. She tried to keep clean, to prioritise hygiene, but it wasn't always easy to get to a bathroom, let alone a shower, and most of the supermarkets in town had too many cameras and security guards around for her to pick up antibac gel off the shelf unseen. More than once this year, she'd suffered through bouts of thrush and athlete's foot, her cunt burning in her underwear and her toes itching in socks that never seemed to stay dry, even in the absence of rain.

She hadn't washed her clothes in weeks.

So... an infection, then.

A virus.

Probably.

———

She spent the rest of the day in the central library, huddled up in a corner of the reference section with a Ray Bradbury collection. It was quiet there; safe, familiar. At lunchtime, one of the librarians – an older, grandmotherly woman in a faded pink sari and a grey cardigan even Ally thought had seen better days – shuffled over to her with a cup of sweet tea and a wrapped cheese sandwich from the Costa next door, laying both on the desk of Ally's carrel before Ally had a chance to object.

"Gets cold out there, love," the old woman said, with a brief but meaningful squeeze of Ally's shoulder. "You want something to put in your stomach."

Ally bit down on her scabbing lip to keep from crying.

When the sunlight streaming through the skylight windows turned to grey, then blue-black, and the library began to empty of all but those with nowhere else to go, she took off for the Civic: what had been the city's biggest theatre, shuttered and derelict for at least a decade now, its steps and exterior doorways and the Brutalist warrens of its elevated walkways given over since to the tents and sleeping bags of people like her. It rose above the rundown shops around it like a miniature Skid Row, indistinguishable visually from the concrete multi-storey car parks that must, Ally assumed, have inspired its design – its ugliness repelling all but those in need of the shelter it offered.

Generally, she avoided it: it was too busy, too loud, too crammed full of people wanting to *talk* to her, to unburden themselves of a portion of their emotional baggage. She was neither a talker nor a listener; preferred instead to take her chances in the alleyways and side-streets, where the walls were quiet and the human traffic minimal.

But there was safety in numbers. And after the night before, she thought, she could probably do with a little safety.

Pig was there, where he always was: camped out on the second-storey walkway next to what had been a fire exit, cooking something that looked like sausage and smelled obscene on the rusty little gas stove he carried with him everywhere.

He seemed pleased to see her: beaming at her through yellowing teeth half-obscured by a wiry red beard, and rising to his feet to wrap her in a hug that sent fresh oscillations of pain along her aching ribs.

"You alright, Allybob?" he asked her, when he noticed her wincing. "I hurt you?"

"It's nothing." He relaxed his arms, and she extricated herself – slowly, trying to minimise any further contact with the sides of her body. With her wrists, and sharp points springing out from them under her hoodie. "Got a bit of a booting from a couple of twats out on the piss last night, that's all. Be fine in a day or two."

The toothy smile fell away.

"Motherfuckers." He squinted at her, scanning her for other injuries thus far undisclosed. "And you don't want to go anywhere to get looked over? There's a pop-up walk-in clinic in the town hall square tomorrow. Opens at 9."

"No need. It's all good, promise."

He squatted, and turned the maybe-sausages on the tiny grill with his fingers – strands of gingery hair falling down into his eyes. "Happening a lot lately. Bastards laying into us on the street."

"Guess so."

"Though that's what you get, when you give a fascist the keys to fucking Parliament and let him charge his megaphone in the Commons canteen."

"Must be," she said, noncommittally. He was gearing up for one of his political rants, she could feel it.

"What were they even thinking, letting a cunt like Barker in? Beggars fucking belief."

She nodded, hoping a show of agreement on her part would slow him down, if not stop him in his tracks entirely. Any sign of debate or dissent, she knew from experience, would do nothing but rile him up.

And she *did* agree with him, mostly. She wasn't a particularly political person, not the way Pig was, but there was no denying Hal Barker's run for MP – and his subsequent capture of the Leicester Central constituency – had made life harder for her, for all of them. *Clean Up*

Our Streets was the guy's whole platform; literally the slogan he'd had printed on his flyers, and Christ knew Ally had had enough of *them* shoved in her face while he and his team were out campaigning ahead of the election. People like her – "street people," in Barker's lingo – were the reason the local economy was collapsing, or so the campaign's argument went. *They* were why families avoided coming into town to go shopping, and why so many of the shops themselves were shutting down; *they* were the reason jobs were drying up in retail, entertainment, hospitality.

They were putting Leicester out of business. Taking money out of ordinary working people's pockets.

Because really: who'd want to look at *that* on every corner, or huddled up in stinking coats at every roundabout and bus stop? Who'd want to steer their kids around that many filthy tents and rattling cardboard cups on the way to get a decaf latte and a Big Mac?

Barker's word had rippled out across the voting populace, their impact felt immediately – by Ally, and Pig, and the hundreds if not thousands of others like them around the city – in the pursed lips and scowling faces of the strangers who passed them on the pavement; in the insults and the curses spat from mouths newly emboldened to say aloud what they'd long been holding back.

Tramp. Dirty bastard. Fucking parasite.

Inexorably, the violence followed: a knee to the stomach here, a boot stamping down on unprotected fingers there. Rains of urine, beer and spittle on them as they slept; slaps and kicks and punches thrown so liberally it seemed to Ally lately that every day another acquaintance from the Civic or the streets sported a black eye, a cut lip, a limp they hadn't had the night before.

She'd suffered a few herself, even before *Paul* and his cheerleading girlfriend.

"But you've been okay up here?" she said, gesturing to the steps and walkways.

"Oh, yeah. Little fuckers wouldn't *dare* come up here. Cowardly cunts." He squinted; cast a look down at her arm, the sleeve of her hoodie. "Here, you sure you're alright, Allybob? Is that you bleeding?"

She followed his eyes; saw the sleeve was sodden.

"Just a splash of water," she lied, thrusting her balled fists into the pockets of her jeans, the wrists facing inwards. "Nothing to worry about."

———

It wasn't water. But nor, she saw – when Pig had passed out for the night and she'd bedded down in the next doorway down from his, sleeves rolled up to her elbows and the Civic's still-functioning security light gathering her into its halo – was it blood.

It was... something else. A clear fluid, faintly viscous, seeping from the place in her arms the spikes had sprung from. It smelled of nothing; tasted of rose and lemons and vinegar, sour and bitter and sweet.

Pus? It didn't *look* like pus. It was transparent, after all, not yellow or green. But she wasn't exactly a doctor... and pus and seeping wounds went hand-in-hand with infection.

So maybe it *would* be worth her swinging by the walk-in clinic in the morning.

But... early. Before Pig came to enough to notice her go, and ask where she was heading.

———

At 9.03 AM, her rucksack on her back and her sleeves crusted stiff with whatever had oozed from her arms in the night, she slipped out of the Civic and across to the walk-in clinic. It was, as Pig had said, a pop-up, four big white marquees erected around the foundation in the town hall square, and each tent signposted according to its function: Registration, Waiting, Assessment, and Aftercare.

A quick glance through the entrance flap of the Waiting tent confirmed what past experience had led her to suspect: it was heaving, each line of folding chairs crammed with coughing, sweating, scratching bodies, many with sleeping bags and rucksacks of their own at their feet. At least a few were faces she recognised; men and women she'd seen around the Civic and the Clock Tower, though none she knew by name. None who knew *her*.

Hood up, she trudged to Registration; took a number – 86 – from the bored-looking nurse at the trestle table masquerading as a reception desk, and trudged back to Waiting, sinking down into the only empty seat she could find, between an old Black guy in a beanie hacking phlegm into his hand and a younger white man with a shaved head and so many weeping scabs around his mouth and nose it made her wince.

"You alright there, bab?" the old Black guy asked her, his Brummie accent thick. He pointed down at her leg. "Get bitten, did you? Bedbugs everywhere lately, I'm telling you. Everywhere."

Only then did she realise she'd been scratching – clawing – at her shin. Gouging at the flesh through the coarse, dirt-streaked denim of her jeans.

And that there was something there, under her fingers. Something sharp and hard, poking up through the skin and muscle, pressing against her fingertips.

She stood up from the folding chair so quickly it made the old man jump and drop the canvas bag in his lap, and every other pair of tired, bloodshot eyes in the tent swivel their way.

"Sorry," she told him, readjusting the hood so that it fully obscured her face. "Sorry."

If he replied, she didn't hear him. And then she was out of there, and back onto the street.

———

In the greasy fluorescence of a chicken shop toilet, she saw it, as she'd known she would. Another spike – longer and sharper than the ones puncturing her arm but curling, corkscrewed, growing out of her calf like a piglet's tail.

This one, it seemed to her, was less thorn than bramble; its pointed tip complemented by a tangle of smaller, jagged points along its shaft.

Her leg, like her arm, was leaking: the same clear fluid seeping from the unblemished and unbroken flesh out of which the spike emerged, leaching into her jeans and drying to a powdery residue on her skin.

She wet a fingertip with the tip of her tongue; touched the finger to the powder, and licked it clean.

It was sweet; sweet as fizzy drinks and sherbet, with none of the sour/bitter notes she'd tasted in the liquid that still pulsed from her wrist like blood from an unstaunched wound.

Sweet as antifreeze, stirred into a cheating husband's coffee.

———

The library was closed on Thursdays; a consequence, as another old lady in a cardigan had confided in her by the reference section only a week before, of the same budget cuts that had taken out the women's shelter and the council food banks. Going there had been her first impulse: getting herself to a computer, typing *what does it mean when spikes start growing out of your body?* into a search engine, and hoping the answer wasn't *you're dying – tough break.*

In the absence of algorithmic anonymity, and whatever slim reassurance a webpage might offer her, she retreated to the Civic, where she might at least be spared the contempt of respectable strangers. She found Pig exactly where she'd left him, fresh spliff between his teeth and a burnt pan of black-speckled eggs scrambling over the camping stove.

"There's something wrong with me," she told him, before he had a chance to push himself up from the concrete.

Perhaps telling him, *showing* him, wasn't the smartest move; perhaps he'd panic, wail his head off or ward her off with the sign of the cross at the sight of the thorns in her arm and the tangle of barbs in her leg. But he couldn't have her carted off in an ambulance, the way a doctor at the walk-in might. And if he did wail at her, or call her a freak – well, what was anyone at the *Civic* going to do about it, when not even the police would go up there anymore?

"Wrong how, Allybob?" he asked her, mouth hanging open and saliva glueing the Rizla to his lip. "What's happened? Not them same dickheads coming at you again?"

She rolled up her trouser leg in lieu of a reply, feeling the denim catch on the spikes.

"This," she said, pointing down. "This happened."

The spliff had hit the ground and begun to extinguish itself on the breeze before she dared look up to meet his expression.

His jaw, previously slack, hung open wide enough for her to see the metal fillings in his molars. "What the fuck have you done to yourself?" he said, disbelieving. "Is that... Did you get that *put* in there?"

"They grew." It was the simplest way she knew to explain things, inasmuch as they could *be* explained. "This, and the other one."

She reached for the sleeve of her hoodie and pulled it, gently, upwards, all the way to the elbow. The thorns were larger now, she realised as they sprung free: the length of a vegetable knife, and equally sharp, though as flexible as a willow branch. Only the thickness of the fabric had stopped them poking out from the sleeve at the wrist – keeping them tucked away, folded in on themselves like an unwanted erection.

Or a switchblade.

"That's not possible," Pig said, scratching at his beard with an anxious knuckle. "You're a person. People don't just... sprout things out their arms and legs."

Now Ally could look at him; stare him down, even. Because it was one thing for him to freak out – to be scared or confused or disgusted. But it was another thing altogether to say that she was lying; that what she'd seen and felt happen to her over the last 24 hours – what she could see and feel for herself *right that second* – wasn't real.

"Well, I did," she said, levelly. "So what now?"

———

"We share something like 1% of our DNA with plants. You know that?"

Two spliffs, a cider and a tin plate of the scrambled eggs in, and Pig was mellower: not quite as expansive as usual, and still throwing wary glances down at her covered arm and leg whenever she forgot herself and scratched at them, but friendly. Gentler.

"Sounds like bullshit." Ally adjusted her position, feeling the bramble jut against the lining of her jeans as she crossed and uncrossed her ankles. They were facing each other across the camping stove, she and Pig; her own tin plate lay, scraped clean of every last remnant of egg, lay empty in her lap. He'd shared the weed with her, but not the cider, though she could probably forgive him for that.

"Not bullshit." He drained the can he was holding – his second – and crushed it to an aluminium concertina with one hand. "I read it."

"Where?"

"Somewhere. Some journal. Back in the day."

He'd been a teacher once, she recalled. *Said* he'd been, anyway. And it wasn't so far-fetched a claim. There were other ex-teachers bedding down at the Civic; ex-teachers, and ex-lecturers, ex-college tutors, in amongst the former care home managers and laid-off nurses and social workers made redundant. You could've built a local council off the back of their collective human resource, diminished through it was.

"And?" she asked him.

"And what?"

"You said, we share 1% of our DNA with plants. Even if that's true, so what?"

He threw the can into the air; caught it again in his other hand. "So, there's a common ancestor. For all us, what do you call them? Eukaryotes. Plants, people, animals, fucking *mushrooms*... we all come from the same source, the same set of cells. And we've all still got a bit of that material in us. That 1%. You look at some cunt in Canary Wharf or the City, some banker or whatever, and yeah, he's probably got more cat or mouse in him than banana. More pig." He grinned, relishing his own joke. "But there's still *some* banana in there. Some fucking...

banyan tree. Deadly nightshade, Venus flytrap. And the cells remember. They fucking *remember*."

"Remember what?"

He leaned in towards her, over her stove, and for a second she worried his beard would catch fire. "When they were part of something bigger. Something with the potential to spin out in a million different ways, to express itself as a cow or a tree or a whatever the fuck. What's the line in that poem? *This is the root of the root of a tree called life.* That's what I'm talking about, Allybob. The root of the root. The tree of fucking life."

"I don't get it," she said, although she thought maybe she was beginning to, that she was picking up the trace of the point he was making.

"Don't you?" He dropped his voice to something close to a whisper, like he was talking not so much to Ally as to himself. "Plants... they're full of defence mechanisms. Fucking have to be, don't they, if they're just sat there all day, waiting for some fucking jackdaw to peck at 'em, or some twat who thinks he's Wordsworth to try and pluck 'em out the grass to put in his lapel. Cunts like Barker, they talk about *defensive architecture*, like building a bench too small to put your feet on is a good way of repelling people, of keeping us from being seen where we're not wanted. But you want to see *real* defensive architecture, something that's properly going to send folk on their way so they don't come back... you want to look at plants. At spiny leaves, and impenetrable shells. Thorns on branches. Fucking *poisons*." He paused; gazed into the stove like it was a glowing campfire. "Show us that leg again?"

Obligingly, she pulled up the leg of her jeans until the cluster of spikes met the afternoon air.

He studied it; extended a hand as if to touch it, then seemed to think better of it and withdrew.

"Cunts like Barker," he said eventually. "Like them ones that laid into you, night before last. They push and they push, because as far as they're concerned, we've only got two choices: we bend, or we break. But they never think there might be another choice, do they? They never think we might adapt." He looked down at his own legs; at his own, smooth hands. "I'm not saying I know how it happened. Why it

happened to you, specifically. But what you've got there, Allybob –
that's defensive architecture. Isn't it?"

———

By night-time, she was hungry again. Pig had taken to his sleeping
bag, lulled by more cider and more weed into an early bed; the Civic
was awake, but barely. Too many of its residents, so loquacious in the
daylight hours, were given to an early night.

Rucksack slung across her shoulders and hoodie – for now, at least
– concealing the spikes in her arm, she descended the steps. The all-
day Filipino buffet by the Clock Tower would be closing up, throwing
its leftovers into the waste disposal around the back; if she was lucky,
she could snag some fried rice and tocino before they coagulated to
inedibility.

Her feet had barely touched the pavement when she heard, then
saw them. Three men, white and bald and older, coke sweat spreading
along the collars of their polo shirts. They were shouting: hurling
strings of incoherence at her from across the road, though she caught
the odd word among the hoots and bellows. *Dirty fucking cunt,* yelled
one; *when d'you last wash them armpits?* demanded another, a hacking
cough digging potholes in the vowels.

She kept her head down. Kept on walking.

They followed her, shouting all the way. A hundred feet or so later,
they crossed the road.

And then they were right in front of her, blocking her path.

"Think you're too good to talk to us?" sneered one of them – the
smallest of the three, a squat short-necked bullfrog of a man with too
many gold rings on his fingers.

She looked around her, scanning the street for passers-by. For
anyone who might be compelled to intervene.

There was no-one. Nothing but boarded-up shops and smashed-up
windows along an empty street.

"He asked you a question," another of them said, spittle flying from the corners of his mouth. This one was lean, hollow-cheeked. Sweat patches glistened around his armpits.

"Please." Instinctively, she laid a palm against her sleeve, feeling the coiled springs of the thorns – the *spikes* – below the heavy cotton. "I'm just trying to get past."

Like a switchblade.

"You go," the bullfrog said, "when we *say* you can go. Rude fucking bitch."

He staggered forward, making a clumsy dive for her wrist, the way she'd half-expected he might.

She tugged at the sleeve; heard the fabric tear as the spike sliced through it.

Just exactly like a switchblade.

The bullfrog clamped a hand around her forearm. A minute later, he was screaming.

———

She left them where they'd found her, the broken heap of them staining the concrete to a poppy red.

The bullfrog might live, she thought, even if the missing fingers and the severed tendons presented some problems in his future. She held out less hope for the lean man with the sweat patches – his guts a leaking mass of purple flesh and too-pink viscera without an ounce of skin to cover them.

There was no hope at all for their friend, though. He'd choked on the blood from the slit in his throat long before she'd finished with him.

Under her sleeve, the spike-thorns pulsed – twisting and length-ening like rose stems in the sun. The bramble on her leg was growing, too; weaving its protection up her thigh and down to her ankle, more comfort now than irritant. Other parts of her would follow suit, she knew… even if she couldn't explain exactly *how* she knew. Other layers of the dermis would give way to carapace and prickles; other stretches of vulnerable softness would harden, cultivating chemical defences just below the surface.

She'd welcome them all, when they came.

She walked for hours, traversing the city: end to end, waste ground to waste ground. Not a single person stopped her. Then, the blood still sticky on her clothes and rucksack, she climbed the Civic's steps – jumping off on the second storey and crossing the walkway to the place where Pig had set up camp. The place had come alive again in her absence: tent-flaps open and fires burning in every doorway, and the thrum of conversation static overhead.

Eyes watched her – a dozen or a hundred, who could tell in that almost-dark of dawn? She ignored them all. And if any of them considered the bloodstains and the spatters worthy of comment, they kept it to themselves.

Pig was up, wide awake and leaning happily against the wall – spliff in one hand, can of stove-brewed coffee in the other.

"Allybob," he said, with a nod. No worry at all in the delighted smile he flashed her, in spite of her face and the state of her clothes. "Glad you're back. Here, you want to see something?"

He came closer, so close he must've smelled the blood on her. Put the coffee on the ground next to his feet, rested the smoking spliff beside it, and – still beaming – undid his coat and pulled up the hem of his sweater, exposing the fishbelly-cream of his stomach.

A triple-row of spikes three inches long and twice as wide protruded from the skin: oleander-pink, and dense as sandbox tree bark.

"What do you think to that?" he asked her.

She considered them.

"Root of the root of a tree called life," she said. And grinned right back at him.

a change in universal flavor

. . .

Hailey Piper

THE WORLD SPAT Raine onto the sidewalk between a condom wrapper and patchwork wads of dried chewing gum, and she couldn't blame it. With a name like hers, she'd been getting spat out for all her nineteen years.

Past the curb, an engine growled.

"This is your last chance," Anderson said, lips curling beneath his auburn mustache. "Do something right for once in your life."

Past him, Stenner sat behind the steering wheel. Aviator shades dangled beneath his badge, but Raine had never seen him wear them. Cops only came for her at night, as if they sprang to spontaneous existence from the darkness the way people once thought mud birthed frogs and old meat spawned maggots.

The passenger side window slid shut, cutting Raine off from the inside of the black-and-white police cruiser. It gave a harsh chirp and then eased from the curb. Its stale aura must have been propping up her secrets. Now she felt the drug baggies loaded in her denim jacket's pocket, and the taped mic and wire sagged from her chest and bra.

Neither weight felt like doing something right, but she started up the sidewalk anyway, eyes peeled for a life to ruin.

Golden streetlights spread pale halos over the damp concrete. They reflected off leaf-choked puddles and glistened across the wet bricks of rundown apartment buildings that stuffed the street from here to the next intersection. The atmosphere hung thick with unseen cigarette smoke and wet dog odor.

And amid the grime and decay, Raine spotted an angel.

She was an unreal shade of chalk white. Luminous spines of light glared behind her head of milky curls, casting deep shadows down her bony brow, black eyes, and sullen expression. She wore a silvery garment, something between a tunic and a dress—Raine didn't know the name.

The angel parted dark lips. "You look like you might be pain itself." Her voice hummed with windchime fragility.

Raine jolted in place, first mistaking that last word for her name. "Pain?" she asked, and then patted her jacket. "I can ease any pain, if you need."

"Pain's transcendence is too great for a single soul," the angel said, and her eyes glanced skyward. "The scale is beyond imagination. There is a throne at the center of the universe. This was not its original shape, but the fountain of will is corrupted, its power spreading in fingers to seize all things. Someday, this will change."

Raine's fingers left her jacket and scratched her scalp-short hair. This angel sounded high already, and Anderson couldn't arrest anyone for that. Someone would have to make a purchase first, and that was only part of his plan.

"If you're looking to hit your head on heaven's door, I got the stuff," Raine said. The pitch sounded flimsy, but she could count it as practice if this woman didn't buy.

"Pain is the doorway to light," the angel said. "That's why I've gathered the others."

Others? That might mean a party. Raine could dump all these baggies in one night, the unfamiliar drugs passing hand to hand until she emptied her jacket.

"May I gather you?" the angel asked. Her breath chilled Raine's face.

"Sure, why the hell not?" Raine stuffed both hands in her pockets. "Let's bring some of that transcendence. Got a name?"

Streetlights glimmered in the angel's eyes. "They call me Angel." No surprise there.

Raine said her name, and then added: "Like the stuff from the sky." Another limp line.

But Angel's sullenness tweaked as if tugged by a subdermal hand. Not a smile exactly, but a pleased look drifted into her eyes.

A pretty look.

She turned and drifted up the street. Raine followed, and reminded herself not to let bodily wants play with her heart again. Such temptations had dragged her into this trouble in the first place. It began with the beers. She hadn't even liked them, but nineteen was underage no matter her ultimate preferences. Next came that time tagging the bus station ticket counter with a purple-painted message she hadn't cared about then and couldn't remember now.

Last came the almost-joyride, cut short when Anderson and Stenner picked her up for the third time. When they turned her into their dog.

And for what? Monica Albridge? Her family had the money and influence to snatch her from prison, and she didn't have thoughts to spare if she encouraged someone like Raine, with nothing, to bleed a little chaos into their small city.

So much mayhem and suffering, all for a straight girl. Raine needed to focus tonight, with her heart and sex drive on a leash.

Same as the cops now kept her soul.

At a chipped concrete stairway, Angel steered them into a seen-better-days apartment building and led them up a jumble of clanging steel steps. Their destiny awaited at the top in loudening chatter and music. Raine couldn't turn back now. She should follow Angel inside and warn everyone to steer clear of drugs and cops and Monica Albridge, to learn from Raine's mistakes.

Except helping them would mean hurting herself. No matter what became of anyone else, she was caught in a pig snare, more toothy and gnarled than any bear trap. She could either side with these strangers or grasp desperately for some kind of future.

There was really no choice at all.

A rust-colored door screeched open, hurting Raine's ears, and a guy in a plaid shirt opened his arms in welcome.

"The angel graces us," he said, eyelids drooping. Half-sarcastic, half-hammered.

"We may begin," Angel said. She nudged Plaid Guy out of her way without her lifting a finger. "I will need forty minutes of waiting."

Plaid Guy laughed. "Take the night."

Raine hurried behind Angel before the door slammed shut again. Its screech made her shoulders jerk, and her head bowed as if someone in the far past still shouted at her, still cared. When she lifted her eyes, Angel was gone.

"Forty minutes, chica," Plaid Guy said, sinking into the party's miasma.

Raine scanned the room for Angel. Her presence had put Raine's nerves at ease, and now they writhed to discomfort again in this crowd of unknowns. Partiers sat on bean bag chairs and sofas, or plunked down on the floor where they curled into each other. Beaded curtains draped various doorways, and band posters obscured one wall's splotchy paint job. A velvety red curtain hung half-open between the cluttered living room and kitchen. Hints of sweat and beer danced in the air.

No sign of Angel—fine. She had already done her part in leading Raine. Now came time to make sales, and to make sure they showed up on audio.

Supposedly Raine was part of a larger plan to—what, catch a local drug lord? Raise the crime rate? Anderson hadn't explained it well, or maybe Raine had been too terrified alone in that cold interrogation room to properly understand. She had only watched Anderson's eyes bore through her while Stenner stood to one side and played with his unworn shades.

But she knew to find people, and here she was, scheming to convince these punks and nobodies to buy from her. Say what, *Hey, want some drugs*? Which tactic had talked that first illegal beer into her hands?

Monica Albridge. Doubtful Raine could wield such charm against any of these people.

But Angel's words might work. The guy at the door had been waiting for her, and everyone else might have come for the same reason. Raine slid toward a living room corner where a couple sat with their backs to either wall, both wearing leather jackets bulleted with steel.

"Pretty cool to transcend, yeah?" Raine asked.

"That's why we're here, hon," one of the women said. Her mascara had smeared, but whether from crying or rubbing at her face, Raine couldn't tell.

"To cry for miracles," said the other.

Raine opened her mouth to follow up, but their bold confidence threw her off. She found the same vocal wall at the next group she neared, and the next. Everyone's chipper attitude seemed fortressed against influence, at least until Angel's return, and their heedless enthusiasm repelled Raine at every approach. She had no idea how anyone could be so certain of the words pouring out of their mouths. These people didn't need drugs; they were high already. Raine was undercooked for this crowd.

"You alone?" asked someone with a sandpapery voice.

Raine turned to find a lanky man smiling at her. His eyes hinted at a growing pool of alcohol in his gut, one he could scarcely hold.

"I'm not into dudes," Raine said, her tone flat.

She tensed for resistance, but the lanky man nodded. "Cool, me neither," he said, and then staggered off in search of someone else to smile at.

Raine's mic must've picked that up. Anderson and Stenner would have wanted her to turn the lanky man's interest into a sale. Not like they could put themselves in her position. No one would trust them enough to chat, let alone buy their baggies of poison. They were probably busy with their own cop games—Anderson twirling his mustache while Stenner tied some shrieking woman to distant railroad tracks.

Raine's thoughts faded along with the crowd's ambient murmur. Her head turned almost in unison with theirs to face the velvety red curtain, now mostly shut against the kitchen light except one spot a few feet off the floor, where it cast a halo around Angel's head.

She rose on the pads of her feet, growing taller as lights dimmed down the living room. Her silvery garment sagged down her chest, froze in the air until the apartment sank into true silence, and then shed away from Angel's nakedness.

Raine's chest tightened, nerves tugging at their leash. She hadn't realized the white curls of Angel's hair fell across her small breasts and down to her waist. A similar pale nest encircled the gentle member between Angel's legs. Above that, Angel clutched a tremendous sword, its hilt spiking in all directions like a blazing sun of bronze.

A voice of chimes and melody shattered the silence. "Tell me you're my pain, and I will reach inside," Angel said.

Seconds passed before Plaid Guy flinched from the crowd on some unspoken cue. "I am your pain," he said.

Angel tilted her sword and spoke again of the throne at the center of the universe and its fountain. Raine listened closer this time, wondering if she'd stumbled into a slam poetry show—except no one else looked prepped to perform.

Only Angel's head glowed with heavenly light. Only her sword looked ready to cut a slit in the night.

"A broken light is a rainbow, wearing the light's death in many colors," Angel said. "Tell me."

"I am your pain," Plaid Guy said, and this time a small chorus joined him.

"None will commit this murder to flesh." Angel raised her sword overhead, baring her marble-white nakedness under the shadow of her blade. "But I wear a self-pain."

Every word thrummed in Raine's ears as if meant for her and no one else. Her heart pounded—fuck, her clit pounded—the pair beating together in a steady drumming thunder. She wanted to hear more. Or black out. Or explode. If Angel didn't keep going, Raine might break into the poem's deathly rainbow.

Angel shifted the sword until it ran a line across her face. "Tell me."

"I am your pain," the partiers said together.

"I am your pain," Raine echoed, and it was a heavier promise than anything she carried beneath her clothes.

Angel drew the blade close to her face, against the skin, until it pressed the flesh beneath her black eyes.

A sting lit Raine's face. She pawed at her cheeks, and her fingers drew back, painted with crimson raindrops. The sting lingered beneath her eyes, and she wondered if this was the agreed-upon pain.

She glanced around the room. The studded jacket couple both wept crimson. Same for Plaid Guy, the lanky man, and everyone Raine had tried speaking with—their cheeks ran red as if gently cut by Angel's sword.

"A broken light is a rainbow," Angel said again, and lowered her sword. "My thanks for letting me gather you."

Soft applause circled the living room as Raine wiped red streaks into denim sleeves. Her heart thrummed on, ready to pump blood through the wounds beneath her eyes, and then she wouldn't have to worry anymore about the great hungry night.

But first, she had to speak to Angel, desperate as if checking a mirror to be sure she still had a face. No one else stood by the curtain or seemed concerned if Angel had hurt herself, or how she'd hurt everyone else. Not a blemish ran beneath her eyes.

"When you talk about the throne," Raine said, sidling closer. "Is that where you want to go? Center of the universe?"

Angel's eyes lingered on her sword. "It will take much more pain."

"What then?" Raine wanted to understand, or at least convince Angel she understood "This corrupted fountain—going to cure that?"

"Change it," Angel said.

"I get the scale now." Raine pantomimed stirring a spoon through liquid. "It's like Kool-Aid."

Angel at last glanced up from her sword. Her natural sullenness bent in confusion.

"The pitcher's full of water no matter what," Raine said. "But you choose your little powder packet. Is it cherry? Strawberry? Right now maybe it's watermelon-flavored, but you want it lime."

Angel blinked in silence, but she didn't disagree.

Raine aimed a finger at the sword. "Can I touch it?"

Angel weighed the sword back and forth in one hand, as if interrogating it for evil intent, and then placed it across Raine's arms.

A heavy weapon, yet somehow lighter than Raine's mic, wire, and baggies. Maybe the sword was purer. She avoided the blade, yet for some reason the sun-shaped hilt's glimmer seemed more dangerous. Sharp objects knew their power, but bronze sunshine might have aspirations to greater threats. Raine slid the sword back into Angel's grasp.

Two fingers crossed the back of Angel's hand. Her skin was cold silk. How could anyone feel that soft and sleek?

"Thank—" Raine began, but cut herself off at glimpsing her reflection in Angel's gaze.

On the street, she'd thought the shadows cast by Angel's brow painted her eyes black. This close, with nothing to obscure them, Raine realized the irises matched the pupils, made distinct only by tiny white cracks of frozen lightning. She leaned closer as if she might fall into their darkness.

The kiss was an accident, lips grazing lips.

Raine jerked back and clenched her teeth, still tasting Angel's cool breath. Had she learned nothing from Monica's chaos? She would die by these impulses if she didn't smarten up, and fast.

But Angel's curious expression, so fresh and vulnerable, stopped Raine from regretting the moment entirely.

And she had never tasted anyone so sweet.

She forced herself back into the throng of partiers and had almost forgotten she wasn't alone with Angel. Now Raine stared at every face, a reminder these people were real. She caught them laughing, wiping blood off their cheeks with napkins or sleeves. The gathering never weakened across the passing minutes, the hour. They wouldn't drift away post-performance and spare themselves the chance of becoming Raine's victims. They instead clung with their friendly expressions and damn open hearts.

These weren't prey for a pig snare. Just people, full of quirks and unpleasantness and life.

The baggies in Raine's jacket swelled to boulders and buckled her knees. She asked where to find the bathroom and then stormed across maroon tiles to a rickety porcelain toilet, where she lifted her top and then froze. If she killed this chance, there wouldn't be another.

But if she kept the wire, it would root itself in her heart, and the pocket baggies would feed it. She couldn't guess what that would make her, but she wouldn't be Raine the next time she looked in the mirror.

There was really no choice at all.

Her fingers clawed the wire and tape off her bra and chest. She coiled it around the mic, and it dropped like a thin black worm into the toilet. The baggies plunked a raindrop rhythm beside it before Raine flushed everything down the pipes in a gurgling roar.

Tank top still rolled to her collarbone, she washed her hands and then scrubbed the tape's stickiness and regrets off her bra and skin.

Her relentless scream charged from deep inside. She could only clasp both hands across her mouth and let it beat breathy fists against her palms. Its force almost blocked out the party chatter, running water, and the bathroom door's opening-shutting creak. Her scream fizzled as she turned to see who had stepped inside.

A mane of curling white hair circled Angel's face. She wore a silvery robe, its weak-knotted sash dangling beneath the V of her chest.

Raine's fingers crawled across her cheeks and nose until they covered her eyes. She couldn't stop Angel from seeing her, but she could stop herself from seeing Angel, and any reflection in her black eyes.

Gentle fingers clutched one wrist and drew the hand from Raine's face. She let one eye flutter open to darkness, the other to light, and then stared into Angel's blinding glory before welling tears stewed the bathroom into hazy maroon and white.

Angel first wiped tap water from Raine's chest, and then tears and dried blood from Raine's cheeks. Raine quivered harder each time Angel's thumb slid under an eye. She would collapse any moment.

"Raine," Angel said. "It was too much pain."

"No," Raine said, voice cracking, but she didn't know how to explain.

Angel's sullenness deepened. "Sometimes I believe the light is whole, and we are broken in ways too vast for pain."

Raine shook her head, but was there a right answer? A choice? She didn't know.

"But I also believe together, we can find a change." Angel spread her arms to either side. "May I gather you?"

Raine half-stepped, half-fell into Angel's chest, and then her body lifted from the mess of tiles. Letting herself go was easier than speaking. The world melted around her eyes, bathroom light giving way to a dark ginger-scented room of Christmas light-circled windows and a row of lava lamps.

And a bed, where Angel laid Raine. Her fingers danced across Raine's body as she settled onto the sheets, into them, and helped Raine undress. She brought a welcome angelic touch.

Except a thorn pierced Raine's heart, the cop wire's emotional parting gift. She needed to shake it out before Angel pricked her finger.

"Wait," Raine said, tears crystalizing again. "I have to tell you—I didn't come here for you. I came to do something bad."

Angel leaned across Raine, one hand hovering over her chest. "But all this pain you take." Dark lips whispered music in Raine's ears. "Are you here for me now? Are you the throne's finger, or my pain? Tell me."

Raine quivered with familiar words. "I am your pain."

And Angel reached inside her. They grasped at each other as Angel's robe spread open in a pair of protective wings, and tender fingers explored damp secrets. Muscles corded down their bodies. A new, different scream bullied its way up Raine's throat, and she had to bite into Angel's shoulder to keep it from thundering out.

The same sense of teeth sank into Raine's flesh, too. Not an angel bite—her face searched Raine's neck, finding unique un-kissed places and kissing them for the first time. Every returned touch slid cool brilliance across Raine's body. Each place where Raine kissed the sweet taste of Angel, she felt tasted. Everywhere Raine's throbbing muscles crushed against Angel, Raine felt likewise crushed, as if Angel were a mirror of sensations. Deeper than under-eye slits and teeth, pain and pleasure fought a war across blurring territories.

Or maybe this was pain alone in its truest form, a knowledge that beyond tonight, this kindness Raine gave and received might be the last she would ever feel, and she wouldn't know what to do with all the horrid emptiness to come.

They slowed, and then Raine curled into the circle of Angel's embrace and listened to her breath ease toward sleep.

Raine wished to sleep too, but her thoughts ran wild. This moment was finite, no matter what Angel said about the universe. Raine needed to leave this bed, party, and apartment before she lured a fresh hell here.

She wouldn't be Monica Albridge. She would be better than all the Monicas in the world.

Anderson and Stenner would be waiting. They would be all scowls and teeth, ready to drag Raine into a harsher pig snare, one without next chances or hope.

But at least if she left now, it was her move in this game of choices and chances. Maybe she wouldn't want to see her face in the mirror, but she could look and pretend she saw herself in Angel.

Raine dressed again, kissed Angel's brow, and drifted from the bed.

The apartment melted into a sloping hollow, ready to spit Raine onto the sidewalk if she didn't hurry herself down the clanking steel stairs and out the door where she belonged. She couldn't blame it. Life had been spitting her out for nineteen years.

Damp air squeezed her skin as she traipsed the empty sidewalk. Streetlights flickered, frail against the darkness, but no one haunted the street. Maybe Raine still had a chance? She stuffed her hands into now-empty jacket pockets and started toward the far intersection.

A familiar chirp jumped through her nerves. She didn't have time to run.

The black-and-white police cruiser growled from the darkness between two wet-bricked buildings. It settled against the curb, its lights flashing red and blue in Raine's eyes. Long silhouettes climbed featureless from either door, only crystallizing into Anderson and Stenner when they stood side by side between Raine and the car.

"Thought we didn't watch where you went?" Anderson asked. "That we wouldn't wait for you to come out?"

"Did you think we didn't hear it?" Stenner asked. His dangling aviator shades rattled against his chest. "What you did."

Anderson's earthworm-pink lips curled in a wet sneer. "You really fucked up, kid."

"I know," Raine said. Defeat formed a wet lump in her throat.

Anderson yanked her against the cruiser and clapped steel cuffs around her wrists. His hands patted her down, checking for secrets he already knew she'd flushed down the drain. She wondered if tonight had really been part of some grander plan. Had it even been an official operation? Maybe she'd fallen into a common cop game, played on private cop time through cop imaginations in which Anderson's and Stenner's pig snare tied Raine a little tighter to life's railroad tracks. For the fun of it, nothing more.

They were Monicas with badges. Maybe worse.

"You do not look like pain," a fragile voice sang into the night.

Raine clenched her teeth and glanced over one shoulder. She hadn't heard a door open or footsteps near, but there stood Angel, as if she had descended from the high apartment on invisible wings in silver robe and bare feet.

And holding her sun-hilted sword.

Anderson lifted from Raine's spine in a cloud of stale heat. She spun around to look as Stenner joined Anderson, their rigid shapes crowding the curb. Angel's dark gaze pierced between them toward Raine.

"She isn't yours," Angel said, her tone suited for sweetly explaining to a small child why they couldn't steal another kid's toy.

Anderson's holster gave a leathery click as he drew his black pistol. Stenner's did the same, as much a mirror to Anderson's movements as Stenner himself. They each aimed at Angel.

Raine surged from cruiser to curb. "Wait, wait, don't." Her wrists tugged at the cuffs behind her back. "I'll do anything."

Stenner crashed a hard elbow into Raine's sternum, knocking her against the cruiser. He aimed for Angel, the pistol trembling in his hands.

"Drop the weapon," Anderson said, almost growling.

"Drop it!" Stenner shouted, and his echo shot down the street. "Hands in the air!"

Angel remained a statue, the sword clutched against her lap. Coils of pale hair tumbled from her shoulder as she glanced back and forth.

"Don't hurt her!" Raine cried. "She doesn't know what's going on all the time, she's special, she's, she's—" The words she needed were strangers; she couldn't call them for help.

Anderson and Stenner couldn't hear, or didn't want to. Their faces squeezed tense, blood pounding too loudly in their ears to catch Raine's pleas as they watched the sunlight sword.

"You can't take her," Angel said, her tone forever soft. "She is my pain."

"We'll be your fucking pain in a second if you don't drop the weapon," Anderson snapped. "Now."

"Right now!" Stenner shouted, arms shaking.

Angel's black eyes drank the night. "You'll be my pain?" she asked, perplexed and awed. She eyed her sword, motionless beneath her waist, and then glanced from Raine to Anderson and Stenner. "So you are."

One bare foot slid from the sidewalk as Angel's leg stretched from her robe. The sword tilted across her body, flashing the cruiser's lights across its blade.

Muzzle flares cast fresh halos around Anderson's and Stenner's heads as gunshots exploded in Raine's ears. She had never stood this close to firing pistols, and she crouched down and hunched her shoulders around her ears too late to block out the first rounds. Her panicked shrieking joined the second rounds. The third rounds. Both cops poured bullets across concrete.

Angel became a statue again. Her eyes narrowed, almost in pleasure.

Wet hot drops sprayed Raine's face as red ringlets burst from Anderson's chest. Another storm struck her skin when Stenner mirrored the bloody eruption, and crimson geysers burst from both their necks. Anderson jostled backward, and his head whipped sideways against the police cruiser, flashing a dark chasm where something quick and hard had driven through his left eye. Stenner twisted in place, his guts opening in a bright fountain. His blood-flecked shades sprang from his chest, and the dark lenses shattered over the pavement in a tinkling glass hailstorm.

Both men fell to the ground. Anderson's leg quivered, but for once Stenner didn't take his lead, lying still between the sidewalk and the street.

Angel drifted partway behind Raine. Her arms jerked as the sword snapped the cuffs, and she could at last hide her face in her hands again. She'd never seen dead bodies, didn't want to. She would see darkness instead and hope no cops grew here to haunt her.

Tender fingers gripped Raine's wrist and guided her hand down. The freed eye fluttered open on Angel's bright sweetness.

"Open both eyes." Angel drew down Raine's other hand. "I want you to see."

"What?" Raine whispered, her voice frail after all the screaming. "See what?"

"Beyond the broken rainbow," Angel said. "A change in universal flavor."

She closed her fingers beneath Raine's jaw and guided her sight between dead Anderson and dead Stenner. Their growing blood puddles slid toward the gutter as if filling the street's trough. Neither cop would hunt Raine again.

Angel kissed the blood from Raine's cheeks, and her nose, and then her chin and brow and eyelids. Her dark tongue licked up the metallic taste, and maybe inside someone unique like her, she could make its flavor sweet.

"We should run," Raine whispered. "There'll be more of them, bad as these."

"As these?" Angel glanced down her sword as if asking it questions and then eased onto the curb, her feet planted in the pooling blood. "Then I will wait for those who commit murder to flesh."

"Angel—"

"You may go," Angel said. "You have led me to new pain, and a chance for the broken rainbow. My thanks for letting me gather you."

Raine flinched back. Tension slid from her skin; she'd been released from her burden as Angel's pain when so much more pain would soon arrive. Wasn't this easier? Couldn't she almost hear the coming sirens? Best to walk away, run if she could, let the night take her in and spit her out on some undiscovered future. Wasn't she used to that yet?

Raine clenched her teeth and dug her heels against the sidewalk. This wasn't fair. She deserved better than a world eager to spit her out. She deserved to be gathered if she wanted. Yes, she could run.

But a mirror couldn't act alone. One needed somebody to reflect.

Raine could return to Angel's side and sit with her on the cold damp concrete. She could be that reflection. They could squeeze close, tuck their heads together, and watch past the sword's end for a roar of sirens and flashing lights to fill the far intersection. The cacophony would pound in Raine's ears, but she'd endure, and she wouldn't leave Angel's side. They would wait, sword ready. Maybe with enough pain, those lights could shatter like in Angel's poem and bring a murder in flesh—a death in many colors.

And maybe a change in flavor, this time the universe flowing sweet as an angel's kiss. All these things could happen, or none of them. For once, there was a choice.

Raine only had to make it.

plague daughter

. . .

S. H. Cooper

DARLING MOTHER AND FATHER,

You must think this laughable, reading a letter written and received from only the floor above your heads. Even while writing this, I can see your expressions. Mother sighing softly with a shake of her head, Father's chin creasing into two as he suppresses a smile, both wondering what their daft girl is up to now. And I am such a daft girl, aren't I? Why write this instead of simply descending the stairs to speak with you in person?

To be honest with you, my dearest parents, as I have always tried to be, there is nothing simple about what I must now tell you.

Often you have proclaimed your pride in me, and I have made no secret that it is that very thing I hold most dear to my heart. Your approval has always been more precious to me than all the gold in all the world. You can imagine, then, how I must ache in this moment, knowing what I know, and what you are soon to know.

I beg of you, do not think less of me. Or if you must, and I believe *you* will believe you must, do not make it known, for it would wound me in ways from which I might never recover.

I am, as I'm sure you've already concluded, dallying, and again I see you, your expressions shrinking as your concern grows, for how could you be anything but concerned when I have presented myself thusly?

Oh, sweet Mother and Father, do not fret. I implore you, keep reading, and I will lay myself out plainly without further delay.

As difficult as it is to do so, I must ask you to turn your minds to Lottie. How like a daughter she was to you, and a sister to me. My love for her burns brightly still, though its flame pains me now in a way it never had before, undulled by the time that has passed since we first received word from her poor mother. Already we near the first dreadful anniversary. How could it be so long, yet not so long at all? Wipe your eyes, my gentle mother, I do not reference her to renew the hurt in your heart; only because that is where this all began.

With Lottie.

They said it was complications that took her, as take so many. Perhaps I could have tolerated such ambiguity, lived with the vague implications and found a way to carry on, as everyone else seems to have done. After all, the risk is part of womanhood and one she undertook willingly. She knew and accepted every outcome, though I know she would have preferred a different one than that which she got. I would have, too. She would have been a wonderful mother, so like my own. She wanted to be. We all wanted it for her.

But there were complications.

I do not think I was ever meant to know anything beyond that. Certainly it's not the sort of talk I take any pleasure in, nor did I seek it out. It found me by way of Sable, following Lottie's service. I'd sought a moment alone in the garden, attempting to quiet the grief that threatened to overwhelm me, and the girl was there, seated upon a bench beside Mrs. Besmouth's geranium beds. I knew her only in the faintest sense, the youngest sister of Lottie's husband, whom I'd met once at the wedding and heard of more often in passing. Initially I took the circles around her eyes to be the same as mine, the black marks of tears uncounted, but then I noticed the swaddling filling her arms, for there was not much to fill, her being only fourteen years of age and hardly more than a child.

Oh, my good parents, you can only imagine how the sight of that small, wrapped babe stole the air from my lungs. Immediately I loved it as it was part of Lottie, but I was horrified by how I hated it, too. This…complication. Still, I composed myself for Sable's sake and took a seat beside her, offering to hold the infant, for the child looked bone weary. She handed it - him - to me with a grateful exhale that slumped the whole of her. As I gazed down at the babe, noting his eyes were almost the same shade of blue as our Lottie's had been, I heard myself ask for his name.

Bernard, like his father.

It did not strike me as unusual; many a proud father has bestowed his own name upon his son, and truthfully, even in one so young, I did find him to have the look of a Bernard, though if you were to press me, I would be unable to say what, exactly, such a look is.

Again, I fear I am allowing myself to wander from the point at hand. Forgive me, it is easier to dwell on such mundane details than reveal my truth.

We spoke idly, Sable and I, commenting first on little Bernard, then the weather, then nothing memorable at all, until I remarked how exhausted the girl looked.

"Why," I remember Sable saying with some measure of tired contempt, hand flapping at the baby, "it's because of him."

I did try to sympathize, recalling when Madeline brought Ambrose to visit during his first months, and told her of the long nights spent listening to my nephew's cries.

She does not just listen, Sable revealed to me most sourly; she looks after little Bernard day and night as if she, herself, were the boy's mother. When asked where her brother, the baby's father, was in all this, she exclaimed he is too busy to raise his child. It is a woman's duty.

I will never forget what next she said.

"He made the choice, but I'm the one who has to live with it."

As you can imagine, I quickly pressed her for the meaning of such an odd statement. The choice of fatherhood? Surely there was some argument for that, but it was not as if he'd planned for his wife's passing.

But oh, my tenderhearted parents. Oh! What she spoke next. I felt as if I'd never been closer to hearing the Devil's own words.

There were complications. The doctor asked him to choose. By then they knew it was a son, but he was coming out wrong. Stuck. Only one would make it out of that birthing bed.

There were complications.

And he chose.

And Lottie, our Lottie, was lost.

If Sable had taken a knife from beneath her shawl and carved all the love out of my chest, perhaps it would have hurt less than knowing Lottie's life had meant so little to the man she'd sworn herself to.

I know you might disagree. A child's life is priceless; no one, not even me, is arguing that. But what of Lottie's life? What of Sable's? What of baby Bernard's, growing now under the care of a child who already resents him, without his true mother or the attention of his father?

Why didn't the doctor ask Lottie what she wanted? I'm sure she would have chosen her son, but then it would have been *her* choice. It would have softened her death no less, but I could have made peace with *her* decision. Why was her husband allowed to make it for her? Why did he have a say in how they sliced her open while she screamed and bled and died?

How I turned this quandary over in my head. How it still turns.

Perhaps you had heard me in my restless nights, my pacing upon the floor, my descent down the stairs after dark, into dark. Under more usual circumstances, you would have stopped me, I'm certain, for what business does a lone woman have outside her home after sundown? Even on an estate such as ours, where a chance encounter is rare even at the height of day, much less during the depths of night, it is unseemly and raises questions regarding one's morals. Or perhaps you did not hear, did not know. The more I think on it, the more I am sure it must be the latter, for such caring parents as yourselves would have followed after to ensure my wellness and seen me back to bed.

Here is where I see your eyes grow large and round, confounded by where all this is leading. Perhaps it would be best if Mother laid this letter aside here and let Father carry on alone, providing her only the most necessary details to spare her constitution. I know she will not, that even now her attention is dragged down the page, to its backside, following this tale to its sordid end, and again I must apologize, for here is where I prick your heart most completely and press until it breaks in two.

When I say I did not mean it, know it pertains only to the pain I am causing you now.

Everything that came before was dealt with the utmost sincerity.

Lottie walked with me on those moonless nights, when I left our gardens for the woods to sing my lament to the trees. I cannot say what drew me there; only that for each step I took, she was beside me, dressed in her nightclothes, though the white was stained through with red and stuck to her legs, giving the macabre impression of trousers. From whence she came, I do not know. We did not speak. She was cloud gray in skin, eyes dull, her hair hanging 'round her face like a mourning veil. But I did not fear her, grotesque as she had become. As she had been made. To the contrary, I held her hand in mine, trying to squeeze warmth into her frozen digits. None passed.

I spent many nights this way, absconding after you took your leave to bed, walking until she was beside me, taking her hand and trying again in vain to trade some of my life for a little more of hers. I wept as we walked. She made no sound at all.

On the sixth or seventh day, exhausted and so full of grief it poured into every other aspect of my existence, I called upon the vicar, hoping he would possess some wisdom that would allow both myself and Lottie to find rest. I told him what had been done to her, how her life had, in essence, been stolen. He cupped my hands between his and patted them most empathetically, before telling me it was God's will that man oversee woman, especially his own wife, and that Bernard's decision *was* Lottie's decision. It was what she would have wanted.

How do you know, I asked him, for no one had asked her? And he tutted in the way that men who believe they know things tut, advising me to pray and that in praying, I would find the peace I was so clearly after.

I went to him thrice more after with the same queries, and thrice more received the same answer, each delivered more dismissively than the last.

I did pray. I still do, for I do not believe God has abandoned me. He knows my heart. He knows I have done what I have done out of love.

I, who asked Lottie first what she would want that night when we met next.

She did not speak. She did not have to.

In the woods where I had wandered, where my tears salted the earth and my anguish caught like cobwebs in the branches, with Lottie at my side, I found the book. It was a plain thing, looking no more descript than a gentleman's private journal, left lying on a tree stump as if waiting to be found. There are some certainties that cannot be explained, and this moment of discovery, when I was moved with the fierce knowledge this was left for me, was one of them. Nor can I explain how, upon opening the book once I'd returned home, it contained writing in my own hand, though none of it was my doing.

A smarter woman might have been afraid, but as we've already established, my sweetest parents, I am but a daft girl, and instead of fear, I felt curious, and I read, and I did the thing that men fear most.

I learned.

And I became a complication.

I shan't ever forget that Sunday, seated beside you in the pew with our prayer books in hand. It was here I knew that God saw me for all I am and loved me still. He would never have allowed it to happen in His house otherwise.

The vicar in his pulpit, arms raised with the climax of his sermon, so full of righteousness. I had been reading from a very different text only that morning, following its instruction with careful precision, reciting my own righteous words. I think we all noticed the stain before he did. The growing strip of red across his fat belly. He was too distracted by the pain. I watched the color drain from his gospel-flushed cheeks, the way his lips pulled and his teeth gnashed, the dropping of his arms to clutch the rail. His robe bulged, pushed outward by his entrails as they slipped between his parted skin.

Before you think me a most horrible creature, I did not take any enjoyment in the way he fell to his knees and scooped at his innards, trying to replace them in his belly.

Satisfaction, that I cannot deny, but it turned my stomach all the same.

All that blood. His screams, above all others. A tremendous display of suffering.

I can see you looking at each other now, all too aware of the vicar's violent demise, and silently asking yourselves if this can possibly be true. Am I really responsible for his death?

Yes, my beloved parents, I am. And I am not sorry for it.

Why him, you will ask, to which I will say it had to be. To prove this book, with its secrets written as if by me, was real, that the promises it made could be believed, that God Himself would allow my actions, I had to start with His servant most holy, who believed a woman's body, choice, and life belonged to man.

I wonder if his opinion would change, now that a woman made the choice for him?

I can hear you asking each other what this book is that I found, where it came from, who left it. I will further disappoint you by having no answers. I can only say it is mine now, and I have, as you already know, made good use of it.

Bernard came next.

I gave him more a chance than I did the vicar. Not out of any love for him, but for Lottie's son, who is already without one parent. Perhaps, in the time since her service, he had taken more to fatherhood and honoring his wife's memory. I orchestrated our running into one another outside his place of business one afternoon, and he did appear genuine in his delight in seeing me. Without Lottie to bind us, we had not stayed in touch, and he had had some busy months since losing her. Little Bernard was growing well (*where is he now?* I asked, forcing him to admit Sable remains his primary caregiver). He himself had received a promotion, and (this he had the good sense to state with an air of shame), he'd recently begun courting a young woman outside of our mutual circle. I did ask her name, and he gave it from a stumbling tongue, but I have since let it slip from my memory.

I understand life must go on after death. I understand it is not unreasonable that a widower should take a second wife. I understand he is still in his prime years.

Just as I understand Lottie might still be here, in her prime years, had she been given the choice.

I returned to my book. I repeated the words. Performed the steps.

Our meeting allowed me to arrange another, when I arrived at the Besmouth residence under the pretense of visiting with Sable and little Bernard. The girl had almost the same amount of color in her as Lottie in her present state and dragged herself as if her burden was an anchor instead of an infant. I asked after her health, and she gave some half-true answer, claiming she was well, only tired, though her hair was in sore need of a brush and her clothing, an iron. I asked if she had any help with little Bernard and she answered with a vinegar grin. Her mother had already raised her children and simply did not have the energy for another, and her father knew nothing of the business of child rearing. It was, after all, a woman's work. They did not hire a nanny, for they had a complete staff already, and Sable was there already. Bernard was too busy with his job and his new courting companion, though there were some evenings he could be convinced to hold him for a time. The moment he started to become fussy, which was often and for long periods, however, he came straight back to Sable.

I rocked that baby for the next hour while Sable slept right there on the sofa, gazing at his cherubic cheeks and button nose and seeing so much of our Lottie in him that I could forget who his father was.

Mrs. Besmouth discovered us in the drawing room and insisted, as her good breeding demanded, that I stay for supper. Of course I obliged. It was why I had chosen that particular hour to make my appearance.

I sat across from Bernard Besmouth, eating daintily, smiling vacantly, waiting for the right moment. It arrived when his son began to cry from his bassinet and no one except Sable made a move to comfort him.

Unlike the vicar, he did not lose color, but turned the most vibrant shade of purple. It grew from his neck and spread into his cheeks, swollen with desperate puffs of air. Truthfully, I did not know a human being could become so like a plum. Initially, all thought he was choking, and his father slapped him most vigorously upon the back, until Bernard shoved himself from the table and staggered to his feet, pulling his clothing up to his chest. I dare not try to guess what organ was peeking through his bloodied fingers, clasped against his ruptured stomach. His mother screamed and ran to him as he fell, his father shouted for their maid to call upon the doctor. Only I had the presence of mind to shield poor Sable's eyes from the sight of her brother as he writhed upon the ground.

He frothed at the mouth and convulsed in terrible agony. He reached for his mother with one stained hand, staining her as well. As his grip upon his belly loosened, so too did what he'd been holding, and lengths of slimy flesh and horrible, hot odor spilled upon the dining room floor.

The last I saw of him before I was ushered out was his twitching body birthing his slithering insides through a deep slash across his lower abdomen.

Though the Besmouth family has tried to keep the ordeal as free of gruesome detail as possible, I'm sure you've heard questions surrounding his death floating through town. Was it the lamb they'd just eaten? Was he ill? Had he caught it from the vicar?

There is some truth to the last. The vicar was one of the greatest mouthpieces for the role of men in women's lives, spreading a foul disease.

I could have stopped there, I suppose, having repaid Lottie's debt, but these musings of a catching illness brought to mind a new idea.

It's easier than you would think, learning whose smile is a mask for a much crueler soul. Walk through the park, sit in a tearoom, any place where women congregate, and you will hear their tales. Did you know Mr. Thomlinson strikes his wife? Or that Dr. Parker steps out with other women while Mrs. Parker tends to their children? I will not repeat what Mr. Harrington does to his daughters after he loses all sense at the bottom of a bottle.

Which all brings us here, to present day, and you reading this letter written and received from only the floor above your heads. You understand now why I could not share this with you in person, my cher ished parents. I could not bear the expressions of horror I know you're both wearing at this moment, nor the ones you will wear in the next, when I make my final admission.

I have already left. Not out of guilt for what I've done, for I do not feel any except for the pain I have left you in my stead. I take with me only the clothing I can fit into my carpet bag and the book gifted to me in my grief by the woods. Do not look for me. You will not find me. It feels wicked to ask anything more of you, who have given me the kindest life and utmost love, but here I will make my final request: Hold fond memories of me close, and let not these latest actions, or what is still to come, repaint me in your hearts.

These are not the doings of a woman driven by malice or cruelty.

Our town is indeed sick, and I will answer plague with plague.

Forever and always,
    Your daughter

phoenix rising

. . .

R. J. Joseph

PETRA STOOD JUST outside the spa doors for a moment to catch her breath. She had parked her dilapidated car around the far corner of the parking lot so no one inside would see the death trap that was her only transportation. As she caught a whiff of the fuel fumes clinging to her clothes, she realized her clandestine actions had likely been for naught.

Besides, when they saw her, they'd still know she didn't belong at a place that provided luxury services to anyone: she was a mess.

Her hair hung limply in the self-styled twists she had last done a month ago, dull and lifeless—almost as washed out as her dark skin that managed to impossibly look pasty and overly greasy at the same time.

Her clothing was clearly two sizes too large for her, and her shoes were half a size too small. She teetered slightly when she walked, trying to make the best of the situation but making herself drag more than she wanted.

She reached for the door handle with a shaky, dry hand tipped with ragged nails and a black discoloration around her marriage ring finger. Garrett had never been bothered to buy her a wedding ring that didn't make her finger turn colors, even though he insisted she wear the cheap one until the infection gave her a permanent mark and had cost them a doctor's visit that resulted in the destruction of the ring to get it off her enlarged finger.

He even made sure to buy an expensive one for himself after that, rather than purchase a new, better one for her. The point of that escaped her—she knew he rarely wore it, anyway. Yet he continued to harangue her for not wearing a wedding ring. As if anyone would take a look at her or want her when he, himself, didn't.

Petra could become lost in the misery that was her marriage. Getting a chance at a new job or promotion at work was the only thing she had to look forward to, if she ever hoped to build up the resources and courage to leave Garrett. None of that would ever happen if she never walked into the spa to get the simple manicure and pedicure she came for, despite the knowledge she would pay for the small expenditure twice: at the spa and at home afterwards, with her not-so-nice husband who hated for her to spend any money he didn't approve of prior.

She couldn't muster up any fear, anxiety, or any other emotion over Garrett. Petra had exhausted all her tears and hopes in their years together. She only looked forward to leaving the bondage that wasn't even torture anymore.

———

Petra's energy was dedicated to navigating her workplace. She worked in a loan processing center where there were at least four levels of promotions available, each coming with a hefty raise she could sorely use. Families in the middle echelons of Houston society often sent their Texas princess daughters to work at the bank. What they actually did couldn't be called work. They typically stepped into the data entry department with no degrees or other qualifications and typed prettily while entering the bare minimal number of loan applications they could. They maintained well-coiffed hairstyles and impeccable manicures through their light performances.

And their actions were definite performances. These princesses weren't at the center to work. They were there to get a husband who worked in lending and finance. Sure, they often got promoted to the lending department, anyway, without having gained any expertise that qualified them for the entry level lending assistant positions, but the women weren't in lending to work, either.

There was much to be said for the lending department being all men in current times, but the women who started out there didn't last long in the department before leaving for the benefits of marriage. Petra wanted to be the first female lender in the department. But she knew she had to go above and beyond the general job requirements to get promoted. Then she'd have to go through all the steps from data entry to lending assistant to junior lender to full lender. She had no aspirations beyond that. Life as a Black woman in Texas had taught her she'd always need more experience and more education and just had to be...more...to get to minimal progress within the bank.

To that end, Petra ran rings around everyone in the entire department with her work numbers, accuracy, and customer interactions. After she had consistently exceeded the data entry department standards for months, she requested a meeting with the manager of data entry and lending to discuss a new opening as a lending assistant.

"Mr. Harris, thank you for meeting with me." The manager gave her a curt smile and didn't offer the usual correction of, "Please call me Gary," he extended to other visitors from the departments he managed.

"Hello, Petra. How are you today?" He offered a general greeting instead. When she nodded, but before she could answer, he added, "What did you want to discuss today?"

She wasn't there to ingratiate herself to him, so small talk was unnecessary. "I'd like to talk to you about the new lending assistant opening."

Harris tented his hands in front of his face as Petra detailed her performance and resume to him. To his credit, he nodded a couple of times, as if he was really listening to her.

She knew he wasn't really hearing what she said; instead, he was biding his time before addressing her.

"Yes, there is a lending assistant position open now. We're inter-viewing candidates as we speak. But there's a different opportunity I'd like to talk to you about." He then launched into an explanation about how the recent merger with other lending centers required that the data entry department align itself more closely with the same type of managerial structure as the other centers.

"This means we've now created the brand-new position of Quality Control Specialist. The job isn't listed yet and is a pay grade above where you currently are in data entry." He then turned on the brilliant, fake smile that kept him in lending management. "I immediately thought of you for the position."

Petra struggled to refrain from allowing her disappointment to show. She took the position, and the subsequent "brand-new" posi-tions he created after she mastered that first one, because she under-stood the writing on the wall: he controlled access to the upward movement in those two departments and he would never allow her to progress the way she wanted.

Only Texas princesses would get that progress, theirs to discard when it no longer suited them.

Oh, to have that power!

———

The woman who greeted her just inside the heavy double doors of the spa did so as quietly as a whisper on the wind. Petra barely heard the lilting question emanating from behind the medical mask the other woman wore underneath kind, wide eyes.

"Hello. How are you today? How may I help you?"

The woman waited for her to answer, seeming to be genuinely interested in her answers. Even in the presence of such kindness and authenticity, Petra wanted to escape back outside to what she knew: her car, her home, her exhaustion. The beauty of the spa beckoned her to walk deeper into the room, instead.

"I…may I have…" a soft scent encouraged her to continue. "I'd like to have a basic manicure and pedicure. No polish, please." Polish cost extra, and Petra didn't have extra time or money.

The woman smiled and invited Petra into a side room. "I can give you exactly what you need. Here, we help each other."

Petra stood in the doorway of the room and gawked at its opulence. Every metal surface shone with the burnished glimmer of real gold; not the obviously cheap, shiny reflector pieces, gaudy and shouting their faux, temporary value—but the muted, almost understated glimmer of everlasting sumptuousness.

Each client station was enclosed in tall dividers made of a shimmery fabric that begged Petra to touch it, if she dared. A peek inside one station revealed a large seat, covered in the same material as the dividers, and a well-stocked bar. Petra couldn't identify the fragrance suffusing the large room, but it calmed her and made her feel she could relax fully in the space.

The woman led her to a station and invited her to put her purse down and remove her shoes. A large bowl at the bottom of the chair held fragrant bubbles Petra could hardly wait to soak her aching feet in. She sat and hesitated before removing her shoes. The cheap material made her feet sweat something awful and before that moment, she hadn't thought about the logistics of removing the shoes and unleashing the rancid scent.

"It is fine." The simple words from behind the mask held honesty. Petra obliged and sighed when she submerged her feet in the water.

The chair molded itself to her body and began a gentle warming massage in just the areas where Petra needed attention. The woman reached underneath the bar and retrieved a neck warmer and placed it around Petra's neck.

"Wait a minute," Petra started. "I can only do the basic pedicure and manicure. I...I won't be able to do the extras."

"No worries. You came on the best day, when all our services are buy one, get the rest free."

Petra frowned and considered the offer. It seemed too good to be true. But how would she know if the woman was telling the truth? Honestly, she couldn't. Since she'd not been to such a place before, she didn't know what the pricing was regularly like.

As the other woman pressed a wine glass into her hand, Petra decided that particular worry didn't matter in the least. She would take the good fortune handed to her and she would enjoy every minute of the ride, relishing the experience she'd likely not return for any time soon.

Petra leaned back in the chair and finished her wine. The technician placed a face mask over her eyes. The soft music and massage quickly put her in a light trance. She felt other techs join them, one doing a much-needed facial, another starting her manicure. The person doing her pedicure had magical hands, and worked every ache out of her sore, mistreated feet. Delicate fingers ran through her twists, lightly scratching her scalp and working through the new growth.

She dozed lightly, her senses filled with release and restoration. The incense called to mind visions of light and flowers. Beautiful things. Happy things. For those hours, Petra allowed herself to enjoy that beauty—to pretend she was a part of it.

She awoke in the candlelit room, unsure of how much time had passed. She felt disoriented but better than she had in years. Better than she ever had, really. The door opened.

Petra recognized the kind eyes she had only seen above the medical mask when she first arrived. The woman no longer wore her mask. A brilliant, genuine smile greeted Petra.

"How do you feel now, Petra?"

"I feel good. I feel..." her voice drifted off as she caught a glimpse of herself in a mirror on the wall. "Oh!"

There were no candles. The flickering light Petra had seen came from her body. She gazed at her reflection, running long, sparkling fingernails along the shimmering skin on her face. Her twists danced, rising of their own volition, standing proudly atop her head, inter-twining themselves into a crown.

She stood from the chair, the glimmering light shining brighter as she did. She fingered the elongated fangs protruding from her fuller lips, beneath eyes that sparkled with multiple pupils. She watched, astonished, as tingling in her back produced lush, black wings reaching high towards the raised roof of the spa.

Petra was no taller or bigger than she had been—but she was

somehow *more* than she had been. She turned a questioning gaze to the other woman.

Breathtaking tentacles emerged from the woman. They slithered towards Petra, arranging her feathers and twist coils, caressing her face. She remembered their touch from her services. There had been only one technician, the one who put the finishing touches on her client.

"I feel powerful. How?"

"I can only work with what is there. We help each other here. You are powerful. You are a goddess." The words of affirmation floated through the air from a line of thought into Petra's head. They resounded quietly. Matter of factly.

I am a goddess. The entire room lit up and Petra laughed.

"You don't have to suffer. We have power. We will use it."

Petra fluttered around the spa. "I can see so much."

"You have always seen. Now you can see the entire picture."

"My skin is so sensitive. I can feel the energy around me."

"You have always been perceptive. Now you can manipulate what you feel."

"And I can fly!"

"Your wings are no longer bound."

"My nails and teeth are so sharp. I'm hungry."

The other woman wrapped Petra in her tentacles, a gentle and encouraging hug. "You can fuel your spirit's every desire. Fill yourself. Then, fill yourself again and again."

The woman sent new thoughts into Petra's head. They weren't the only goddesses. Others like them lived and loved and filled their own spirits, dream after dream coming.

So much power!

Petra understood what had brought her to the spa that day. Broken-spirited and downtrodden, she entered as a shell of her true self. She would now emerge, triumphant, to bend her life to her divine will.

A goddess would always be more powerful than a princess—and goddesses didn't need low level jobs or unworthy husbands.

my pretty little psycho

. . .

Elizabeth J. Brown

THE FIRST THING Sienna Moore did when she woke up was scream.

The second was run at the door.

Neither helped.

That was yesterday. Today she sat on the stained mattress, squinting against the shafts of sunlight slanting in from outside. There was nothing else in the locked, dingy white room—nothing but the mattress, the bars on the window, and the woman in the corner.

The woman sat with her knees drawn up to her chest, watching Sienna with dark, unblinking eyes.

Sienna hadn't noticed her at first. She'd been too busy pounding her fists against the door. Too busy screaming until her throat was raw. But now, slumped back down on the mattress in defeat, she saw her. The thought of not being alone should have brought comfort. It didn't. Because no matter what Sienna asked, no matter how much she pleaded, how much she begged, the woman didn't answer. She just watched.

Sienna shook her head and picked at the hole in her tights, worrying at the frayed edges with her ragged fingernails. They were her only pair. She'd bought them especially for the interview.

She clenched her jaw, the pressure behind her teeth pulsing in time with the throb in her head.

All she'd wanted was a job. To prove that she could be a functioning member of society, just like everyone else.

Marla Blackwell. That probably wasn't even the interviewer's real name. Just like "Social Media Assistant" hadn't actually been a real job. It'd been too good to be true. Entry level, perfect for someone fresh out of uni like Sienna. Someone with anxiety issues. Someone who needed to take Olanzapine every night before bed just to keep it together. And the interview had been going so well, too. Low-key, in a cosy little coffee shop—just right for keeping her nerves in check. She and Marla had hit it off straight away. But then, about twenty minutes in, she'd become drowsy, disorientated. Marla had suggested they go outside, get some fresh air.

It must've been the water. That slight salty taste. Sienna had thought it was from the glass, where it had come out of the dishwasher. She hadn't wanted to say anything—hadn't wanted to seem difficult, not during the interview. So she drank it anyway.

Fuck.

With a bellow, she slammed her fist into the mattress.

'Someone's coming.'

Sienna jumped, gaping at the woman in the corner.

The woman stared back, shifting her position so that she was sitting cross-legged, and tilted her head. A slow grin spread across her gaunt face, pulling the greyish skin taut over her sharp cheekbones.

For a moment, Sienna couldn't bring herself to speak.

'W-what did you say?'

The woman pressed a skeletal finger to her cracked lips.

Then Sienna heard the footsteps.

The metallic scrape of a key turning in the lock was followed by the door swinging inward. A man stood in the doorframe, his bulky form blocking sight of what lay beyond.

Sienna leapt to her feet, her face set in a snarl.

'Who the fuck are you? Where am I?'

The man didn't answer. Instead, he ran a hand through his stubble and smirked, stepping into the room as Sienna instinctively took a step back.

Marla appeared behind him, her gaze sweeping the room with apparent disinterest before settling briefly on Sienna. 'Ten minutes.'

The man grunted in response. The door locked behind him.

'Marla! Marla, let me out of here!' Sienna shrieked.

The man ignored her. 'Lie down,' he said, jabbing a finger at the mattress.

'Fuck you! Let me out of here! Marl—'

His hand moved in a blur. A crack of pain exploded across her face, her vision flashing white. Sienna staggered back, pressing a trembling hand to her mouth. It came away bloody.

'Don't make me tell you again, bitch.'

The words barely registered. The sting in her cheek, the coppery tang of blood, the pounding of her heart—none of it mattered. Not when all-consuming fury roared through her.

With a cry, Sienna launched herself at him. She clawed at his face, nails raking deep, then drove her knee up, aiming for his groin. He twisted away with a growl, taking the impact to his thigh.

'Fucking whore!'

Before she could strike again, he drove his fist into her gut.

The blow sent her sprawling, her back hitting the mattress with a muffled *thump*. Pain exploded through her abdomen, a vicious, jagged thing that stole all thought, all movement. She gagged, forcing herself to roll onto her side, every inch a gruelling effort. He was on her before she could get up.

His weight crashed down, crushing the breath from her chest. She tried to scream, but there was no air, no space, just suffocating pressure. Her arms jerked as he seized her wrists with one hand, slamming them above her head with ease. His grip was a vice, fingers biting so hard she thought the bones might snap.

'No! *No!*'

She struggled beneath him, thrashing, kicking, trying to shove him off, but he barely flinched. His free hand fumbled beneath her skirt. She bucked wildly, but his weight pinned her down.

'Help me!' she screamed, whipping her head toward the woman in the corner. '*Help* me!'

The man's gaze followed hers. His brow furrowed. The woman didn't move, didn't so much as lift a finger.

Fabric tore. The sharp rip of tights splitting at the gusset.

Cold air. Bare skin.

Sienna's pulse roared in her ears. Her mind refused to process what was happening. It *couldn't*.

She shrieked again.

Still, the woman said nothing. Just stared back, her expression empty.

For a moment, his hand disappeared. A fleeting, terrible hope surged—maybe he'd stop. Maybe—

A sharp yank. Her underwear wrenched aside.

Then pain.

White-hot, blinding, *ripping* pain as he forced himself inside of her.

Sienna screamed.

The sound was raw, guttural, bursting from her lungs in a wretched wail. He grunted, his body shoving against hers, harder, faster, each thrust sending fresh agony lancing through her core.

Her cries cracked into strangled sobs. She turned her face away, throat tight, chest heaving—there was no escape, nowhere to go, nothing she could do.

The woman in the corner watched her.

She didn't move. Didn't speak.

Just watched.

Watched while the man rutted on top of her.

When he was done, he clambered off her without a word and left the room.

After a long while, Sienna sat up, slowly. Minutes. Hours. She couldn't tell. She wiped between her legs, the motion numb and mechanical, then dragged her hand across the mattress, smearing every last trace of what had happened along its surface.

'Why didn't you help me?' her voice broke.

'Wouldn't have made a difference.' The woman blinked, then ran her palm across the track marks scarring her arm. She picked at a scab in the crook of her elbow. 'You should try and pee. Don't wanna get a UTI in a place like this.'

Sienna turned her head slightly. The bucket in the corner sat untouched, its foul stench tainting the air, thick and putrid. She closed her eyes and curled into herself. The ache wasn't just in her body. It was deeper. Everywhere.

Were her parents worried? Were they looking for her? Would they be lying awake tonight, wondering where she was?

She hated this—this helplessness, this brokenness. She hated the woman in the corner. Hated the man who'd defiled her. But most of all, she hated Marla Blackwell. Hated her for lying to her. For manipulating her. For dragging her into this hell like she meant nothing. Like she wasn't even a person.

Biting down on the inside of her cheek, Sienna let the rage simmer within her. Let it warm her. Let it burn away the pain, the desperation.

The hours dragged on, the bleeding sky surrendering to darkness. She drifted in and out of sleep, but her anger remained—a steady pulse beating against her ribs—even when her body couldn't quite hold on to the fight.

She woke with a jolt.

Her stomach cramped—a gnawing, hollow mix of nausea and hunger. She wasn't sure whether she was starving or about to vomit. Her mouth was dry, her tongue thick like cotton. She hadn't eaten or drunk anything since yesterday, and dehydration scraped her throat, rough as sandpaper.

A shadow skittered across the moonlit wall just in front of her face, accompanied by the faintest whisper of scuttling.

Sienna jerked back.

A beetle? No. Too fast. Too erratic. A spider.

She pushed herself up. Another scurried past. Then another darted from beneath the blistered paint, its legs twitching, its body bloated.

Her heart lurched. She scrambled back, kicking herself away from the mattress, landing hard on the floorboards.

More legs. More bodies. More spiders.

Thousands more.

They cascaded from the ceiling in a tide of black, the mass shifting and swelling, their spindly legs scratching against one another as they poured down the walls.

Sienna's breath hitched. She clawed backward—

The spiders surged toward her, swallowing her whole.

A scream clawed its way up her throat. She batted at them, raking at her own skin, but they poured into her mouth, their tiny legs scrabbling against her teeth as they forced their way down her throat.

Thick. Writhing. Choking.

They were everywhere. Skittering over her arms. Burrowing into her ears. Crawling beneath her eyelids.

She gagged. Gasped. No air.

They pushed deeper—into every orifice, working their way under her skin. Her lungs burnt. Her chest spasmed.

Dying. She was dying.

The world tilted. Her body went slack. The pressure inside her skull built, unbearable, like her head was about to split apart.

Then—

Nothing.

The weight lifted.

No movement. No sound. No spiders.

Just silence.

Sienna lay on the floor, chest heaving. Her quivering hands rose to her face, feeling the raw sting where her nails had torn into her flesh.

A broken whimper escaped her lips.

She sobbed.

The woman in the corner regarded her with interest, head tilted, her expression caught between curiosity and amusement. 'What the hell was *that*?'

Sienna didn't answer. Her breath rasped through her sweat-slicked body as she fought to pull herself back together. Piece by broken piece.

Finally, she swallowed and muttered, 'I need my pills.'

The woman snorted. 'Pills? They give you heroin here. Stops you fighting back. Makes you need it. Need them.'

Sienna eyed her warily. 'Not that. My medication.'

'Why? What's wrong with you?'

With a groan, Sienna pushed onto her hands and knees and crawled back to the mattress. It reeked. But the floor was worse – grime caked deep into the boards, sticky with filth. At least the mattress was soft. Sort of.

'I've got schizoaffective disorder,' she said. 'And... some personality stuff.'

The woman let out a slow, exaggerated whistle, circling her finger next to her temple. 'So, you're crazy.'

Sienna flinched.

'Trust me to get stuck with the nut job.'

'I'm not.' She took a breath, lowering her voice. 'I'm not crazy. I just... I hallucinate. And sometimes, if I stop taking my meds, I can get... aggressive.'

The woman's interest sharpened. 'That's what that was? A hallucination?'

Sienna nodded.

'Jeez. I mean, it looked pretty rough. What did you see?'

'Spiders.' She pulled her knees into her chest, shivering against the chill.

'So, what, you've spent your whole life seeing spiders?'

'No. Sometimes. It's not always the same.' Sienna rubbed at her forehead and winced, her fingers coming away slick with thin streaks of blood. She frowned at them, absently smearing the red across her palm. 'It started when I was little. I had an imaginary friend—'

The woman scoffed. 'We all had imaginary friends.'

'Mine told me to do things.' Sienna's voice dropped, throat tightening. 'Dangerous things. Violent things.'

The woman didn't reply.

'My parents thought it was a phase. I saw... a lot of specialists. Doctors, psychologists, therapists. Nothing helped. Not until I was a teenager and they put me on Olanzapine.'

'And then?'

'Then she went away.'

A pause.

'She?'

Sienna exhaled slowly. 'My imaginary friend. Matilda. Like in the Roald Dahl books.'

'Right.' The woman said nothing more, seemingly losing interest. In the pale streaks of light, she almost looked less gaunt—the silver sheen softening the shadows under her eyes, filling out the hollows of her cheeks.

Sienna stared at her for a while, listening to the rhythmic sigh as the woman breathed through her mouth. She was in constant motion, twitching and fidgeting like a coiled spring on the verge of snapping. Her fingers picked and scratched at her skin in repetitive, almost frantic motions.

It was annoying.

The woman's head snapped up, gaze locking onto Sienna's. 'And what would Matilda tell you to do now?'

Sienna took a moment, her eyes narrowing. Familiar heat detonated in her chest—the anger she'd been stoking roared up like an inferno, blistering through her core.

'She'd tell me to hurt that bitch Marla. Make her beg. Make her scream.'

The woman's eyes blazed, her lips pulling up in a grin. 'Best you get started then.'

Sienna smiled back.

But how? They were trapped, and the room was devoid of anything useful. No makeshift tools, no sharp edges, not even a lightbulb. Just a rank old mattress and a bucket of piss. Nothing to work with. Nothing to do any kind of damage to the door whatsoever.

She prodded the mattress. Springs. Maybe if she could tear it open, she could pull one out and use it to pick the lock on the door. She dug her fingers into the fabric, scraping her nails against its rough surface, but they only snagged uselessly. With a growl, she yanked at the seams. The material held firm.

Gritting her teeth, she pulled harder, frustration fuelling her strength. Her palms were slick with sweat, fingertips raw, but the mattress remained unyielding. The springs stayed hidden, out of reach.

'Fuck!'

Surging to her feet, she grabbed the mattress and threw it across the room with all her might. It landed a couple of feet away, dust and dirt spiralling in puffs around it. The impact was agonisingly pathetic, her unsatisfied need for destruction igniting something deeper in her—a fury so visceral that her body quivered with the force of it.

Her eyes snapped to the door.

She launched herself at it. All of her weight, all of her rage, slamming into the wood. The rebound sent her stumbling back, nearly knocking her off balance, but she drove forward again.

A feral howl ripped from her throat as she gripped the handle, twisting it violently. Her muscles strained as she pulled, fingers burning as she yanked, anything to make it open. She felt the handle give way, the metal screeching as it tore from its fixture.

She stepped back, breath ragged, heart pounding, eyes wide. She was still clutching the handle, but the door remained locked, mockingly intact.

Even so, she smiled. Because glinting in the wan light were four, very sharp-looking screws.

'Not much of a weapon,' the woman said. She was standing now, hopping from foot to foot like she was caught in some delusional game of hopscotch. She leaned forward, craning her neck to look at them. 'Hardly gonna do much damage.'

Sienna scowled back at her. She was right, though. What *could* she do with them? Gouge them into Marla's eyes, maybe? The thought sent a giddy thrill racing through her.

But that wasn't her biggest problem. She was still trapped. And if she stayed here much longer, she'd be too weak to fight back—even if an opportunity came. *No.* She had to make someone come to her. Make them open the door.

The woman moved closer, staying just out of reach. For a moment, her face rippled, skin melting like wax, sliding down her cheeks.

Sienna blinked rapidly. The room snapped back into focus. Everything was as it had been.

I really need my meds.

'What you gonna do?' the woman asked.

Sienna licked her lips, her gaze darting around in the near-darkness before landing on the bucket. A slow grin tugged at her mouth.

'I'm going to teach those cunts a lesson.'

The woman giggled, swiping at her hair with a quick, jerky motion.

Pulling the screws free, Sienna discarded the rest of the handle and set them carefully on the edge of the mattress. Then, she grabbed the bucket and flung its contents across the floor in front of the door. Cold urine splashed up her legs, the ammonia stench hitting the back of her throat. Dropping the bucket, she snatched up the screws, pressed two into her right palm, the tips protruding between her fingers, and curled her hand into a fist. She did the same with her left. It wasn't much, but it would have to do.

Time to spill some blood.

Sienna started screaming, stamping her feet against the floor like a woman possessed.

The door burst inward.

He stood there, silhouetted against the blazing artificial light from the hallway, chest rising and falling. She recognised that shape, the way he held himself. *Him.* The fucker who'd pinned her down. Who'd ignored her screams. Who'd violated her.

She could see the glint of his teeth as a feral grin split his face. Wider and wider, until it ripped from ear to ear, his jaw yawning open to reveal a long, oozing black tongue that lashed out at her.

No. Focus.

She blinked hard, fingers tightening around the screws. The metal dug into her palms, grounding her.

He stepped inside, boots splashing in the puddle of piss. His face twisted in disgust—like *he* had any fucking right to be disgusted.

Sienna lunged.

She smashed her right fist into his face, electric pain jolting up her arm. The screws tore free of her grip, embedding deep in his cheek. He howled, staggering back, pawing at his face.

She swung again—left fist this time. He flinched, stumbling, boots skidding in the slick mess. His arms flailed, grasping at empty air.

She launched herself at him, slamming into him with everything she had.

He went down hard. His head cracked against the doorframe with a sickening crunch.

His body twitched. *Still alive.*

Sienna stood over him, breath sawing in and out of her lungs. Her vision hazy.

'You should probably kill him,' the woman said. 'Otherwise, he's going to be proper fucked off when he wakes up.'

'Help me move him.'

'No.' She shrugged in response to Sienna's glare. 'Too weak to help.' Then, with a sudden spin, she twirled in a quick, dizzying motion. 'And too pretty.'

With a growl, Sienna grabbed the man's legs, and dragged him further into the room. Her muscles burnt, arms trembling from the strain, but she held on, heaving until his head was flush against the doorframe.

The man gasped, his eyes flickering open. His fingers twitched, reaching for her.

No you fucking don't!

Adrenaline tore through her like wildfire.

She grabbed the door with both hands and slammed it into his skull.

Again.

And again.

And again.

The wood shuddered. But she didn't stop. Not until it was cracked and splintered. Not until her arms shook. Not until his head was pulp and his blood ran slick into the piss-streaked floor.

Chest heaving, pulse pounding, she released the door. It swung loose, creaking on its hinges.

She looked down at what was left of him, her lip curling. Then, with a sharp sniff, she spat—a thick glob of saliva—right into the ruin of his face.

She turned to the woman in the corner and smirked. 'Well? You coming?'

'Does a bear shit in the woods?' She flashed a grin and followed as Sienna stepped over the corpse, vanishing into the darkened hallway.

The building was a maze of locked doors. Grunts, screams and pitiful whimpers stalked them as they crept across the warped floorboards. Every squeak and groan sent a jolt of fear lancing through Sienna's chest.

Just how many women were trapped here? Had they all been snatched, just like she had? Their promises of a better tomorrow ripped away by that bitch Marla?

Neither one of them spoke, not until they reached a kitchenette.

'Water!' Sienna rushed to the sink, fumbling with the tap until it spluttered on. She thrust her face under the stream, gulping down greedy mouthfuls. When the ache in her throat finally eased, she switched it off.

'Look, knives,' the woman said, her voice high-pitched with excitement as she clapped her hands together like a child in a toy shop.

Somehow, under the harsh fluorescent light, she looked healthier than before—her skin less grey, her eyes less sunken. Even the bruises and crusted scabs on her arms seemed to have faded. It made her look younger.

A knife block sat beside a collection of chopping boards, a kettle, and caddies for tea, coffee, and sugar. The sight of it, so ordinary, so domestic, felt almost obscene after the bare, squalid room they'd been trapped in minutes before. Sienna reached for the biggest knife, fingers closing around it. The whisper of steel made her smile as she pulled it free.

'The fuck? How'd you get out?'

Sienna's heart leapt into her throat. The knife slipped from her grasp, clattering against the counter as she spun toward the voice.

A man was staring at her, his shock twisting into something sharper —something predatory.

Two things happened at once: the man lunged for Sienna, and Sienna for the knife.

He seized her by her shoulders, yanking her around to face him.

'Look, you little—' His words cut off when Sienna rammed the blade into his gut, driving it up and in.

They stared at each other, wide-eyed and breathless, before the man let out a ragged, wheezing gasp. His back hit the fridge, legs buckling, blood pooling across his t-shirt.

Mouth gaping open and closed, he pressed a hand against the wound, fingers tracing the handle as if unsure whether to leave it in or pull it out.

'Go on, put him out of his misery,' the woman said. She hardly glanced at the man before practically skipping to the knife block, a hum slipping from her lips as she pointed. 'This one. Use this one.'

Sienna shook her head. 'I just want to get out of here. To go home.'

'You know he's one of them, right? The ones who take girls like you. Who find the men willing to pay—to be locked in a room with them. Ten minutes of sordid pleasure.' She licked her lips, the tip of her tongue flicking out. 'Or ten minutes of hell. But then... you already know about that.'

Heat flared through Sienna's body. She glared down at the man, her fists clenching as she relived the searing pain that had burned between her legs during her assault.

She reached for the knife the woman had pointed at. Just as her fingers met the handle, the steel writhed, twisting away from her grip. A fanged head emerged, jaws unlocking with a hiss as it reared back, poised to strike.

Sienna yelped, snatching her hand away just as the creature snapped at the empty space where her fingers had been. It swayed in place, its silver body undulating, glinting in the harsh light.

'I *need* my meds.' She squeezed her eyes shut, pressing her knuckles into her temples.

When she opened them again, the knife was just a knife.

It wasn't worth it. If she didn't find her medication, didn't escape before it was too late, there'd be no telling what was real and what wasn't.

Making up her mind, she turned to leave. And that's when she came face to face with Marla Blackwell. How long the woman had been standing there, she'd no clue. But as Marla's startled gaze flicked from the man muttering incoherently on the floor to Sienna, it didn't make a difference.

Marla's eyes widened. She bolted.

Sienna lunged, fingers knotting in the interviewer's hair, yanking her back with enough force to send them both crashing to the floor. Marla shrieked, thrashing beneath her, nails scraping at Sienna's arms as she fought to break free. Sienna tightened her grip, shifting her weight to wrap an arm around Marla's throat. But before she could lock in the chokehold, Marla's elbow rammed back into her face.

Pain erupted through Sienna's skull, stars bursting across her eyes. Blood poured freely from her nose, filling her mouth. She gagged, coughing a mouthful of crimson across the tiles. Marla took advantage of the moment, clambering to her feet.

Not a fucking chance.

Sienna snarled, diving to grab Marla's ankle. She yanked hard. Marla pitched forward. She hit the floor, her wrist bending at an ugly angle beneath her weight. A scream tore from her throat. Sienna was already moving, crawling toward her. If she could just keep a hold of that smug, lying cunt, she'd smash her face into the tiles until there was nothing left but mush.

The heel of Marla's ankle boot slammed into her ribs, knocking the breath from her lungs. Sienna reeled backward, her side flaring with sharp agony. Her shoulder hit the cupboards, wood cracking under the impact, splitting at the hinge.

Marla groaned, cradling her wrist as she struggled onto her knees. She was slower now, weaker.

Good.

Sienna's eyes flicked to the damaged cupboard. Something gleamed in the darkness beyond the broken wood. She shoved her hand inside, fingers closing around cold metal. A pan. Heavy-bottomed, cast iron.

With a guttural scream, she hurled it.

The pan slammed into the back of Marla's head with a deeply satis-fying *clang*. Marla crumpled, her body hitting the tiles.

Out cold. But definitely not dead. *Yet.*

Chest heaving, Sienna sat back, wiping the blood from her own face with a trembling hand. Her nose still throbbed, radiating through her skull. She gritted her teeth and reached up, fingers pressing against the broken cartilage.

She took a deep breath and snapped it back into place.

Agony exploded behind her eyes. A bellow ripped from her throat. Nausea rolled through her gut. She let the pain settle, let the fury boil over it.

This was Marla's fault. Every last bit of it.

'That looked like it hurt.' The woman crouched down in front of her, smiling that infuriating smile.

'You know,' Sienna hissed, 'you *could* help.'

'I am helping.'

'How, exactly?'

The woman's smile widened as she bounced up and down on the balls of her feet. 'Moral support.'

Sienna grunted, pushing herself up. Every movement sent fresh aches through her body. Clutching her ribs, she shuffled to the counter and flicked on the kettle.

'Hardly seems time for a cuppa.'

Ignoring her, Sienna reached for the same knife as before, pulling the serrated blade free from the block. Grasping it tightly, she knelt in front of Marla and yanked her head up.

Marla let out a groan, her eyelids fluttering open.

Sienna bent close, lips brushing Marla's ear. 'Where's my stuff? My bag? My pills?'

Another groan.

She wrenched Marla's head back further, forcing a strangled noise from her. 'I said, where's my stuff, bitch?'

The glassy-eyed daze gave way to fear. Marla started struggling, weak and useless. Sienna pressed the jagged blade to her throat, and she stilled, eyes bulging, spit bubbling on her lips as she huffed out a pathetic sob.

Sienna exhaled sharply, biting down the frustration before it could explode. Instead, she moved the knife to Marla's cheek and pressed down. The notched steel snagged at her skin, pulling and tearing as it carved her face into a bloody mess.

Marla shrieked. Tried to twist away. But Sienna still had her by the hair, and with her wrist shattered, escape was impossible.

'Downstairs!' she spluttered. 'The room just inside the front door.'

The kettle clicked off.

Sienna stood, tossing the bloody knife onto the countertop with a dull *clink*. Her fingers closed around the kettle's handle, its plastic still warm from the heat inside.

Marla sobbed, clutching her cheek.

Sienna tilted the kettle forward.

Scalding water cascaded over Marla's head.

The reaction was instant. A howl—raw, animalistic—tore from her lungs as steam billowed in thick tendrils. Her body convulsed violently. Her hands clawed at her face in blind panic, ripping at the burning flesh as skin peeled away in grotesque ribbons that revealed the quivering tissue beneath.

The stench of cooked meat filled the air.

Boiling water streamed down her scalp, across her neck, her collarbone, searing deep, angry welts that blistered and burst with each shudder. She kicked weakly, gagging on her own screams, but the damage was done. Her face was unrecognisable—distorted, swollen, a pink, sludgy mess.

Sienna's lips parted slightly as Marla gave one last, jerking spasm before unconsciousness claimed her.

She considered picking the knife back up. Dragging it across Marla's throat. Watching her life drain away.

But no.

A slow, cruel smile curled her lips.

Living would be worse.

Marla would wake up to a nightmare that never ended. A face she couldn't escape. The horror, the self-loathing, the revulsion—every time she saw her reflection, it would be waiting for her.

Sienna snorted and turned away. The woman followed.

It took longer than she would have liked to find the room. The pain slowed her, pulsing through every bruise, every cut.

The woman skipped beside her, looking less like a junkie and more like a child with every passing moment. Sienna shared none of her energy. Only the simmering furnace of rage kept her moving.

When she finally shoved open the door, she stumbled to a stop.

Bags.

Dozens of them. Stuffed into corners, piled against walls, slumped in heaps on the floor. Different shapes, different colours—but all worn, all telling the same story of broken innocence and stolen lives.

She stepped inside, fingers trailing over cracked leather, torn fabric. A handbag with a charger still tangled inside. A suitcase, the tag still attached from its last journey. A little rucksack with a unicorn keyring dangling from the zip.

Sienna swallowed hard.

The woman nudged past her, tipping out a handbag and rifling through its contents. 'This is fun. Like a lucky dip.'

Sienna ignored her, scanning the room until—there.

Her bag.

Crushed beneath the pile. She hauled it free, unzipping it with shaking fingers. It had been rummaged through, her purse empty, but her things were still there.

Her heart gave a painful *thud* when she found the Olanzapine.

She wrenched the bottle open. The little tablets clattered inside. One swallow away from quieting everything. From numbing the rage, the noise, the hallucinations—

She lifted a pill to her lips. Just one swallow, and she could leave. Escape this shithole. Go back home.

A muted scream drifted through the building.

High. Panicked. Young.

Sienna froze.

'You know what happens next.' The woman was watching her. The sores on her skin were gone. Her hollow cheeks filled out. Her eyes— wide, bright, alive.

She looked sixteen.

The age Sienna had first started taking her meds.

The scream came again, louder this time, slicing through the walls and into her very being. It awakened something inside her. Something primal, something dark, something that bayed for blood.

She launched the pills across the room.

The woman grinned wide. 'There you are. I've missed you... missed the fun we used to have, my pretty little psycho.'

Sienna exhaled. Her chest ached. Her vision blurred. But for the first time in years, she felt awake.

'I've missed you too, Matilda.'

Then she snatched up the heaviest thing she could find—a rusted padlock still attached to a length of chain—and stalked toward the sounds of the screams.

This wasn't over.

to love and obey

. . .

Sarah Jules

CARMILLA WAS RUNNING out of time. If she listened carefully, she could hear the incessant ticking clock of her ovaries, a stark reminder that she was failing. Failing at the one thing women were 'supposed' to do. A woman who wasn't a mother was worthless. And, to guarantee the cleanliness of the future of humankind, women were forbidden to reproduce after they turned thirty-five. It was well-known that after the age of thirty-five, a woman's eggs became scrambled and any offspring 'spoiled'. Low IQ, developmental delays, and a whole host of physical disabilities and difficulties would mar the population, if *old* women were allowed to reproduce. Politicians were starting to reintegrate the word 'retardation' regarding children who didn't fit into the 'Universal Standards of Health', as outlined in the hundred-page document advocated by the current government.

It was a woman's job to further the development of society. To produce offspring before the age of thirty-five, and to provide a stable household (both in terms of a decent income and a marriage certificate) in which said offspring would be raised. It was a man's job to raise the next generation. A stronger, superior generation.

Carmilla had two years to birth a child. Two years. Two years until the white van picked her up for failing to contribute to society. Irrespective of the business she'd built. The charities she'd supported. The taxes she'd paid.

Carmilla had it all.

A dream job: big-time CEO of an all-natural make-up brand. A dream house: a Tudor-style mansion with plenty of land for animals. A good group of friends who stuck by her through each failed relationship. Though those friendships wouldn't last into her impending incarceration at one of the nation's Spinster Camps. No friendship could ever survive that.

It wasn't like Carmilla hadn't tried. She'd dated countless men, many of whom appeared perfect on paper. Inevitably, though, the relationship would crumble when their true views came to light. They'd pretend they were okay with the life of a submissive husband, the kind of husband all good, powerful women wanted. Then, the perfectly curated mask would slip, and the relationship would perish.

Societal standards were such that the woman would head the household. It was the way things had always been. The wife would provide, both births and finances. The husband would keep the house and take care of the children. Men were *natural* caretakers. Women were *natural* leaders. It was the *natural* order of things. Why else would women have evolved to bring life into the world? Only something close to mythical, god-like, could germinate a new being from within their body. It was a task reserved for the holiest of holy beings. Unless they didn't become mothers.

Then they were worth nothing but the product of their forced labour at the Spinster Camps.

And Carmilla only had two years to fulfil her duty.

Having a baby outside of the sanctity of marriage was worse than not bothering at all. She'd always thought she had time. Time to build wealth, a career, a life, before she fulfilled the government-sanctioned role of bearing a child. Despite a woman's superior place in society, her worth vanished should she fail to marry and produce children. Anything that had come before, everything she'd worked so hard to accumulate (ready for her future family) would be stripped from her and handed over to the state.

And so, she put out the advert.

A desperate attempt to find somebody who lived up to the standards she needed from a husband and the father of her future children. As far as she could tell, she had a couple of months to find the perfect trophy husband before she resorted to settling for any man willing to marry and impregnate her.

The advert was placed in an online magazine for single people. She ignored her instinct to do so anonymously. While she was a 'public figure', it wasn't like she was an A-list celebrity. Some people would recognise her, of course, but the vast majority wouldn't.

———

Wealthy, accomplished woman seeking traditional husband.
Must meet the following criteria:
Aged 25-40.
6ft – 6ft 5in.
Fit and healthy.
No children.
No ex-wives.
MUST be traditional home-making husband.
Eager to obey and be submissive to wife in all things.
Eager to marry within the next 6 months. And have children within the next 18 months.

-

Ad placed by:
Carmilla Marianna Lynch.
33 years old. 5ft 6 inch. Athletic. Fit and healthy.
CEO of a billion-dollar company.
Forbes 30 under 30; and 40 under 40.

Carmilla had five applicants. Only five. She stared at their profiles. Their smiling faces. The mirror-selfies (*immediate no*). The fishing photos (*also an immediate no*). It left Carmilla with one candidate.

Julian Anderson III.

Born into a socialite family.

6ft 2 (*and a half*).

Six pack abs.

College educated (*men's studies*) and then worked for mummy's business.

His photos showed him with dogs. A good sign.

With children (*nieces and nephews*). A good sign.

Blonde hair perfectly coiffed.

T-shirt perfectly pressed.

Erratic butterflies exploded inside Carmilla's stomach. *This* was her future husband.

———

The first date went well. As did the second, and the third. Julian was the right amount of coy, flirty, bubbly. He wore a tight shirt that accentuated his chest. Tight jeans that hugged his body in all the right places. He wasn't the sharpest knife in the draw, but that was perfect. A husband didn't need to have an award-winning IQ, he just needed to do as he was told, and *want to*. The *want* was key. You couldn't force that. You couldn't catalyse that. It had to be there: the desire to please. He also had to look like Julian did. A modern-day Ken doll.

On the fourth date, he allowed Carmilla to defile him. She took him back to her mansion, led him to the bedroom, and had him kneel before her. Julian acquiesced, willingly and enthusiastically bringing her to orgasm.

On the fifth date, they didn't leave the bedroom. *That* was where Carmilla could work her magic, where she could teach him exactly what was expected of him. She was in charge. His job was to serve, and serve he did.

On the sixth date, Julian proposed.

They married on their tenth date. Carmilla had tested him at every possible juncture, forcing him into situations that should show any signs of potential dissent. He scrubbed the toilet with a toothbrush wearing only his skimpy underwear, while Carmilla sat back and admired the view. She forbade him from talking to female friends, and he agreed without hesitation. She asked for the passcode to his phone; he didn't flinch before he told her. The password was the anniversary of their first date.

And when Julian promised to love and obey, at the altar in front of friends and family, Carmilla felt the ticking of her biological clock quieten.

———

The baby did not come.

Months of *trying* (*which simply equated to scheduled sex, and that wasn't difficult when you were married to somebody who looked like Julian did*) led to a barren nothingness. The ticking clock crescendoed. Carmilla saw babies everywhere. Each chubby-cheeked smile caused rage to flush through her body with red-hot intensity. Julian spent nights crying in bed. He longed to be a father. It was all he'd ever wanted. In his despair, he started eating. Not just eating: *binge eating.* Ice cream. Family-sized chocolate bars. Anything he could get his hands on. It was disgusting. His abs began to vanish beneath a layer of fat. His once-perfect skin broke out in raised red lumps. When Carmilla pointed it out, rather sensitively, she thought, he ran from the room in floods of tears and drank an entire bottle of blood-red merlot to himself.

Julian didn't realise how lucky he was.

Carmilla was the one who would be ostracised if they failed to produce a baby. The one who would be banished to the camps and forced to work. The one who would lose everything. And despite the threat of that hanging over her head, Carmilla was the one who still had to work every day in order to keep a roof over their heads and food on the table. Carmilla was the one this affected. All Julian had to do was keep the house clean, cook dinner, and ejaculate on command. How hard was that?

He began to nauseate her.

Whenever she looked at him, she felt sickening revulsion. Her stomach churned and bile flushed into her throat. Yet, she fulfilled her duty. She did what she needed to do. She allowed him to climb on top of her every night. She didn't recoil away from him when he kissed her. She said thank you when he put dinner in front of her.

She made him go to the clinic to get tested.

A woman didn't get to her age without knowing whether or not she was capable of having children. Those who weren't didn't get a free pass. It was unwomanly to not be able to carry your own children, after all, but knowing in advance gave them a chance to escape the promise of a Spinster Camp. To flee the country, leaving everyone and everything they'd ever loved, for a chance at freedom.

She should have had Julian tested before they started dating, she knew, but she'd gotten caught up in the fairy tale. He was young. Fit. Healthy. His body had screamed, 'I'M FERTILE! LET ME IMPREG-NATE YOU!'

The results of the fertility testing said otherwise.

Oligozoospermia.

A word that didn't even look real.

In layman's terms, a low sperm count. So low, in fact, that the doctor had said that Julian's semen was as good as useless.

Julian cried, great heaving sobs in the doctor's office.

Carmilla seethed. Julian had just signed her death sentence.

———

There hadn't been a reprieve from Julian's flood of tears since the doctor's appointment. Not when Carmilla had told him about her plan. A plan that would save them both. A plan that resulted in Carmilla's rounded stomach filled with her saviour. It wasn't like she'd forced Julian to watch as she was impregnated. She'd graciously allowed him to run from his failure, rather than face it. He'd hidden downstairs, drowning his sorrows in merlot while a man, who looked remarkably similar to how Julian had before he'd let himself go, deposited his seed within her (*for an extortionately large fee to guarantee his secrecy, of course*). It wasn't an ideal situation. If anybody found out, the baby would be ripped from her, *destroyed* like a dangerous dog, and Carmilla would find herself in that white van and on her way to a Spinster Camp.

It had been her only choice. She couldn't lose everything, not because of Julian's inability to provide her with a child.

Julian withdrew from her.

He no longer touched her.

He never once rubbed her stomach or dreamed of their baby's future.

They kept up appearances in public. Holding hands, laughing, acting. The second they were alone, their hands separated. They retreated to different wings of the house.

And then Julian did the worst thing a husband could do. He threatened to tell his wife's secret. He was a man. He could start fresh. There were no consequences for him for not producing offspring. Carmilla's jaw unhinged when he told her he was going to the authorities and confessing her crime.

He couldn't live with the lie. This wasn't the marriage he'd signed up for.

Didn't he realise how ungrateful he sounded? She'd saved them. Saved their marriage. She'd fulfilled the task he was supposed to achieve. How dare he be so thoughtless. So self-centred. After all Carmilla had done for him, he was ready to strip her of the life she'd built because *he had failed her*, and she'd had to take matters into her own hands.

The rage burned white-hot inside her veins. Her skin was on fire.

Julian didn't see the knife until Carmilla had buried it to the hilt in his fleshy stomach.

———

Julian stared up at her with baleful eyes. The pairs of handcuffs attaching him to the wooden chair held him tightly. Handcuffs that had once been used for a different purpose. Once they brought pleasure; now they brought pain.

Carmilla stared back at him, refusing to avert her gaze. She struggled to decide whether to kill him or to spare him. He'd been so ready to end her life. He was lucky she'd even stopped to consider whether to end his. He didn't deserve her grace. He was her husband. He'd stood before friends and family and promised to love and obey her. He'd made a mockery of her. Of the sanctity of marriage. Of the very system meant to protect the future of humankind. All children deserved a mother and a father who were joined in wedlock. They deserved to have a father who would nurture and raise them. They deserved to be born before the mother's eggs became rotten and ruined. That was all Carmilla wanted to do. It was what Julian had promised her. And what Julian had failed to provide.

She begged to know, why would he risk their future together? Didn't he love her? He'd left her no choice. Didn't he understand that?

Julian shook his head. Tears formed a thin skin across his cheeks. Mucus seeped from his nostrils, dripping to his knees.

She demanded that he answer her questions. Why, after all she'd done for him, was he so willing to end her life?

He refused to answer.

The slap resonated from the cellar walls. Her hand stung. Julian's head snapped to the side, blood shooting from his mouth with force, spattering across the floor.

Her skin was hot with fury. Her eyes burned raw and red and dry within their sockets.

Her words barked out, ragged, spittle-lined, that it was his fault. That all of this was his fault. He'd broken his vows to her. He was her husband. He was supposed to obey her. To provide her with a child so that she could keep the life she had built for herself. That was all he had to do. He was a man. His life was easy. Men never wanted for anything. They went from their mother's home, to their wife's, to the grave.

Women had to provide. They were the breadwinners. Not only that, but they were responsible for birthing the next generation from the space between their thighs. Failing to do so meant they failed society.

And so, society banished them. Didn't he understand the crippling pressure society placed on women? Their social standing didn't depend solely upon their ability to be financially stable (although they were judged immeasurably if they weren't); it depended on their ability to marry and have children. And if they didn't *want* to marry and have children? That was inconsequential. Without children, their only worth was in the Spinster Camps. Didn't he understand that?

Julian's refusal to acknowledge her meant that Carmilla was able to soliloquise him. With each word, each syllable of injustice, her rage grew hotter, brighter. Painfully incandescent.

It wasn't fair. None of it was fair.

Why should she lose everything she'd worked so hard for when her husband was to blame?

People said that the world was built for women, but that wasn't true.

The world was built against them.

The knife was in her hand.

When had she picked it up?

The handle was cold against her flushed skin.

Julian began to beg.

The slobbering, sorry excuse for a man.

She couldn't believe she'd ever been attracted to him. He was nothing. No one. He'd ruined her life. In a world where *he* had everything, he'd been determined to take everything from her. She wouldn't allow him to do it.

The knife raised. Her wrist tilted. The knife sliced.

The clean cut didn't bleed at first.

Blood began to bubble. To ooze. And then to spurt.

It drenched her. Covering her in a slick, metallic layer of crimson.

She tasted it.

Coppery.

Powerful.

It was everything.

The knife fell to the floor. She rubbed her hands against her body. The blood spreading and spilling between her fingers. And she knew what she had to do.

She wouldn't accept what society was offering. She deserved better. Women deserved better. Fuck, even men deserved better.

They deserved a choice.

Her hands found her stomach and cradled the sleeping babe within.

She bent, awkwardly around her protruding belly, and picked up the knife. Pointing the tip at her abdomen, she pressed lightly. Testing. The knife pierced the skin. A sharp exhale escaped her mouth.

She had a choice to make.

picking up the pieces

. . .

Candace Nola

"JUST PICK UP THE PIECES," my mother said. "Life goes on." She tapped the end of her cigarette on the edge of the ashtray, blowing out smoke through pursed lips, steely gray eyes looking down her narrow nose, disdain for me apparent in her stare. "My God, Jane, you would think you're the only woman that's ever been dumped. Get over yourself."

I sat across the table from her, in the outdoor patio of the trendy cafe she frequented. She liked it because she was a "regular" here. They knew her, knew her order, and always got it right. "They respect me here, Jane. They know their place and they stay in it," she was fond of saying. The truth was, she once berated a young barista so badly that the poor girl burst into tears and quit on the spot. The remaining staff was terrified of my mother; quite honestly, so was I.

"I mean, honestly, what did you think was going to happen? You're not pretty by any means, you could lose a few pounds too. You're not very interesting either, dear." She took another drag from her cigarette and blew it out, tapping her stiletto against the wrought-iron table leg. One long manicured nail swept her platinum blonde hair back from her face. Her fancy sunglasses were perched trendily on top of her head. "Gregory was far too good for you, anyway. He's intelligent, appreciates fine art, has excellent taste in clothes. I mean, really, darling, he's a gorgeous hunk of a man and you're just... plain." She smirked. "Good old Plain Jane."

"I should have named you that as a baby, Plain Jane. Even then, you were disappointing. I honestly don't know why your father doted on you so much. Of course, he was just as pathetic as you are." She sneered at me. I sat hunched over in my chair, trying to disappear. I hated these meetings. I hated her. My whole life with her was like this: degrading, humiliating, and frightening. My every move was wrong. I spent my childhood tiptoeing around her. Heaven forbid if I made a noise or made a mess. "Just pick up the pieces, Jane. Stop sniveling, you're making a scene for Christ's sake!"

"Sorry, Mother," I said meekly. "You're right. You're always right."

She sneered at me as she took another drag on her cancer stick. "Of course I am." She exhaled, smashed the cigarette butt out in the ashtray. "Now then, what do you want from me? How is Mommy dearest supposed to save you now? Money? A lawyer? A place to live? You know you can't live with me. I won't allow you back in my house, ever."

"No, Mother, of course not. I don't need any of those things. I just thought I should tell you." I was dying inside, unshed tears making my eyes glassy. No way could I tell her that I just wanted her to be a mother for once, to show a smidge of compassion for her only child. I didn't know why I had bothered showing up today.

Another dose of public humiliation was not what I needed right now, not after seeing my husband escorting that woman out of our favorite restaurant: the one where he had proposed, the one place where we celebrated every special occasion. They both had looked at me and smirked, the blonde kissing him on the lips before she got into her cab. He just looked at me and said, "I told you to wait at home." Then he walked past me to his car while I stood there, shattered on the sidewalk.

My mother stood up and sighed. "Well, if you have nothing of interest to say, I'm not going to waste my time here any longer." She gathered up her leather satchel and her cell phone. "I do have a life, you know, important matters to attend to." Narrowing her glare at me, she continued: "Do try to pick up the pieces and move on. It's not like you were in love or something." She turned on her heel and walked away. Her neat gray suit trimmed in dark red with her red stiletto heels fit her perfectly. Her hair glistened over her shoulders as she shook it out and settled her sunglasses back over her eyes.

I sat there for a long while, feeling miserable and broken, ashamed and worthless. Then, suddenly, I was seething. My blood was boiling hotter than it had ever had. Thirty years of anger, hurt, and constant rejection finally rose to the surface of my stunted emotions. I was furious and fed up with this cold-hearted bitch that I had been forced to call Mother for the last 30 years.

"Pick up the pieces? Oh, I will, Mother, I will." I said the words defiantly, out loud to no one. I would do exactly what she said. No one would humiliate me again. I'd be damned.

I stormed out of the cafe, head held high. I knew what I had to do, and I did not need Mother's help or her approval. I made several stops on the way back to my home, carefully selecting the items that I would need for tonight's dinner. After all, I was still the meek little housewife that Gregory expected to greet him at the door, with his dinner on the table.

Arriving at home, I parked my car, grabbed my bags, and went inside.

In the kitchen, I started dinner for my cheating husband. *"Mustn't keep Gregory waiting, dear,"* I could hear my mother's words in my head. Seething inside, I chopped meat and vegetables. Putting the pot roast in the oven, I tossed the salad and set it in the fridge to chill. Then I popped open a nice Merlot to let it breathe.

Moving into the dining room, I set the table for three, using all of my finest crystal and china. Polishing the silver, I laid them out properly next to each place setting. I released the heavy golden drapes from their hooks and pulled them closed, then I lit the candles on the table and the mantle. It was perfect. The setting truly looked like it belonged in a magazine.

Picking up my phone, I dialed Mother. Two rings and she answered it, asking snidely, "What is it now, Jane? I really am busy." Calmly, I replied, "I'm sorry, Mother, forgive the intrusion. I wanted to thank you for today, for setting me straight. Won't you come to dinner tonight? I've made Gregory's favorites. I'm sure you'll approve." I hated the pleading tone that appeared in my voice.

She sighed deeply. "Very well, I'll be there at 7:30. But then, you pick up the pieces, got it? He doesn't want you anymore." I made my voice contrite and soothing. "Yes, Mother, of course." Hanging up the phone, I went upstairs to shower and dress for dinner. Two hours later, dressed, primped, and polished in a satin gown, I was ready for the evening.

I studied my reflection in the mirror. Thick blonde hair fell to my shoulders in waves, my gray eyes focused and determined. The gown showed off my figure, full breasts and hips with a narrow waist and flat belly. My long legs were tanned and toned, enhanced by the slit in the gown. My arms were sleek, like the rest of my body. Mother said I could lose a few pounds, but I disagreed.

I refused to listen to her insults any longer. My whole life had been spent in her shadow, never good enough to be seen by her side. My eyes flashed with anger and resolve. Floating down the steps with a smile on my face, I readied the wine: red for them, white for me. Then I filled their glasses halfway and set the roast on the cutting board to rest. I heard the door open and went to greet my darling.

"Gregory, dear, there you are. How was your day? Was it dreadfully busy? I know how you despise those long days." I took his coat and hung it up in the closet, all the while smiling cheerily and chattering about my lovely coffee with Mother.

He looked a bit shocked, but then steadied himself. "Jane, you seem pleasant this evening."

I smiled sweetly. "Yes, dear. I've had such a grand day. I've made all of your favorites for dinner and Mother is joining us. Isn't that delightful?"

He looked pleased. "Well, how nice? That will be a treat. But I thought you were upset about Gwendolyn?" He had the decency to look uneasy saying her name.

I tittered perkily, swallowing the bile in my throat, "Oh, that. Boys will be boys, Mother always said. Time to pick up the pieces and move on, isn't that so, darling?" I handed him a glass of wine. "Go relax while I carve the roast. Mother should be here shortly." I floated off to the kitchen in a swirl of gray satin.

Back in the kitchen, I carved the beautiful roast and settled everything on the serving platter. The doorbell chimed just as I finished bringing dishes to the table. Quickly, I walked to the entryway and opened it. "Mother. How lovely to see you. May I take your coat?" She shrugged the fur jacket off into my waiting hand and walked into the living room. I could hear her greeting Gregory as she did so.

I returned to the living room and announced dinner. Gregory still looked shocked. "What's the occasion, Jane dear? You have outdone yourself tonight."

My mother snickered. "Yes, you've actually set the table properly for once."

Gregory helped her to her chair, then sat at the head of the table.

I sank into my chair and lifted my wine glass. "A toast then, to picking up the pieces," I said. I drank deeply, relishing the full body of the wine. They followed suit, looking a bit perplexed, but they emptied their glasses soon enough, the dark red Merlot vanishing in an instant. Quickly, I stood to refill them and then slowly began to serve the food. As I did so, they talked to each other and I became invisible.

When their speech began to slur and their heads grew heavy, I pulled out the roll of duct tape that I purchased on the way home. After they passed out from the drugged wine, I pulled their chairs away from the table, facing each other, and taped their torsos to the chair backs. I wove the tape around and around their bodies and limbs. Then, I readied the small saw I had bought and went to work.

Mother came to while I was still attending to Gregory. "Jane! What have you done? What are you doing? Stop this instant! Oh, my God, is he dead? Did you kill him?" Her voice became shriller at every question. I backhanded her, leaving a bloody handprint across her face. "Do shut up, Mother. You're making quite a spectacle of yourself."

I gave her a disgusted look as I finished sawing off Gregory's left leg. "I'm just taking your advice. I'm picking up the pieces." I tossed his leg onto the table with his other limbs. Grinning, with blood dripping down my face and coating my gown, I picked up the bloody saw once more. As I stepped over to her, she began to scream. Her tongue would be the first to go.

roses for his garden

. . .

Ai Jiang

YOU ARE IN THE GARDEN, cleaning up the weeds—with needle-like pricks that even the thickest of gloves couldn't prevent from penetrating you towering over your head, and needing to be hacked away with a large scythe. By the gate, you hear your husband's voice on the other side. You freeze, eyes sliding to their corners to peek at the navy fabric of your husband's polo shirt through the staggered slits between the wooden planks, like parted lips hissing in sharp inhales. His dress shoes scuff against the damp stone of the narrow pathway lined with overgrown grass leading to the front of the house.

"My wife… is the most terrifying when she's silent," your husband says in a low voice.

"Why? Didn't you say you wish she'd stop talking?" The neighbor. You always thought she was kind, but now you wonder what she thinks about you behind that smile she offers when the two of you cross paths sometimes, during the afternoons. What your husband has said about you when you weren't listening.

"… did I say that?" Your husband sputters a laugh. He kicks something, and you hear a small rock clatter down the path.

There is a flash of flesh, and you imagine your husband raising his hand to scratch at his stubbled chin. He often comes home late from work and leaves early, almost always forgetting to shave. "When she's talking, that's when I know she's okay, that *we're* okay. But whenever I mention the roses, she just… becomes silent, so silent I can't even hear her breaths, and so still I think I'm back at the gallery, considering one of my statues."

"What made her like that? Fall silent, I mean."

Your husband hums, the sound thoughtful, faraway, and you know his eyes are glazed over—the same expression he has as he contemplates his next masterpiece, staring into your garden from his home studio while tapping a finger against the block of stone in front of him.

"Roses. It was the roses."

"Ah…"

The pair of *them* fall silent, but you dare not breathe until they disperse. Then, you're back at the weeds, slicing at them with such fervor the scythe almost slips from your hand and flies across the grass. Standing there, you feel like a reaper who has lost control of life and death, even though you know, in the end, the choice to give or take is still yours—so why does it feel as though it's otherwise?

———

You stare at your husband, long and hard, scrutinizing the small changes in his expression – from the slow dip of the brows before they rise, then fall once more, even deeper.

They say eyes are the windows to the soul, but at this moment, your husband's are pitch with a dull sheen, opaque, and you can't even see your own reflection, much less a glimpse into his soul. As though he has poured ink into the well of both his irises and pupils – cement over a dead corpse – to prevent you from seeing the bones hidden beneath.

But you don't need to see them. You already know.

He wants you to grow a rose in your womb.

It can be beautiful, yes, but it also has thorns. And you're not ready for the thorns.

"When will you ever be ready?"—a question he always asks.

"Do I have to be? Ready?" you say.

"Yes. So we can have a garden."

"We have a garden."

"We don't— We can't— We can't have a garden without—" your husband stammers, but you interrupt him.

"Without roses? And why is that?"

"Because— Because…"

He can't even give you a straight answer, and you almost want to laugh in his face at his determination, because it is a frustration without cause. At least, that is how it seems to you.

"Because?" you prod him further.

"Yes. Because."

"Is that what your mother told you? Your father? Your grandmother?"

He doesn't answer, but he doesn't need to, because you already know what he would say.

Your husband has lived his entire life believing that he needs roses to have a garden, or else he has failed. Believing that he needs you to tear your body apart for him to have a rose that you are not willing to offer. And then he has the audacity to tell you that you have no choice, that you would be worthless otherwise.

"Why would you not want to water the buds waiting to blossom within you?"

"Because I would have to feed those same buds with my life. With my blood. And as soon as they flower, I would have already wilted."

"But look at — how she glows, how like sunrise she has become." He's talking about our neighbour.

"But I'm not her. I wouldn't become a sunrise; I would become a sunset."

"How do you know for sure?"

"I don't, but this is not something I am willing to find out."

You turn from your husband with your scythe in hand, and he leaves out the gate.

He doesn't return.

———

You're heading into your garden when your friend calls to tell you about your husband's new garden, one with a woman named Mela, one that already has three rose bushes and continues expanding. All you can think about is the number of thorns that Mela will have to tend to, that will slice through the woman's fingers, and you wonder if your ex-husband will help Mela, because he never helped you, even when it was only the weeds and grass.

With your scythe over your shoulder, you begin your day as you always do, tending to your garden—and somehow, you've become more content with it, even with all the weeds, even without any roses, now that your ex-husband is no longer in it, if he had ever been in it at all.

the savage other

. . .

Leigh Kenny

A BITING wind swept through the village, rattling the huts and teasing the smoking bonfire into an eruption of golden sparks. It shook the skeletal trees that surrounded the small encampment like a barrier and sent a spray of long-dead leaves dancing around William's bare ankles. He shivered, the movement causing a reciprocating ache to shoot through arms that were stretched taut and tightly bound above his head.

The village folk were gathered before him in the throes of celebration, and the atmosphere was a strange blend of menace and jubilation.

Mary was right. He should never have agreed to come to this place. Had he listened to his dutiful wife, he would be home now. Across the small sea in Britannia. Warm and safe.

But instead of listening to Mary, he had backhanded her.

Offering up a silent prayer to God, William swore that if he made it out of this wretched place, he would never raise a hand to anyone again. Not to Mary. Not to their five children. Not even to any of these savages or their ilk.

As though hearing his internal pleas, a hush began to fall over the crowd.

Up until now, they had largely ignored him, content to fill their cups and rut with each other in plain sight. It was a spectacle that in any other circumstance would have easily aroused him but bound as he was, a prisoner to these Hibernian savages, he felt helpless and very much afraid. No amount of naked flesh cavorting before him could dislodge the thought that this was likely his last night on God's earth.

The crowd began to chant, a quiet, barely discernible sound that compelled him to raise his eyes to watch. The villagers parted, bowing their heads in reverence, and a woman, small but perfectly formed, stalked between the people. William's eyes widened as he watched her slow approach. Pinning him with her gaze, she held his eye like a challenge until he could no longer stop himself from looking away. His eyes returned to her almost instantly though, drawn not by her large, dark eyes but by her body.

She moved with a certainty he had never seen in the women back home. Her hair was dark and flowing, a crown of thorns and branches affixed upon her head. The delicate features of her face were painted in startling shades of white and crimson in loops and swirls. Her full lips parted in a cruel smile as she stopped a few metres from him, allowing him to drink her beauty in. Despite his fear, his eyes continued to track along her body, taking in not the strange pagan symbols that adorned her flesh, but the flesh itself. She stood naked and proud, and William felt a stirring in his groin as she began to move again, her breasts swaying, her dark nipples teased to a point by the biting cold, her hips undulating as she began to dance.

From the crowd, two men came forward and began to sway with her, grasping at her flesh, then at each other as they began to fight one another so close to his suspended body that he could feel the blood spatter against his face as the victor rained blows on his opponent. The woman moved closer to William, her hands roaming along his body. She was so close he could smell her, and it was almost intoxicating. She smelled of earth and fire smoke and excitement. William watched half-aroused, half-terrified, as the unfortunate loser's skull was smashed into the ground by the foot of the grinning victor. The man smeared the blood of his opponent onto his face before turning to the painted woman and smearing the fluid across her bare chest. He howled into the ember-streaked sky, and the woman laughed in delight. Her laugh morphed into a bloodcurdling shriek. The glistening crimson slick staining her breasts caught the light of the bonfire, appearing almost black in the warm glow of the hungry flames.

She turned to William and forced her mouth against his, her naked flesh pressing against him. He was grateful for the warmth and kissed her back, his own excitement becoming evident.

The woman began to stroke him, his breaths coming ragged and harsh. He closed his eyes and drowned out the sounds of the villagers as they hooted and jeered at this soft, weak stranger in their midst. Crying out, he ejaculated, then winced at the sudden pain in his chest. Opening his eyes, he whimpered at the thin crimson line that bloomed upon his skin. Blood began to trickle from the wound and he watched in fear as she lifted the bone blade and ran her tongue along it. With a satisfied hum, she lifted a tiny bowl to his chest, allowing the blood to trickle in.

Another girl with similar, but less intricate symbols on her body came forward and took the bloodied bowl and another small container from the painted woman. The second bowl, he realised, contained *other* fluids from his body. He watched in trepidation as the girl carried them to a makeshift altar in front of the bonfire.

The shrine had been there since his arrival to the village.

He had known the moment he had first laid eyes upon the strange effigies that had hung from the trees that this was not a place that welcomed outsiders, and his mind had instantly conjured those stories from home of cannibal Celts. Manoeuvring his horse closer to the small straw dolls and wooden symbols that had decorated the trees, he had scoffed. No savage nor their strange ways would frighten a man of his standing away.

He shouldn't have been as surprised as he was when the savages attacked, the fur-adorned men falling upon him as he had dozed by a small fire. The folly of a man who should have known better than to let his guard down in this godforsaken land of wild people. William was not a physically impressive man. Short in stature and soft of flesh, he was no match for the small band of warriors who surrounded him in the clearing. They bound his hands and forced him to walk behind his horse at a pace that was ill-suited to him. One of the Celts sat proudly atop his black mare, and William acknowledged that he was likely going to lose a good horse. As the surrounding forest grew thicker, and the strange symbols and dolls began to reappear, suspended from bare branches that stretched to the sky like monstrous fingers, he conceded that losing the horse could be the least of his problems. As they approached the village – no more than a small encampment of huts made from sticks, dirt and animal hides surrounding a central firepit – more of the Hibernians began to appear. The men in their furs growled at him, words that he had never heard before.

Crom Cruach, they rasped, their eyes cruel and their sneering faces mocking.

The women – some with little to no material covering their skin – laughed each time he flinched or stumbled. The children hissed and threw stones as he passed, their grubby, cherubic faces at odds with the feral light within their eyes. Around the village, more of the straw dolls and wooden symbols were evident, most notably at an intricately carved shrine that he watched the men carry to a flattened space by the bonfire. The worn ground suggested that this was a regular part of their savage rituals, and William had watched them nervously from his place on the edge of the surrounding forest, lashed to a tree by his arms. He had stood there for a long time, his body first burning with pain, then eventually becoming numb as the cold and the dark washed over the settlement. His eyes had traced the symbols a thousand times, and he realised that he had been restrained in such a way that to these savage onlookers, his silhouette likely mirrored the effigies that swayed from the trees.

The thought made him uneasy.

Every time he tried to speak to one of the heathens or to catch their attention, they responded by spitting or hitting him. Only one sound was uttered by them, the same one each time. *Crom Cruach*.

The words had whispered in his head at intervals, as though the villagers had spoken it to him often enough for it to take root like a plague. William winced as the words came again, his eyes still on the girl who carried the bowls of fluid. She had no sooner positioned the offerings on the altar when a young man appeared at her side. He dipped a finger into one of the bowls, then dragged the fluid across her bare skin. There was no shadow of a scarlet darkness visible, but even from this distance, William could see the glistening trail of his ejaculate the man's finger left as they traced along her. Giggling, she pulled him to the ground and the pair began to writhe beneath the flickering flames. He shivered in disgust at their brazen display, but continued to watch as their bodies moved together, the man thrusting into her beneath the watchful eye of the savage altar.

Glancing around, William realised with dismay that most of the villagers had begun to come together, some fornicating in groups of three, four and five. The women were clearly the dominant ones here, just another show of savagery in the eyes of the bound and pious man. Never had he seen such sexual aggression before from the fairer sex, and he couldn't begin to imagine what Britannia would become if such customs were allowed to thrive so close to his homeland.

While most of the villagers were in the throes of passion, others were in the throes of battle: blood, hair and teeth arcing through the dark night, visible only because of the raging bonfire. And he realised that it was no longer a small smoking fire, but a glorious inferno that even from this distance heated his skin and lifted the bitter chill from his bones. A final mercy before they killed him, because if he was sure of anything in this godforsaken place, it was that he would die among these savages tonight. Still, he would rather die than be forced to live like them. Shame washed over him as he recalled the feeling of the woman's soft hands against his skin, in places not even Mary would touch him. He felt a fresh stirring of lust and began to weep, tears sliding down his face in glittery tracks against the firelight.

"Have you forsaken me, My Lord?" he whispered through his tears. All of the wrong he had done in his life, every cruel action and word that had come from him now assaulted his thoughts. He felt a great sorrow, but also anger. "I came to these savages to spread your word," he spat, hoping God was listening. "I am in this den of sin for *you*! To bring these wicked people into your loving arms. But you have forsaken me. Left me at the mercy of these devils and this wicked enchantress. This savage other." His whispers had built to a roar, but the final words were choked as a fresh wave of grief washed over William.

The crowd around him fell silent again. He raised his tear-stained face and saw the painted woman watching him. Her brows knit together as her expression shifted. He could not discern her intent. She blindly held an arm out towards the crowd and a cloak of fur was thrust forward. The woman shrugged it over her shoulders, covering the devilish curves that he found so alluring. He sagged, relieved that he no longer had to look upon her flesh. He had sinned already tonight, more than once; he would not sin again.

"Who is this god you speak of?" she barked at him.

William's eyes widened in surprise. Nobody had told him that the savages could speak anything other than the coarse Celtic dialect that was impossible for outsiders to understand. Those words resounded in his head once more. *Crom Cruach*. Had he known, he could have tried harder to speak to them. To tell them of the need to change their wicked ways. It was the entire reason he was here in the first place. His position was that of an emissary. This was his first stop, and he hadn't expected things to go as they had. He was supposed to stop, to preach the Lord's word and warn these sinners to repent their ways. If they resisted, a band of soldiers on horseback would be here within days to burn the encampment and all its inhabitants.

Assimilate, or die.

Those had been the bishop's words to a room full of emissaries during his final speech before they each set out in a different direction. The land of Hibernia was small, no more than a large island, but the Celtic people who inhabited it were fiercely resistant to William's people. They didn't understand that Britannia could offer them a new way of life.

A better way.

Instead, the people clung to their old gods and strange customs. Rumours back home were rife. *The Celt men pillage and rape. The Celt women are naked and lustful wildlings. Most of the Celtic tribes murder strangers on sight, and worse again, they eat them.* He could not imagine eating a fellow human. The very concept twisted his gut. These people were savages. Too different to ever really fit in with a civilised society.

And that is why he had hoped to avoid them completely. He had intended to spend a few days trotting leisurely upon his reliable mare through the wilds of Hibernia. His eye straying to the carved symbols on the wooden altar, he recalled the uneasiness he felt when he had first stumbled upon those effigies in the forest, hanging from branches the colour of bleached bone. How he wished he hadn't stopped. He should have just returned to the soldiers' station with encampment locations and see them all burned. There was no redemption for sinners such as these.

It seemed there might be redemption for William, though.

The painted woman stood before him, her mouth set in a hard line. Her eyes though, how they danced with curiosity.

Perhaps this beauty could be salvaged, he thought.

In a heartbeat, William had imagined a whole lifetime. Plucking the painted woman from this place and leaving the rest to burn. Training her to behave like a lady. He imagined how she would look in the modern clothes that filled his wife's cupboard. Then he imagined her without them. Desire filled him again, and he wondered idly if the bishop would allow him to keep her as a second wife. A prize of sorts. Filled by his own sense of grandeur and superiority, he raised his face to the woman, his mouth lifting into a sneer.

"My God is the one, true God," he replied, his voice carrying through the silent crowd.

The villagers gasped.

William stared out into the sea of faces, inwardly shocked that the entire village appeared to understand him. Outwardly though, his face remained serene as he gazed coldly at the gathered savages.

"Allow me to leave this place and I shall ensure no harm comes to your people. I will see to it that you are taught of God's love. That you are taught how to be a civil people. To love properly, in accordance with Our Lord's wishes." He directed his appeal to the painted woman who stood watching him, her head cocked slightly as she considered his words.

"Civil?" she eventually replied. "What need do we have for your civility? Our people have lived on these lands for all time. It is you who has come to take what isn't yours, as your people before you have. As they will again. Our gods protect us. They see us provided for. And all for an honest price. You and your god want to see us eradicated or worse, become slaves. What will your soldiers do to our men? What will you do to our women? Will your god intervene? I think not."

His cheeks flamed red as William surveyed the woman angrily. How dare this savage woman question him or God. "And do you think your false gods will intervene?" he spat. "Do you think *they* can protect you from the wrath of Our Lord? You live like animals. You live in sin."

The woman moved closer to him until they were almost nose to nose. Despite her small stature, she radiated power, and William found himself holding his breath in her presence. As she lifted her arm to stroke his face, the heavy fur cloak fell away from her bare skin. Her exposed nipples hardened instantly in response to the chilly night air, and he swallowed heavily, stricken by the fresh stirring in his groin. She narrowed her eyes as she drank in the warring emotions on his face, brought into animation by the flickering firelight. Then she smiled, a salacious grin that suggested she understood the power she held over him.

Over most men who encountered her.

She moved closer, her calves stretching as she raised herself upon tiptoes. Her mouth grazed his ear. Her breasts grazed his chest. A groan escaped him.

"My gods will always intervene for me," she whispered in his ear. "Tonight, we honour one of my gods. You are a gift for Crom Cruach." William's eyes darted to the wooden altar. Stricken, he looked from the offering bowls to the crowd of villagers who had started to sway, their voices mingling in a shared whisper as they chanted that name he had heard far too often in this place. *Crom Cruach*. Realisation dawned on him.

He was to be a sacrifice.

With a soft moan, he pulled against his restraints, knowing it was futile. Knowing he had tried a multitude of times already. The painted woman stroked his face.

"Despite what you think, we aren't savages. It would have been quick. Almost painless. And you would have known great pleasures." Sucking in a breath, he couldn't pull his eyes away from her face as her hand travelled lower again. A feather-light touch along the length of him, gone as quickly as it had arrived, left him reeling.

He was excited.

He was terrified.

He was ashamed.

Each emotion swelled within him, slithering across each other like snakes, reminding him of how human he truly was. How fallible. Just as savage as this enchanting creature before him.

Tears pricked at his eyes as he struggled to accept that death was coming for him. Her hand stroked his face once more, and he found himself leaning into her touch, desperate to leach whatever contact he could before his light was snuffed out.

"But Crom Cruach deserves better than you, holy man."

His restraints tugged and William closed his eyes, squeezing tight, waiting for the killer blow to be delivered. Would they smash his skull in with something heavy? Slit his throat? He wondered how it would feel to choke to death on his own blood. The woman moved from in front of him and the heat of the bonfire touched his bare chest. His eyes opened in a sudden panic. They would burn him! His gut twisted in fear as he imagined the flames licking at him, his skin bubbling and bursting in the fire.

And then he was on the ground, the restraints no longer holding him in place. The ground was cold. Gravel and thorns dug into his flesh everywhere it was exposed. His arms burned as blood began to flow back into them. A hand on his back, and then she was whispering in his ear.

"Go, holy man. Into the woods with you. The Crom Cruach will take you, but the glory is gone. You are no longer an offering. This is no longer a sacrifice. It is a hunt."

And then she threw back her head and screeched, her long dark hair flowing down her naked back, her crown of thorns silhouetted against the great red inferno. The sound was inhuman, and as though in answer, like pack animals, the gathered villagers began to howl and shriek in response.

William watched in terror for a moment as madness seemed to descend upon the encampment. The copulation began again in earnest, but this time there was a darkness to it. A violence. Three different men descended upon the painted woman, her animalistic screams becoming moans of pleasure. The sound was at odds with the grunts and angry cries of the men as they thrust into and against her, covering every inch of her skin with their hands, their mouths, their teeth. Her eye caught his, and between shuddering gasps she pointed a finger at him. "Go," she roared, the sound elongating and becoming more high-pitched as she reached climax.

Without another glance, William stumbled to his feet and fled into the woods.

Darkness swallowed him as the trees welcomed him into their shadowed depths. He didn't stop as the sound of the savages rutting en masse faded into the withering, distant glow of the bonfire. It no longer assailed his ears, but still he forced his legs to keep moving. Not an hour ago, he had considered himself a dead man. God had given him another chance.

God had protected him.

In his mind, he could see the dark pools of the painted woman's eyes as she shuddered and moaned among the bodies of the savage men. The ecstasy upon her face. She knew true power in that place. *She* had set him free.

On he ran, until his body gave out and he collapsed to the ground panting. The weakest of dawn's light had begun to bleed through the sky, though it had yet to penetrate the forest, where the trees grew close and crooked. Curling into a ball between a moss-covered boulder and a silver birch tree, William tried to put the painted woman from his mind. He thought of Mary, and what she would say when he told her of this adventure. He imagined her face, enthralled by her husband's tales. Would she consider him a hero? Would her flesh burn for him? Would she touch him as the painted woman had? The fantasy played out in his mind as his body shivered in the morning chill, but it wasn't Mary who rocked against him naked, breasts heavy and swinging in the throes of passion. In his daydream, the painted woman bucked against him until he reached his own climax. The sudden wetness pulled him from the fantasy, and he looked at the dark patch on his tattered trousers, shame washing over him once more.

William wept softly to himself as he tried to curl tighter into the sheltered space between the tree and the rock, pressing his hand against the mossy surface for better leverage to turn his aching body. With a hiss, he pulled his hand away, sighing as fresh blood bloomed on his palm, the result of a sharp indent in the stone that had been hidden by the silvery lichen. He wiped his hand against his trousers, the material becoming a dark soup of bodily fluids, and settled himself down to rest.

Soft shafts of dawn light crept closer to his huddled form.

So too did another.

The forest seemed to come to life around him, and William found he could not settle. The feeling of a thousand eyes burned into him and nearby branches began to clack together like old, dried bones.

Squinting his eyes, he peered into the murk and gasped as a dark shape separated itself from the surrounding shadows. His body tensed, anticipating an attack from the savages.

Perhaps they had found him. Perhaps he should have kept moving.

But the figure appeared to be alone, no others detaching from the gloom to join it.

Whoever was out there moved in an odd way. No footsteps sounded. No crunching leaves or breaking twigs announced its progress, and yet he could see the distance between them grow smaller.

A female form – only identifiable by the curve of a breast – approached him, unusually tall and thin to the point of gaunt, and with a crooked, lurching gait. The figure, shrouded in a billowing cloak the colour of dirty rainclouds, moved with purpose, its body contorting with each step. The closer it got, the faster William's heart hammered in his chest, the air around him still and stale – as though this woman was absorbing the very atmosphere around them. A cacophony of forest sounds accompanied the figure's approach, each bird, animal and insect screaming a warning. As though nature itself was dying. Or proclaiming the arrival of death.

William watched, frozen in place as the figure stepped from the shadow of the trees, the weak light illuminating its features. His skin crawled as he gazed up at the creature, for a creature it was. This thing was no woman, though it looked like a poor approximation of one. It had limbs and skin and a face, but everything was skewed enough to leave William's insides lurching. The skin was translucently pale and forked with veins as dark as night, its eyes almost entirely black. It smiled at him, a sinister leer that held the appearance of a wolf baring its teeth at the lamb before striking. Its teeth were small and sharp, encased within gums the colour of ash. Mere steps away, it raised one elongated, twisted arm and pointed a yellowing talon at the trembling man. The warring sounds of the forest creatures cut off instantly, and a momentary silence ensued before it spoke.

"I am the savage other."

Its voice came not from its throat, but from what seemed like every-where. It seeped from the trees, from the ground, from the boulder behind William's back. From the ants in the dry grass beneath his feet; from the owl that watched in the branches above his head. It flooded his ears and his mind. He was sure he could feel it reverberating in his very soul.

Blinking, William screamed as the landscape around him changed in an instant.

No longer was he in the forests of Hibernia, surrounded by damp and greenery. The creature still stood before him, but now the grass was a black pit of tar, the trees a writhing mass of shadows with teeth. The watery morning light had become a blazing inferno that hung suspended above a sky of crimson and ochre. The creature's body contorted as it fell to all fours and began to crawl, closing the short distance between them.

He blinked again, and the Hibernian landscape returned, but still the twisted creature crawled towards him.

Another blink, and those long, crooked limbs were touching him, but the Crom Cruach's face was different – no longer pale and hairless but painted with a crown of thorns atop a head of long, dark hair. Two dark pools gazed at him, and William found himself falling, relaxing into the warmth of the painted woman as she heaved herself upon him. Squeezing his eyes shut tight, he knew his god did not exist here. He could feel her breath against his ear, the weight of her breasts against his skin. Opening one eye, he whimpered. The creature's sharp teeth dripped gore, its abyssal eyes looming, watching him. The smell of carrion, of death, of decay and the very earth of the forest floor hung heavy between them. The god-creature's angular frame – the weight of everything and nothing all at once – twisted and writhed as it moved in for the kill, each sharpened nail tugging and tearing at his skin. Crying out, he closed his eyes again, grateful as the warped limbs and cold skin morphed against him once more and became soft, warm flesh.

William cried out.

The painted woman rocked against him.

The Crom Cruach stripped the flesh from his bones.

The forest accepted his unwilling sacrifice. The branches became one with his bones.

Corrupted and consumed, he ceased to be.

a suitable punishment

. . .

Lisa Hutchinson

WEDNESDAY 11TH MAY *1904*

A deafening explosion rocked the village of Darley, hurling confused villagers from their homes, spurring them into the ensuing commotion and toward the pillar of smoke that rose ominously over the northern outskirts of their village.

The pit…

Wives and daughters shrieked the names of their loved ones, but not Violet Cook, who led the charge. She ran silently, praying that all the men and boys had escaped the depths of the pit before the explosion.

Beneath her, the ground shook. A second explosion erupted from the pit entrance, arresting the villagers in their path, spewing black billowing smoke into the clear sky as gravel flayed their faces. Still, Violet continued forwards, undeterred.

As the pit came nearer, she finally saw them: dozens of miners crawling around the entrance, smoke and dust belching out from inside the mine and cloaking over and around them.

Two miners whom she knew, William and Edward, were on their knees, their bodies coated in black dust, a young boy on the ground before them, as they attempted to revive him. Violet fell to her own knees beside them, frantic for answers. William, the younger of the two men, gave up trying to rouse the child, and fell back to the ground.

"William! What happened?" Violet asked, her voice trembling.

Before he could answer, yet more panicked villagers arrived, their gasps and screams echoing around them, cloaking Violet and the men in fear.

"John! Oh, dear God! MY BOY!"

Pushing Violet aside, a woman… Cynthia Green – though through the soot covering her face and dress, she appeared almost unrecognisable – began to shake her child's unresponsive body. "Where is the blood coming from?" she cried, weeping, pushing her face into his soot-covered shirt. "He's only thirteen. Please God, don't take my only son!"

Violet stood on unsteady legs, surveying the faces and chaos around her. She reached out a steadying hand to Charlotte Miller who ran the local public house with her husband, and asked her to assist with Cynthia and her boy – then left them grieving and stumbled to the other miner, Edward, who had helped carry John from the pit.

He sat back against a tree, huge chesty coughs erupting from his lungs. Even through the coal smeared across his face, his ghostly white complexion shone like a beacon against the soot.

"Edward," she said, holding the man's thick forearms. "Please, what happened in there? Did you see George?"

He wiped the spittle from his lips with a bare, dirt-covered arm. "I'm sorry, Vi, I didn't see him anywhere. The explosion happened below us. Hell, it shook the whole damn place. The seam started to collapse, and we all panicked and ran. I only saw William, and young John there." He nodded to the unmoving boy, still in his mother's arms. "William was trying to carry him out – the young lad had been hit by falling timber. So, I grabbed his legs and we ran like our lives depended on it. But… he's gone. We were pulling a corpse."

His words were a knife to the stomach. Suddenly unable to keep herself upright, she fell, landing hard on her hands and knees, gravel biting through her dress into her skin. "Please," she said, looking up at him, pleading with him to give her hope. "Tell me there's a chance… people could still be alive in there…"

He let out another volley of rasping coughs, doubling forward with each bark, but didn't – couldn't – answer her, and after a moment, Violet got to her feet and ran from him, towards the drift.

A larger group had assembled around the opening, attempting to fight their way through the debris to the mine, but the surviving miners blocked them, holding steady. It was too dangerous to go searching for loved ones, they all knew it – but that didn't mean anything when it was your family trapped below the earth.

A gut-wrenching wail rang through the crowd, and Violet turned to see Cynthia cradling her limp son in her arms, screaming her grief into the soot-choked air. Some of those around her tried to comfort her, but Cynthia pushed against each one, as if drowning and frantic, leaving bloody handprints on their shirts and dresses as she clung tightly to her son.

This is death.

Violet's heart broke for her, but what could she do? There was no way for her to lessen Cynthia's pain.

Eyes hardened, lips thinned, the crowd turned. It was as if the smoke itself made them violent, their anger erupting. Violet's own hands clenched into fists. Other women threw themselves on the miners, who faltered, fear on their faces, and perhaps they would have caved, but exactly at the moment Violet herself had committed to violence, an almighty voice called out.

"Stop this madness at once!"

Joseph Wood, the mine manager, stood at the opening of the drift. Despite being of smaller stature than most men, most would not dare step up to him. He fought dirty, and they all knew it.

"No one is to enter the pit 'til we can assess the damage. If you enter, you do so at your own risk, and I for one won't follow you in."

Cries rang through the group; the threat of Joseph's words not quite enough to ease its collective desperation.

"You can't expect us to stand here while our loved ones may still be alive down there!" said a voice amongst the crowd. A chorus rose in agreement.

"I am telling you, for your own safety, DO NOT enter the pit. The explosion has made the shafts unsafe, the whole mine is at risk of collapse from the explosions. I know it's hard, but the best solution is to wait 'til the disaster team arrives."

More angry cries rang out – then stopped abruptly at the sound of frantic footsteps from within the drift. Joseph disappeared into the gloom, the miners holding back those villagers who attempted to follow him.

Another round of commotion, and a small group of miners exited the pit. Desperate family members fought to see through the crowd – to see if it was *their* loved ones emerging from the pit. The group was led by Joseph and a miner Violet couldn't recognise, a man so covered in soot, even his eyes seemed black. They held a badly burnt man between them, smoke rising from his arms and legs, his clothing already burnt into his skin. Behind him, another miner carried an unmoving woman in his arms like a sleeping infant.

"Help!" the burly man called out. "I found this screens lass pinned to the wall by rubble." Miners rushed forward to help their brethren. Straining to look closer, Violet's heart rate grew frantic, the hope that her husband would follow burning like a fever in her throat, but no one else emerged from the depths.

The lucky ones, those who'd managed to make it out, were now in the arms of their families. Those whose family members hadn't emerged from the pit sought comfort in one another, or screamed into the smoke, refusing to admit their own worst nightmares.

A sudden numbness clutched Violet's chest and throat, a dead weight which threatened to collapse her lungs as she struggled to breathe, each breath hitching as she collapsed to the ground and fought for air. Nearer the earth, where the air was clearer, her raging heartbeat calmed a little, even as she took in the devastation.

Cynthia cradled John, his head buried in her chest. She rocked back and forth, fingers idly stroking his blackened hair away from his face. Hair that had once been blond, but was a dark as coal.

The screens lass who had been carried from the mine looked lifeless and had evidently been discarded. She lay, bent, her knees sticking into the air – only her dress, caught below her body, holding her legs partially upright. She stared, unseeing, into the sky, arms open to her sides, as if trying to fly.

The burnt man who had been brought out was conscious but incoherent. His wife was trying to keep him subdued, even as he attempted to get up and re-enter the pit. A cloud of brown smoke rose from his limbs, yet he ignored it, seemingly beyond pain.

The turmoil was broken when Joseph spoke again. "I need everyone to move back. We have no way of knowing if any other explosions may come, so I implore you all: head toward the treeline. We have sent for help.

"It is only a matter of time."

———

Sitting in the chair that still held her husband's scent, Violet placed her head in her hands. It had been over a month since the explosion, and the whole village grieved.

"With child? Are you sure, Violet love?" Agnes asked, gently, placing a hand on Violet's shoulder.

"I am almost certain." Violet's response was muffled by her hands. She raised her head to look up at her friend. "My monthlies are late, and my breasts tender to touch. Oh, Agnes, how can I raise a baby as a widow? I can barely attend to myself with the grief of it all. How can I care for a little one?"

The older woman cupped Violet's face in her rough hands, wiping her tears. "Now you listen to me, Violet. Our village is mourning. Many of us will never be the same again. But we grieve together, each supporting one another as well as we can. Same as when your little one comes. You will never be alone."

"It's all George and I ever wanted. A family of our own. He would have been so happy, Agnes. It kills me, knowing that his baby will never know his love."

"But it will have your love in abundance. This baby is a ray of light." Violet's eyes softened. "Twenty-nine people perished on that

God-forsaken day, Vi. As much as it pains me, we need to move on from the tragedy. It was a terrible accident that could not have been foreseen. But we need to carry on." Agnes grabbed the arm of the chair Violet sat in to support herself as she stood, her knees audibly popping with the effort.

"Don't you leave your elder struggling now," she winked. "Now, come on. My house is so quiet without the boys. I just can't bear to be there. I'd much rather help you, here. So let's get this place spick and span."

In that moment, it hit Violet that she was not the only one grieving; her friend had lost her own sons, her own husband in the accident. Violet reached out and gave Agnes's arm a squeeze – and, with a reassuring smile, wiped the remaining tears from her own face.

A pounding at the door startled both women. Standing, Violet looked to her companion, but felt the blood rush from her face, feeling suddenly dizzy.

Agnes pointed to the chair. "You look a little peaky, love. Sit down, I'll just go see who it is."

The knocking came again, seemingly more frantic this time, and Agnes frowned, her lips thinning, as she ambled to the door.

"Mary!" Agnes greeted the teenager who stood beyond the door. 'You frightened us, pounding away like that. A knock like that could frighten someone my age to the grave in a time like this. Whatever's the matter?"

The young girl crossed the threshold, cautiously looking around as if to check that they were alone. She twirled a ringlet of wavy blonde hair around her finger as she fidgeted on the spot.

"Mrs Wilson, Mrs Cook – I'm so sorry to arrive unannounced." She looked frantically from one woman to the next as she tugged at her dress. "Please, you cannot tell my father that you have seen me, but my mother has requested to see you both.

"Urgently."

———

"Another whiskey before you head home, Joseph?" called the portly man behind the bar.

"Aye, Daniel. Make it a double, and I will leave peacefully," Joseph called back, sniggering at his own joke. He swayed as he positioned himself on a barstool. "I'd ask you to pour one for Albert, but he's never on time."

The landlord let out a bellowing laugh, retrieving the bottle of whiskey and topping up Joseph's grimy glass. "Poor bastard has never been punctual. I guarantee he will be late for his own funeral."

"Aye, late and unorganised. He will be our downfall." Joseph's words dripped with distaste. He picked up his glass and gave the whiskey a swirl.

"Give it time, for all of this to blow over. Then we can resume our business, with people none the wiser," Daniel said, wiping the counter with a dirty off-white bar cloth.

Joseph shot Daniel a look that said *shut up now*. He'd known Daniel for many years, and the man should have been aware of Joseph's temper; he'd seen Joseph pull weapons in fights and beat men nearly to death. He should know better than to shoot his mouth off. He should know, certainly, that Joseph wasn't a man you crossed.

A sharp few raps to the door caused both men to turn. "This will be them now. I asked that Albert gather the others." Daniel walked over to the entrance and, lifting the latch, pulled the heavy door open. "Why – Agnes, Violet, what are you doing here, and at this time?" Joseph's eyes burnt into Daniel's back as intensely as his growing ire.

"We are ever so sorry to bother you," came Violet's gentle reply, "but we saw the place was still illuminated. Since losing our beloveds, we find that sleep doesn't come easy. We take comfort in each other's company. Could you spare us just a drink or two?"

"There's no one left here." Daniel swallowed. "I was about to shut up for the night…"

He turned to look at his friend, to gauge Joseph's reaction to the request. But before he could interpret the glare from Joseph he received in response, the other woman spoke.

"Come now Mr Miller, there is a chill to the air. And you're a terrible liar—we all know that. Allow us to have a drink in the place where our husbands spent so much of their free time. We come bearing money, and we do not care to bother you and whomever you may be with."

"Go on, Daniel," Joseph said, his mood seeming to soften. "Do not leave those women on the doorstep. The fire is still burning away in here. Allow them some warmth and solace in their time of need."

Raising an eyebrow at him in an unspoken question, Daniel opened the door wider to allow the two women entry. Violet made her way in first, glancing around the room, followed by Agnes. Spotting Joseph seated at the bar, Violet gave him a nod, while Agnes thanked both men for their generosity.

"Now get yourselves warmed by the hearth," Daniel said with a smile. "What can I get for you both?"

"Two pints of ale, Mr Miller," Agnes replied.

Joseph's smile broadened. "Well, that sounds to me like two women who know what they want, Daniel. Get them their ales, on me."

"Thank you, Mr Wood. Your kindness is appreciated in our time of loss," Violet said, wiping away the tear that had run down her cheek.

"A tragic accident, ladies. I am so sorry for your loss. I wish we could have done more, but with the structure so unsteady we didn't dare venture too far in. We tried the best we could," Joseph said, as Daniel placed two pints of ale before the women. Lifting his own glass, he nodded his toast. "To those we lost that fateful day," he slurred, swallowing.

And let that be the end of it.

———

The door to the public house opened. Violet was unsure of who the first man was, but recognised one of the other two who followed.

"Vi! What on earth are you doing out at this hour?" Edward

exclaimed, shock evident on his face. Before Violet had the chance to speak, Joseph's voice took over the room.

"Edward, my good man, I didn't know you were already acquainted with our guests! Ladies, you appear to know Edward here. A fine man, and a hard-working one at that. We also have Albert Hilsop, my second in command, and his nephew Bert," he added, indicating the others as they entered the room – the younger man, Bert, closing the door behind them.

"Come now, Violet, we really should get you and Agnes home. It's late," Edward insisted.

"Let us not ruin their night," Joseph slurred. "They came here for a drink, just like us. Pull up a seat at the bar and leave them be." His tone was insistent enough to leave no room for argument. Edward headed over to him without a word.

As the women warmed themselves by the fire, Violet sensed an excited buzz coming from across the room. As the men knocked back drink after drink, they grew rowdier, and their rowdiness made her uneasy. She barely knew these men, or what they were fully capable of. Perhaps, she thought, it would be best to leave…

"Gentlemen, ladies," she heard Daniel say. "I must ask that you finish off your drinks and kindly depart, and that as quietly as possible. I shouldn't have allowed such activity to take place in my public house after hours, so please keep it down as you leave."

The men moaned. Agnes took the opportunity to tap her pint glass against the table, loud enough for all to hear.

"Well then, gentlemen," she said, when they fell silent. "Violet and I would like to thank you for your hospitality. You kindly offered us warmth and good ale. Although I fear it was gifted out of guilt, to appease us poor widows." She grimaced, gesturing to Violet as well as herself. "Did you know I lost two sons in the explosion, as well as my dear Bernard? We had the world, but it was ripped away from us."

One of the men coughed, the noise punctuating the silence like an apology. Joseph raised his hand to cover his mouth. To cover a smirk. Agnes stared down at her hands, spread out on the table.

"Every morning I wake," Agnes continued, "I do not want to rise. The pain rips through me from the moment my eyes open, 'til the minute I lie down to sleep. You cannot possibly know what it is like to feel such loss."

Several of the men had the grace to seem taken aback by her outburst.

"Now, Agnes, love – I think that ale has gone to your head," said Daniel, moving slowly towards her. "Get yourself home and sleep it off."

"Stay away from me! I know what you're capable of. What all of you are capable of!"

The men glanced at one another. Bert licked his lips.

"I think you need to be leaving now… Agnes, is it?" said Joseph, his expression unreadable. "You heard the barkeep. Go and sleep it off."

"We have no intention of leaving, Mr. Wood." Agnes stood tall, unwavering, all eyes on her. "Violet and I came here with intent. You see, when you men have your late-night drinks, you're not always as quiet as you think."

Joseph lurched to his feet. Fearing for her friend's safety, Violet stepped between him and Agnes. He struck out with one hand, catching Violet hard across her face and sending her colliding into the table behind her.

"Bastard!" cried Agnes. She turned her back to flee, but Joseph grabbed her hair and jerked it back, roughly. She screamed as he pulled her towards him.

"LET HER GO NOW!"

Silence once again descended over the room as all eyes turned to see who had called out.

"Mary? What on earth…?" Daniel's brows creased with confusion.

Mary stood silhouetted by the fire – rifle in hand and pointed at Joseph. She'd appeared from behind the bar, it seemed. Through the hatch that led to their home.

"Stay back!" she told Albert, who'd begun making his way towards her. "I will not hesitate to fire."

Joseph laughed, mockingly, still holding onto Agnes by her hair, the woman on her knees before him. "You're but a child. I don't believe you even know how to fire a rifle, let alone hit a target."

"Trust me, Joseph," Daniel said, hand raised as if to keep his daughter from firing. "She can fire a rifle as good as any man. I've had her out hunting with me since she was a bairn. Put it down, Mary. We can discuss this, just… please, lower the rifle."

"DO NOT lower that rifle," came a voice from behind the girl. Another group of women appeared behind Mary, each of them brandishing a weapon.

"Charlotte?" Daniel said, perplexed. "What is this madness?"

"We *know*, Daniel," Charlotte spat, taking a step forward, her machete raised before her. "Mary overheard you all talking one night, about not having the right equipment down the pits. That you, Mr. Wood, had refused payment, at the expense of your workers – our loved ones. All in the name of greed!"

Joseph only laughed. "We have candles, canaries. I refuse to pay for Davy lamps when we have the next best thing."

Violet climbed back to her feet, the pain from her stumble falling by the wayside as the anger coursed through her body. "We lost husbands, sons, fathers, daughters, mothers… And you scoff and talk of money? How dare you! You pass it off as an accident, but you're responsible for each of those deaths."

"Did you know that I went there, nightly?" Agnes said, not raising her head. "Knowing there were survivors trapped, waiting for the help you held away. Even now, I feel I can hear my Louis calling for me. I'm in a constant state of unrest, knowing that my loved ones suffered, and all at your hands."

"They knew the risks," Joseph scoffed. "They might as well have signed their own death warrants." He pulled Agnes to her feet and spun her around, so that she was shielding his body. "Come on, then," he snarled at Mary. "Take your shot. You'll take out the old hag before you kill me. Can you live with that, child?"

A scream emerged from among the small gathering of women, and the group was forced apart. Another pushed her way out from among them: wide-eyed, her knife raised as she raced towards Joseph and Agnes.

Cynthia.

Then… *bang*: the shot rang out, and the grieving mother hit the floor, hard. Violet's gaze turned to the men; to the youngest, Bert, whose gun was still raised, smoke drifting from the barrel.

He swallowed. Then, apparently shocked by his own violence, dropped the gun. One of the women ran forward to check on Cynthia on the floor, the blood spreading out from under her chest.

"Heed that warning, whores," said Joseph, pulling a knife from his jacket and holding it to Agnes's throat. "I suggest you take your friend and leave, before I kill *this* one."

"She's gone," said the woman beside Cynthia.

Violet felt a stab of anguish in her chest. "Monsters. All of you monsters!" she roared. "You don't care who you hurt. All those innocent lives lost at your hands!"

"That's right, Daniel. We know." Charlotte's words were directed only to her husband. "Mary told us – not only did you talk of the explosion, but also of why you were all afraid to go back into the mine to retrieve the fallen."

"What are you accusing of?" asked Daniel, his voice wavering. "I spend my days tending to the bar and our patrons."

A terrible liar, Violet thought.

And everyone knows it.

"The ladies you disposed of in the used-up shafts," she said, with eerie calm. "Those poor souls you raped and murdered – all of you, over the years. Mary heard it all."

None of the men responded to Charlotte's allegations. They only stood, stoic and unmoving.

"That's why we're here tonight," Violet said. "To take our revenge. Not just for our own loved ones, but for those innocent women whose lives you ended, so your dirty little secrets would stay buried. You brought them here, didn't you? Had your wicked ways with them, and then get rid of them like they were shit on your shoes."

"*You* came for revenge?" Joseph laughed, his face split into a smirk. "Weak, mild women – only good for feeding us, tending to us, and for the space between your legs?

"Every one of those women deserved it. Men have needs, you know. And if we don't get them met willingly, we take what's on offer.

The explosion was an accident, *yes*, but it permanently disposed of those dirty whores. The shaft collapsed. They'll rot there, forever.

"That's God's will. That's judgement."

From somewhere deep within Agnes, a roar ripped free... and, before Joseph could react, she pulled a knife from her skirts and thrust it deep into the meat of his thigh.

But he still had her by the hair; there was no time to move away before, letting out his own roar of disbelief, he thrust his own knife into her back, again and again.

Screaming, the women surged forward – swarming the men, their weapons glinting in the candlelight. Daniel turned to his daughter.

Silently, he pleaded for her to let go. But she refused, her grip tightening around the stock.

Violet saw the surprise on her face as the gun suddenly went off, her father's blood spurting over the girl's face as he flew backward, then down to the floor, his throat open and ragged. Mary lost her balance, falling hard into someone behind her: her mother, Charlotte, who held her upright.

Neither shed a tear for Daniel as he lay, dying, at their feet.

A small group surrounded Bert. One woman held him by the hair, while another used her knife to strip his shirt from his body. A third woman had her arms hooked around his shoulders from behind, holding him in place as the knife wielder slashed at his chest and stomach, each cut deep, but not enough to end him. He didn't fight back; just trembled as the knife went in, silently hyperventilating, his bottom lip quivering. Every stab of the knife glinted in the eyes of his attackers. They delighted in every wound on his pale body. Finally, he sobbed and grunted and cried out for help.

No help would come.

Across the room, Albert was forced to listen to his nephew's pleas, prevented from reaching Bert by the young raven-haired woman clinging to his back, her nails digging into the flesh of his neck. He threw himself backward, the corner of the bar catching his attacker hard in the spine. Letting out a wail, she dropped to the floor, and Albert slammed his boot down hard on her face, repeating the action over and over until she was an unrecognisable, bloodied mess. Violet shook from the sight: the raven-haired woman's face now pulp, her hair gore-red.

Daniel lay twitching on the floor, the pool of blood seeping out around him a clear sign that the barman was dying. Albert smashed a whiskey bottle on the bar, then stalked across the pub, stabbing at any woman that came within reach, picking his way around Daniel, careful not to fall in the thick, syrupy blood. A group of the rage-fuelled women huddled in a corner, beating a body that no longer looked human. Reaching out amongst the frenzy was a bloodied arm.

Joseph or Edward? There was no way to be certain.

Bert's pained cries called to Albert like a siren's song. Violet saw Albert swerve to help him. Channelling all his rage, he grabbed the woman with the knife, still fixed on attacking Bert's chest, and pulled her away, throwing her to the floor. The two holding Bert let go, raising their hands in surrender. They had no weapons.

Bert fell to the floor. His uncle grabbed him under his slick armpits and yanked him to his feet.

"Come on, lad." There was fear in Albert's expression. "We need to get the hell out of here, now."

Young Bert's face was a mask of his blood and snot. Snivelling, he allowed himself to be pulled to the door, coils of intestines slipping through the rips in his skin. On seeing Daniel's body, the younger man stopped dead and began to shake uncontrollably. Albert pulled harder.

Violet didn't see Charlotte race forward at first, her machete raised – not until the blade was buried in Albert's flesh, slicing deep into his gut. Eyes wide and stammering, he vomited uncontrollably over his chest; over the handle of the machete. He would have fallen, but Violet grabbed his head from behind, and slipped her own arm around his chest. It took all of her strength to hold him up, but keep his head facing forward.

She wanted him to watch.

The machete slid slowly up his body, his weight pulling him down as Charlotte held the handle in vomit covered hands. His skin slipped apart, the innards within bubbling out and hitting the stone floor with a wet slap. Albert followed quickly behind them, landing face-down in his own viscera.

Bert remained frozen to the spot, eyes trained on the bloody remains of his uncle. Mary seized her opportunity to run the blade of her knife across his throat. Blood poured from his mouth, from his neck as he grasped frantically at the wound – until, coughing and spluttering, he fell beside his uncle.

Charlotte wore their blood with pride. Mary, her daughter, got to her feet from the mess in which she'd fallen, her own arms slick with gore. Violet stood tall. It felt like a rebirth.

Wiping the blood from her face with the back of her hand, Mary tucked a strand of hair delicately away from her eyes, behind her ear.

Something sharp pressed against Violet's throat.

Joseph.

The women turned, as one. "Step away from her, you beast!" Charlotte yelled. "Violet! Where is Agnes?"

Violet flinched from Joseph, even as he pressed closer into her back. He stank of whiskey and sweat. The very act of his caress felt invasive. Though she couldn't yet respond, she clenched her fists.

"That old crone?" Violet heard the grin in his voice. "I ended her. Bitch put a knife in my leg." He spun around, so that Violet could see Agnes's prone form on the floor. Her back was a cross-hatch of stab wounds. "She can be with her husband and sons now."

"You are pure evil," Violet spat through gritted teeth, her words barely audible. "No conscience, no empathy." Though she was one slice away from death, she had never felt more alive in her life. "You use and abuse others for your gain. You are nothing but a coward."

He raised his hand and brought it down hard against her head, the handle of his blade cracking against her skull. She screamed, her legs almost collapsing from under her. The other women tensed, ready to pounce.

"Stay back!" Violet told them.

Joseph's fist ploughed into her face. An unstoppable wagon of dynamite, running over the live wire of her teeth.

It felt like the explosion, all over again.

"Stay down, bitch!"

But Violet did not fall.

Instead, she grew taller, her face raised defiantly to his. Blood poured from her nose.

"You weak, pathetic little man. You leech," she spat, and jerked her knee up, hard, until it connected with his groin.

Something popped.

He dropped. Like a stone. Hands grasping, futilely. His knife fell, blade first, and smacked into the ground seconds before he collapsed beside it, moaning and rolling in agony.

"It appears it doesn't take much to get you to the ground, Mr Wood," said Violet, circling him. His smug expression fled, replaced by pain and fear – things she'd never before seen cross his face.

"You are vermin. A dirty rat that can't stay out of trouble. Well, you know what we do to rats? We exterminate them. Ladies, drag him over to the fire," she added, no trace of emotion in her voice.

Joseph kicked out at the many hands reaching down to grab at him. He screamed, calling out for help even as he was carried toward the hearth. Though the fire no longer roared, it was still lined with plenty of hot coals.

Mary aimed the rifle at his head the whole way there.

"When we thought of a suitable punishment," Violet told him, "we wanted something to match what our loved ones felt, and we decided that fire was quite appropriate. Do you not think?"

"You'll never get away with this," he said. "I am an upstanding member of the community. Others will come looking for me!"

"We'll cross that bridge when we come to it, won't we, ladies? I will see you in Hell, Joseph Wood, because Heaven wasn't made for monsters like us."

In unison, the women lurched forward, shoving him into the hearth. His head hovered above the white-hot coals, the stubble on his chin sparking to life. Instinctively, he put his hands out in front of his face, hands thrust deep into the coals, trying to push them away, his skin blistering and puckering.

Violet positioned herself at his back, pushing him harder and harder into the flames in a mirror of a caress, never allowing him to recoil. The heat and flames licked at her hands, but it felt good. Like justice.

She didn't let go until she heard the death rattle hiss through his blackened teeth.

———

The stench of burning flesh hung heavy in the room as the women went about cleaning up the mess. It wasn't going to be an easy job.

They laid out each of the fallen, covering only Agnes with a white sheet Charlotte had fetched from upstairs. A pang of guilt hit Violet on seeing what remained of Edward, his face slashed beyond recognition, but she brushed the guilt away. Each one of these God-forsaken men, she reminded herself, had been a slave to his urges – and, she knew, had the women not acted, it would have continued.

They worked through the night. It was hard, brutal work, but it pulled them together, as always.

Violet's nose dripped blood steadily onto her slightly swollen stomach.

Tomorrow, she thought, would be a whole new day.

the hunt

. . .

Emerald O'Brien

1.

My sister isn't well, and neither am I, so I've gone out hunting again.

Light gray clouds roll across the dreary sky as I lock the door behind me. The bright glow from the wall fixture casts a faint shadow behind me on the back gate. My steel-toed boots smack against the asphalt driveway, and I pull the hood of my black sweater up, tucking my long brown hair inside.

As I meet the sidewalk, I turn left, and it happens all at once: the cold wind of the early evening embraces me, the headlights shine in my eyes as cars coast down the road, approaching me, and the desperate need pumps through the veins running through me.

This all started because my sister wouldn't give him the time of day, and now, I focus every hour of my life on being the kind of sister she needed. She wouldn't believe how much I've changed. Not that she couldn't, but she'd refuse to. She'd tell me more than enough damage was done, and I shouldn't waste my time—my life—because a man turned me into a hunter.

But tonight, I'm hunting him.

Although I'll never be able to prove it, I know his schedule better than he knows my sister's. And I know he waits for her because he still doesn't know she's gone.

Most of the glowing windows in the houses I pass are closed, seemingly insulated from the dangers that lurk in the darkness between the streetlights. There are no streetlights where I'm headed. It's why he always followed her there. It's why I warned her countless times not to take that route home.

"Go the long way, Mina," I'd tell her.

"And add over twenty minutes to my walk? I'm not going out of my way," she'd say.

We were both right. A bunch of bright lights wouldn't stop him from following her, but they might have given her an opportunity to be seen—helped—when it happened.

Every move we make comes at a cost, and I used to be more risk averse. I'll never know just how much of my life I missed out on, or how much time I lost, or how many opportunities went undiscovered. All I know is that I thought the price was worth it for my safety.

Now, I'm the one going out of my way, the wind in my face, and my pockets full of some of the extra weight I carry since the night it happened to her.

Rambling vines and weeds crawl up the metal fences ahead, lining the secluded pathway—the last place she saw him—the place where I can focus all my fury. My chest heaves with each quick breath I draw, increasing my pace. My heart starts to race.

Passing bushes and shrubs, and trees with empty branches, I'm coming up on the giant crack in the sidewalk that splits it into three from near the center. Broken, yet fixed in place. Intersecting lines; a constant among the madnesses just before the entrance to the path. I stop as my boot covers it, turning to the left, waiting.

A figure approaches from the other side of the road, turning the street corner in my direction, right on time. My breath hitches in my throat before I've had the chance to catch it. I've kept my distance thus far, learning his routine. I'd say it's all for her, but it feeds a part of me now, too; the insatiable part born that night when I got the call from my sister.

I watch him crossing the road, but he doesn't appear to recognize me. He passes by without a glance and starts down the pathway. I'm not surprised. If I spoke to him or got in his way, he'd likely brush me off and remain on course.

He can't be late.

But every move he makes comes at a cost, now that he's in my sights, and I'm no longer making cautious choices.

It won't be long before he understands that and more—before he understands we have something in common.

We'll both risk everything for her.

2.

I want him to turn around and notice me.

Following him down this path while he's unaware of my presence bothers me in a way I can't adequately express. I wonder if he felt like this when he started following my sister, before she realized what was happening, or if the hunt alone fueled him plenty.

It's not enough for me. I want to scare him. I want to know he's afraid. I want him to feel like she did, but I know it'll never be the same.

What I want more than anything else is to make him stop for good.

The blue and gray clouds barrel across the sky as light fades. Mina's shift at the frozen yogurt shop ends in fifteen minutes. Even if I wasn't following him, I bet he'd be out front of the shop before she was set to walk through the doors. Just like he's been for the past two weeks.

He's about twenty yards ahead, and he picks up the pace. I'd like to think it's because he senses me, but I doubt it. He's too focused on her right now. He hasn't seen Mina in days, and if his obsession is anything like I've read online, his patience is running thin. He's growing desperate.

In just a few minutes, he'll be standing in his usual spot, bathed in the glow of the red neon light from the frozen yogurt shop sign. How long will he wait for her before he realizes she's not coming?

Last night, it was almost an hour after her shift before he left. He marched to her house, but of course, she wasn't there, either. He stood outside for hours, watching her place while I watched him from behind a house down the street.

He was there again this morning. He must have wondered if he'd just missed her. I bet not knowing where she is kills him. He might be ready to escalate things. I know I am.

If I could see Mina right now, I'd tell her I won't let him get away with this.

The row of cedars on the right side of the path begins and he reaches them well before I do. The fresh, woodsy citrus notes fill my lungs, mixing with the anticipation growing by the second.

We're steps away from the worn dirt walkway off the main path to the yogurt shop, so when he turns his body around abruptly, his focus finding me, I almost stop walking. I wanted this— willed it to happen —but I didn't expect it. My pulse races as I stare at the dark, isolated path straight ahead, clenching my jaw, keeping the same pace. I'll walk right past him if I have to. It's not time for us to meet, yet, but what if that's not up to me anymore?

I've imagined—tried to guess what he'll do when we come face to face—but I'm not naive enough to think I know what I'm up against.

I stuff my hands in my pockets, my fingers sliding against the bear spray on my left and my butterfly knife on the right. Eager to control my breathing, I take deep, purposeful breaths in through my nose. Each second he watches me; I'm adding up the threats he poses. He takes another step back, still staring, sending chills down my spine.

Ten yards and closing in.

Is he thinking about doing to me what he's done to her? She wasn't prepared like I am. She was just trying to get to the safety of her home after a long day at work, tired and depleted.

He knew it, and he preyed on it.

Will he make the mistake of choosing a new target tonight? Will he keep his focus on me, hoping to scare me? I fucking dare him to try it so I can give him what he should have got in the first place and save myself the time.

I've almost reached his side as I slip my fingers through the Velcro loop. I wrap them around the spray can, turning to look him in the eyes.

I can't make out his expression, but he's not looking at me anymore. He approaches the worn dirt path in the deep blue evening haze. He veers right, disappearing between the cedars. I inhale a shuddering breath, slowing, and stopping at the last cedar before the gap.

Swirl's red neon light glows softly in the parking lot and he treads towards the laundromat. He steps up onto the slab of covered walkway in front of the shops and leans against the cement pillar, the large glass window of Swirl's in his sight.

And my sister steps into mine.

3.

My feet and lower back ache. My hands and face are cold, but I can't move. I wonder if his body is getting stiff like mine as his red-stained face remains fixed in the direction of the front window.

It's been over an hour since Mina's shift would have ended, and my sister stands inside by the front counter. Her shiny dark brown hair is tinted red from the neon lights inside, and she's wearing the red Swirl's polo shirt with their spiral logo.

I make eye contact with my sister. No words or actions are needed to confirm the shared understanding between us.

My fingers remain wrapped around the can of bear spray in my pocket. Bear and dog spray are the only legal forms of chemical deterrent in Ontario—solely to defend ourselves and our pets against animals. If he tries anything, I'll be ready for him and that gives me a modicum of comfort. But he hasn't turned around. Not once.

I sigh, my breath clouding before me in the dark evening air.

The front door of Swirl's opens, and a woman walks out, looking both ways before stepping over the curb. She strides towards the first row of cars, and I wonder if she can sense how close she is to danger.

He steps off the curb as if triggered by the motion, marching towards the front door as it swings closed.

I ignore my instincts screaming at me to follow him—to get inside before he can—and keep my boots firmly planted where I am. Exactly where we're supposed to be.

4.

He stops just inside the doors. The yogurt attendant behind the counter looks in his direction. My sister stares at him from this side of the counter, but he doesn't register her presence. The attendant says something, but I can't read their lips from this far away. He turns around and storms out the door.

As he marches across the lot, towards the worn, dirt path, I step out of view and shield myself behind the cedars to my left. He always makes a left, back down the path, in the direction of her house. If he does, he won't see me through the cedars. If he doesn't, I'll improvise, but there's an undeniable nervous energy swelling in my stomach at the thought of having to do it.

His boots pound on the worn dirt path, and he charges through the open gap in the cedars. As always, he turns left, striding back the way we came with a new determination in his expression.

I wait a few seconds before stepping out from behind the trees, keeping enough distance between us to prepare myself if he should turn around—if he really has sensed me somehow this entire time.

My sister glides from between the cedars, wearing a hoodie. With one look at me, her stoic expression eases my nerves, and she continues down the path without a word, following him. I follow her, keeping the same pace, with a small gap between us.

He makes fists with his hands and releases them, his fingers retracting and flashing out dramatically as he stalks down the dark, shadowless pathway. His jerky, abrupt motions continue as he stares straight ahead, and so do we.

It's difficult to see much down this pathway. No moon out tonight. No time to gaze at the stars, and now I know it makes no difference, afraid or angry. Either way, you can't enjoy them.

We're almost two-thirds of the way down the path when I catch sight of the figure at its end, backlit by a distant streetlight. They must be standing right on that cracked slab of sidewalk.

He glances over his shoulder, barely turning his head ninety degrees towards us before looking back at the figure. They're pulling their hood up.

My sister does the same ahead of me.

My chest swells, my lungs filling with an undeniably intense pleasure.

On exhale, it constricts, and I steel myself for what lies ahead.

5.

The hooded figure remains unmoving at the entrance to the path. He slows down, and I do too, pulling my cell phone from my pocket. The screen glows and I blink against it, tapping my contacts and then the name Josie. I press my phone to my ear as it rings.

My sister stops a few yards behind him as he shuffles forward, turning over his shoulder to face us.

"Hello." Josie's warm, bright tone fills my ear.

"It's happening again," I whisper.

"It's…" she pauses. "Oh no. Hey, are you okay?"

"Mhmm," I tell her, making eye contact with him before he turns back to the figure at the head of the path. "I don't mean to worry you."

"What? No." Her emphatic denial is expected. I'm grateful she answered my call. "Just tell me where you are. Tell me how I can help."

My sister takes a step closer to him.

He turns around and stumbles back to the edge of the path, where the pavement meets the brown, sparse grass.

"What are you doing?" His voice is higher than I expected.

I've never heard him speak.

"Nothing," my sister says, but he's not looking at her.

His eyes bore into me.

"Hey," Josie says in my ear. "Are you there? Hello?"

"I'm here," I whisper.

I'm unsure if it's because our answer was insufficient for him or because he knows I'm on the phone—maybe with the police—but he turns around and continues towards the entrance to the path again, giving me the time I need.

"Josie—" I start.

"Seriously, what the fuck are you doing?" he calls ahead to the hooded figure, less than ten yards away, standing still on the same slab of sidewalk. "Fuck off."

"We're not doing anything wrong." The woman's youthful, calm voice comes from ahead, beneath the hood, and it feels like she's speaking to us as much as him.

"Hey, look, I'm coming to pick you up," Josie says. "Can you get somewhere safe? Just let me know—"

My sister takes another step towards him, and he stumbles off the path, into the dead grass. He backs up against the wire fence, shaken and cornered.

"Just please do one thing for me," I tell Josie, walking towards him in the footsteps of my sister.

6.

I tap the megaphone icon on my cell phone screen and hold it before me in his direction.

"…ever a bother. I told you." Josie's bright voice holds a cutting edge, and we're all captivated. "If anyone hurts you, they'll have to deal with me. I meant it."

"Thanks," I say, tapping her off speakerphone. Pressing it back to my ear, I whisper, "I just needed to hear it. I'm safe now. I'll call you right back when I get in."

I end the call and stop at the edge of the paved path before him. His bewildered expression tells me I'll have to explain myself, but with the presence of my sisters and Josie's display of allegiance, it shouldn't be a problem.

"Did you recognize that voice?" I shout when speaking at a normal volume would have been loud enough. I can't hide the contempt in my tone. He reaches his hand into his pocket. I tuck my phone back into mine, grabbing my spray again. "That was Josie."

He's blinking, likely still in shock, but his eyes widen, scanning the path from me to my sister, to my other sister at the entrance.

An understanding washes over his expression as he returns his gaze to me.

He jabs his finger in my direction. "You stay the fuck away from my sister."

I want to tell him to do the same. I want to spit in his face for even suggesting his family deserves more respect and protection than mine. But in time, I'll show him instead. People often learn more by experience, after all.

"Why?" I ask, instead. "We haven't done anything wrong. That's what the police officers have told you, right? That you haven't technically, legally, done anything wrong. We're just doing what you've been doing."

He scoffs, craning his neck back, echoing incredulously. "We haven't done anything wrong?"

He removes his other empty hand from his pocket, shaking his head.

"You're nuts." He takes a step towards the path, away from me, and then another, towards my sister at the entrance.

I follow slowly as he strides to the street, almost jogging. I brace myself—and the spray in my pocket—as he trudges past my sister at the entrance. He glances over his shoulder and makes eye contact with me. It's not a menacing stare, but it's not quite fear, either. Confusion, maybe, or perhaps the opposite.

He turns around and jogs across the street.

My sisters and I follow.

7.

My knuckles knock three times against the pale blue door. I step back and wait in the dark, cell phone in hand, forcing a sweet smile to my lips.

It would be a lie if I said I wasn't looking forward to this part, but now that I'm here, there's a responsibility to do this right. Some of the excitement I expected from the anticipation is missing, but there's nowhere else I'd rather be.

The porch light beside the door flickers on and I squint to shield my eyes from the brightness. The door swings open slowly.

An older woman I recognize from the driveway to my right fills the space between the door frame and the door. She wore jeans and a cardigan when she took out the trash this past Monday, but now, her blue housecoat hangs open, draped from where her hand remains clutched on the doorknob.

"May I help you?" she asks, her taut tone expected, but a potential barrier.

I might have even woken her up, but I doubt it.

"Is your son home?" My smile widens and I raise my shoulders slightly.

The woman raises her brow, opens her eyes wide, and soon, she's smiling, too.

"Just a moment, dear," she says quickly, and turns on the spot, shuffling towards a door not far behind her. She opens it, revealing a flight of descending stairs, and takes a single step down. "CJ, there's someone at the door for you!"

"Who?" he shouts back.

She starts to look over her shoulder, maybe to ask me my name, or if I'm a friend, but stomping echoes from the staircase. She shuffles away from the door as he climbs onto the main floor.

Our eyes meet and he opens his mouth, seemingly in shock, still wearing the jacket he had on the pathway. Whatever he reached for inside those pockets might still be there, too but my smile never falters. I wouldn't want to disappoint him. I know he likes it. It's what he told Mina to do.

"Aren't you going to introduce me?" the woman asks.

Then, he's rushing for the door with his hand out. Maybe he means to slam it in my face, but I wouldn't if I were him.

"I live in the neighbourhood," I start, looking right at him. "And I've lost my dog."

"Oh dear," the woman mutters, pressing her hand to her cheek.

"I've seen you around the parks and pathways," I say, tapping the screen on my phone and turning it so both of them can see, "and I wonder if you might have seen her?"

They both stare at the picture of my sister, holding our old Springer Spaniel, Macy.

"What a darling little dog. I haven't seen her." She turns to CJ, and I follow suit, waiting for his answer.

He looks up over the top of my phone, into my eyes, with a dirty, defiant sneer.

"Do you recognize her?" I ask.

He shakes his head, maintaining eye contact with me. "I don't recognize the bitch."

The woman swivels her head to look at him with a shocked expression. I'm sure he says those kinds of things in front of her. Even worse. Maybe she taught him better, or maybe she's just embarrassed, but she doesn't say anything.

"No?" I ask, unfazed. "Well, she'd recognize you. You've come to see her over at the park, and on that pathway to Swirl's. You've followed us home before, so I was sure you'd recognize her." I turn to the woman. "Your son wouldn't lie about seeing her, would he?"

Her brows knit together, and she squints at him before giving me an appalled look—not unlike the one she gave him moments ago. "Excuse me?"

Oh, the things your son would do—has done—and it stops now.

He scowls at me, side-glancing at the woman briefly before taking a step forward and reaching for the doorknob.

"I'll be looking out for her," I say, giving him one last look before turning around, and walking back down the pathway.

The door slams behind me. I'm not entirely sure he hasn't followed me out here, but my sisters are watching from across the street, and they give no indication I'm in trouble.

But maybe now, after Mina's unfruitful police reports and visits, he'll realize he is.

Maybe he'll realize that just when he thought it might be over with Mina, we're just getting started with him.

8.

My key comes up against some other part of the metal lock for the third time without finding the hole. It's too dark to see and I curse at the landlord under my breath.

I've reminded him to leave the light on for me, but he doesn't want to waste money on the electricity.

With my back to the driveway at the side door, I'm left easily exposed to any oncoming attack. The longer I'm forced to stand here fumbling around to get inside, the more vulnerable I become.

I used to be afraid. Just last month, in a similar situation, I'd be wondering if someone would sneak up on me—gain control over me—hurt me.

I don't think he understands that feeling. Maybe he's never felt it before, or maybe he has, and doesn't care if I do.

Power is too important to him to waste.

But I don't care about that anymore. After what happened to my sister back in our hometown, the fear has mostly been replaced with rage.

I finally slip the key in the lock and twist it open, stepping into the dark landing before the stairs I descend, careful to lock up behind me. At the bottom, the lights are off in the living room, but the overhead light in the kitchen illuminates the entryway.

I push my boots off and gently set them on the mat before walking to the kitchen and filling the kettle with water. I place it on the stove and turn the burner on. I can't help but sigh before I turn right, towards the bedroom.

Her bedside table lamp is on, casting a golden glow on her sleeping face. Her head rests on the pillow I fluffed for her before I left. The intersecting scars there, from her cheek to her chin, and her lip to her ear will fade. The physical injuries are healing, and she's doing all she can to carry on until she's ready to deal with the rest. Cocooned in the blankets, she's been forced to morph into someone else. She's been like that since it happened.

I stayed there with her in the days after we moved in. The bed was my cocoon, too, and I wanted to be her chrysalis. I should have done more to protect her, but I felt so helpless. Lying in that bed beside her, the guilt consumed me. I couldn't stop him in time. When I saw her in the hospital, I wasn't afraid for her or of him anymore. All I wanted to do was make him pay, but I knew even then, it would never be enough. I was forced to become something else, too.

I hunted down the man who did this to her and took care of him the way my sisters and I are taking care of the man stalking Mina. I didn't emerge from my cocoon a butterfly, but the day I left the bed was the day I purchased my butterfly knife.

Pushing off the doorframe, I skulk back into the kitchen and pull the kettle off the burner before the low whistle becomes a scream. I'll pour my sister a cup of tea once I finish one last task for the night.

I sit on the couch in the dark living room and produce my phone from my pocket. The screen provides a light I no longer need. I've befriended the darkness. As I tap her name and press the phone to my ear, I'm surrounded by it again.

"Thank God," Josie gasps. "I was worried about you."

"I'm safe," I whisper and pull the phone from my ear, tapping on the screen in my picture album. I text her one I've saved and press the phone back to my ear. In mere seconds, her life will change. "I just sent you a photo of the man who's been stalking my sister."

"What?" she whispers and pauses. "I thought he was—"

"She was a new friend, like you." I met Mina at Swirl's when I started working there last month. CJ's relentless pursuit started not long after. It intensified in ways that reminded me of the man who attacked my sister. I witnessed the horrors with Mina in the weeks that followed. "But now, after going through similar things, she's my sister."

"This… this is my brother," Josie says, her voice shaking beneath the weight of the accusation.

It is.

Before Mina became my sister, she already had concerned friends and family, enraged that nothing and no one with more power seemed to help her situation. She told me they felt helpless despite their efforts to keep her safe. I told her it was time for me to do what I wish I'd done for my sister. Mina's friends volunteered to help. We've found a new purpose, just like we'll find new women—new sisters—in need of our specific kind of help.

"Are you sure this is the guy?" she hisses.

"I'm sure."

"I don't know… I don't know what to say."

"You don't have to say anything," I whisper and try to swallow down the lump in my throat. "You don't even have to believe me, but I wanted you to know. Take care, Josie."

I end the call and wander back into the kitchen on tired legs. I'll make my sister her tea and stay awake with her for as long as she needs.

She doesn't sleep much anymore. She only leaves the bed to use the toilet, and she doesn't shower, or brush her teeth. She barely eats, and she won't reply to our parents' calls, but she'll text them to let them know she's okay.

But she's not okay.

My sisters are unwell, and so am I.

But we have each other—and the hunt.

teacups

. . .

Candace Nola

I AM NOT whiskey in a teacup
    I am boiling lava in an open crater
    Seething under kohl and color make-up

Do not tell me how to carry my burden
    When it's not your soul that is hurting
    Do not pretend as if my shoes you have worn
    When it was not your innocence torn

Do not preach me your forgiveness and grace
    When the scars do not mar your body and face
    You carry no right to judge or critique
    When you prey on the tired and weak

I am not daisies and lace
    I am the beauty in the fractured vase

Candace Nola

I am the reckoning, a force to behold
The consequence of your mistake

I am not whiskey in a teacup
I am a fire bright volcano
Ready to erupt

boss bitch

. . .

Megan Stockton

AMANDA'S shaky hands moved the photo of her dog's goofy face towards the edge of her desk. She used the palm of her hand to swipe dust that had gathered underneath it, threw away a few small candy wrappers and a pen that didn't match the rest of those in the cup holder. She stared longingly at the pink gel pen in the garbage, eyes flicking back to the gathering of black ink pens that it had once been kept with. She bit her lip and then removed it from the bin, tucking it in her purse instead.

It had been three months since she had gotten the job at Delacroix Literary Agency: the beginnings of a dream career. She had wanted to work here since she was a child, but the application process was tedious and their employee retention was cutthroat. She eventually wanted to move up to become an agent and editor, but for now she was one of five people who sifted through thousands of submissions, declining those that didn't follow the guidelines and sending the ones that were terrible in the first five pages to be discarded with the slush pile.

She had never met her employer: the elusive Blake Delacroix. His name even sounded like it belonged to a male love interest in one of those cringy dark romance novels. No one talked about him, and it was in the onboarding paperwork that if *any* information about Blake Delacroix was leaked, including photos, the offender would be sued into oblivion. He liked his privacy, and he demanded respect and professionalism. It had been hard for her to not ask about Blake when she'd first started working, but the rest of the employees didn't seem to want to talk to her. The only coworker Amanda wasn't afraid of was Patrick Huelman, the older gentleman in the cubicle next to her. Everyone else looked like they'd spoon your eyes out for a Klondike bar.

Today was the day though. Blake was returning from a trip overseas to meet with a big client. She wasn't sure what took twelve weeks, but it must have been some serious business deal for him to have dedicated all of that time. His absence, however, meant that Amanda had been hired remotely and she had *never* met him. She wanted to make sure she made a good first impression.

Amanda stood, peering over the walls of her cubicle to where Patrick sat. He had a hardcover book open, pages spread with his fingers as he dutifully hunkered over it.

"Pssst."

He looked up at her and smiled, tucking a bookmark in the book before closing it, removing his reading glasses and laying them on top. He regarded her with kind eyes, leaning back into his chair as he laced his fingers together patiently.

"Do you want to eat lunch together?" Amanda asked, voice hushed. "I brought extra."

"What is it?"

"Lettuce wraps."

"I'm in."

"So... I know we shouldn't talk about it." She whispered. "But what's with the big trip Delacroix went on?"

He looked around as though someone might have been eavesdropping, rubbing his left arm. "Paid some people off and is collecting a manuscript from a dead author, or so the rumor is. The wild theory is, Blake's going to publish it – *as* Blake. Claim it."

"That's a lot of rumor for a workplace where you can't talk about anything work related." She laughed. "Where'd you hear all that?"

"Reddit."

They laughed quietly, wheezing noises that they stifled with their hands.

Patrick's smile quickly faded and Amanda's brow furrowed; he sat up quickly in his chair and started unlocking his computer.

"It's Delacroix. Look busy." He said, hyperfocusing on a manuscript on his screen.

As she quickly sat back in her seat, moving the mouse on her computer to bring the screen alive, Amanda heard the ding of the elevator and the sudden hush that fell over the office. The sound of clicking shoes on the floor approached at a steady pace, and she had to fight the urge to catch a glimpse of Blake and whoever might be with him. A shadow fell over her, and the sound of the shoes stopped…

Right at the entrance of her cubicle.

Amanda froze, clearing her throat as she tried to decide if she should turn or pretend she hadn't noticed the presence of Blake beside her.

"What is *that*?" A feminine voice spoke and Amanda slowly turned at the sound.

A woman with shoulder length silver hair stood there, holding the photo of Amanda's dog in her hands. She was dressed in an all-black dress suit, an orange layered scarf around her neck.

"That's my— dog." Amanda blurted out, chest burning with stress. "Her name is Apple."

The woman stared at the dog a little longer, turning it to show it to Amanda as though they may not be looking at the same photo. Apple's smushed face with her oversized tongue lolling from her lips brought a tiny bit of instant joy to her.

"This?" The woman asked. "This is a dog? You let this thing live in your house?"

"I'm…"

"Is that why you don't sleep well?"

"I'm sorry?"

"Dark circles and bags under your eyes, outfit isn't pressed, cup of cold coffee by your computer."

Amanda blinked, looking down first at her blouse and skirt and then touching her hand gently to her cheek just below her eyes.

"I sleep fine, thank you for your concern, Ms. —" She trailed off.

The woman raised a brow, sitting the photo of Apple face down onto the desk's surface.

"You don't know who I am? You don't know your own employer? I'm Blake Delacroix." Her words were venomous, blue eyes threatening to cut Amanda in half with the disgusted way they looked at her.

"Ms. Delacroix." Amanda breathed. "I'm so sorry, I didn't realize."

"Now you do. Too little too late. I want to see you in my office."

"Of course. Yes, ma'am." Her voice shook in terror, knee tapping under the desk despite her attempts to keep calm.

The sound of someone coughing followed by a moan stopped the conversation between the two women. It was coming from Patrick's cubicle. Amanda stood slowly, extending her height by moving onto her tiptoes so she could see into her friend's cube.

"Patrick?"

He leaned back in his chair, face so red that his lips were purple. His mouth was twisted into a grimace of pain, and he clutched at his chest with both hands, like he was fighting off some entity that she couldn't see.

"Oh my God. Someone call 911! I think he's having a heart attack." Amanda screamed, pushing past Blake to rush to her friend's aid. No one else moved. Blake stood with her arms crossed, watching her as she held Patrick's hand.

———

Amanda stood frozen, a somber atmosphere engulfing the room as the paramedics wheeled Patrick's body out of the office. They had him covered with a white sheet, strapping him to the gurney as though he might still try to break free of death's grasp.

He *was* dead, though. He had died right in front of her, clutching her hand like a lifeline. He had been scared, terrified. Amanda would never get those last moments of him out of her mind.

She felt a tap on her shoulder and she flinched, turning to see Blake, her expression cold and unyielding. "Now," she said, her voice like ice.

"Now?" Amanda repeated. "What do you mean?"

"My office."

Was this lady serious? Someone just died. A long-term employee of this company, Amanda was reminded as her eyes moved to the crystal statue that sat on his desk – the one that read TWENTY YEAR ANNIVERSARY. Two men in janitorial garb appeared, raking everything off of Patrick's desk carelessly into cardboard boxes.

"Are you deaf too? Now means at this moment."

Despite her inner protests, Amanda followed Blake. Her legs felt like lead as they made their way to the employer's office, her gut rolling with anxiety. The other employees averted their gazes as the two women passed, their faces emotionless and cold. Blake's office was spacious and well-lit, a large oak desk taking center stage. There were floor-to-ceiling windows offering a panoramic view of the city, just like in the movies.

Blake sat down in a high-backed leather chair, her eyes never leaving Amanda's face.

"So tell me, Amanda. What led you to apply to my agency?" Her voice was dripping with contempt.

Amanda settled herself into a seat on the opposite side of the desk, this one less plush and comfortable. She felt like she was in an interrogation room.

"I'm sorry. Ms. Delacroix. I'm in shock, I think. Patrick…"

"Was fifty-seven years old."

"He was my friend."

"We don't make friends here. Are you going to answer my question?"

Amanda's jaw dropped and her voice came out with an uncertain tone. "I love books. I love writing. I want to be involved in that process."

"So buy some mass markets at the grocery store," Blake said, unimpressed. "Pack up your desk. I want you out of here."

"I'm sorry, Ms. Delacroix. I will improve. I promise to work harder and pay more attention to detail." Her eyes filled with tears, her voice shaking. "Please, I need this job."

"Get out of my office, get out of my building."

Amanda got up and walked to her cubicle, a sense of numbing unreality settling over her as she saw an empty box was already sitting there waiting for her. She raked her meager spread of belongings into the box and made the walk of shame across the office floor. She could feel the eyes of the other employees on her back as she stood in front of the elevator. She put on her winter hat and gloves nervously.

She waited, and waited, but the elevator didn't come.

"Come on... could this day get any worse?" She smashed the button a few more times, but there was still no activity.

She couldn't stand there like an idiot any longer, so she opened the stairwell and started descending the steps to the ground floor, grumbling to herself.

"Stupid bitch. I can't believe this. I have been such a good employee for her. It isn't my fault I thought she was a man and she thought my dog was ugly..."

Two men were coming up the stairs, dressed in black tactical gear. They had masks covering their faces and they were holding guns in their hands. One of them met her gaze, his eyes cold and hard, gun at the ready.

Her heart lurched and she pressed herself into the corner of the landing to let them pass. They did so without a word, and she realized their intent when they went right into the Agency's door. A mixture of fear and curiosity kept her rooted to the spot as gunshots rang out.

"Oh, my God."

She dropped the box of belongings to the floor, sprinting up the stairs. She cracked the door just ajar, peeking through the crack. The office had transformed into a warzone. She watched as the two masked men moved from cubicle to cubicle, pointing their weapons at the cowering employees. Then everything had a bullet hole in it, and blood seeped from the cubicles across the grey floor.

Blake was out of her office, her hands in the air. Facing the gunmen. Amanda took the opportunity to rush inside, hiding behind the wall of one of the desk spaces.

"What do you want?" Blake asked, voice as calm and collected as ever.

Amanda heard the muffled voice of one of the men. "We know you have a box of cash, and a very important manuscript in your office."

"You can have the cash, but I won't give you the manuscript."

The second man raised his gun, pressing the barrel to her forehead, right between her eyes.

"We're the ones with the guns, Ms. Delacroix."

"What do a pair of criminals want with an unpublished book?"

Amanda crept around the back of the desks, making eye contact with one employee who was hiding under her desk.

"One of you come into my office, and I will give you what you want. Only one."

The men exchanged glances and nodded. One of them stepped forward. Blake led him into the office, shutting the door behind her. The remaining man paced the floor nervously. It was quiet for some time, and Amanda found herself just as nervous as the remaining thief. What was going on in there? Would Blake be able to turn the other man against his partner? Had he already killed her?

It was clear these guys weren't professionals. Well, Amanda assumed they weren't. She didn't have any real-life experience with criminals, but they didn't seem confident, like she imagined hardened robbers would be.

Suddenly, gunshots rang out from inside the office, the sound echoing through the silent workspace. The remaining robber, his eyes wide with fear, rushed towards the office, jerking the door open.

He ducked as a pair of bullets erupted from within, both missing him and lodging themselves at the level his head had been at in the wall across the room. Blake emerged, a black and gold handgun glistening in her hand. How was she *always so fucking calm*?

"Hey, hey, hey!" The robber stammered, dropping his gun to the ground and putting his hands up. "Hold o—"

She pulled the trigger again, and the man fell lifeless to the ground, flat on his back: a bullet wound directly between his eyes. Blake laid the gun down on the water station's tabletop, smoothing her hair and pantsuit as she approached the man on the floor, crouching down beside him – to ensure he was dead, Amanda assumed, or to search his body for identification.

Amanda believed in signs, both good and bad. She knew when the universe, or some higher power, was telling her what she needed to do. It had led her to some interesting places in life, but she'd never done anything like she was about to do. Just as she started to approach, Blake stood up and walked back into the office.

But the sign was still there. She'd forgotten her gun, still on the table.

Amanda retrieved it, turning it over in her hands before walking into Blake's office and stopping her in her tracks. The older woman paused, rotating her body to look at Amanda. She had an emotion on her face this time: surprise.

"I'm impressed with your initiative, Amanda." Blake said, nodding her head in approval. "I didn't expect this of you."

"Why'd you fire me?" Amanda whispered. "I'm a good employee."

"You were mediocre at best. You want to edit but you have so many typos in your emails that I have to hire a translator every time I review your communications. You read half the manuscripts the rest of the employees do..." She leaned to look at the quiet office. "Did. Congratulations, though. Now that everyone's dead, you're a top performer."

Amanda's hands began shaking.

"You aren't going to do anything. Disappointing. I can read *you* like a book. Now put the gun down and get out of my fucking sight before I shoot you."

"You're such a bitch," Amanda whispered.

Blake laughed. "Am I? This is just business. All of it. Hiring, firing, pissing people off. Losing employees – whether they quit, you let them go, they die of a fucking heart attack, or they get shot... Those two men thought it was worth dying over a few thousand dollars and a manuscript they couldn't market if they tried." She laughed, tapping the case on her desk. "Laziness. And laziness has no place in business."

Amanda was silent again, finding no words.

"Uh, oh, bu—..." Blake fake-stammered. "Ms. Delacroix is so *mean,* and she isn't scared of the gun!"

She probably shouldn't have, but Amanda pulled the trigger.

"Anything to shut you up."

She sighed in relief, tossing the gun onto the first gunman's body. She pulled the phone out of her pocket and pulled her glove off with her teeth to unlock it with biometrics. Then she dialed 911, working up tears.

"Hello? Please help me. I work at Delacroix Literary Agency and two men just came in and killed everyone. Please hurry. I'm scared."

They said they already had units en route – someone in the building must have heard the gunshots and screams.

Sobbing her gratitude, she ended the call and walked over to Blake's desk, opening the case with her still-gloved left hand and removing a stack of bills and a manuscript. That mysterious manuscript.

She went back to the stairs, picked up the box of her things and returned to her desk to rearrange her desk, positioning Apple's face where it belonged by her computer. Then she hid the money in her purse, climbed underneath the desk and waited for the police to come, the manuscript clutched to her chest.

All it needed was a new title page. One that read: *By Amandu Stillwell.*

return to sender

. . .

Shauna Mc Eleney

THE PHONE'S ALARM BLARED, and Jo reached across the bed to silence it.

Not for the first time, she realised, on noting the time on the display. Evidently, she'd already set it to Snooze. And now, several Snoozes later, she was late.

She threw back the sheets; eased herself out of bed and staggered into the bathroom.

Normally she cycled to work: the distance between the house and the hospital wasn't so far that it left her sweaty and breathless, but just far enough to constitute her daily exercise. Today, though – looking out at the sleeting rain through her kitchen window, morning coffee in hand – she decided to give it a miss. A few times a month she'd give herself a pass and order a taxi; oversleeping on a rainy Monday morning felt like reason enough to do the same today.

She pulled up the on-demand app for the local taxi company, hoping they weren't too busy ferrying school kids similarly intent on avoiding the rain. A few moments later, the confirmation arrived: her driver, Mike, would be arriving in twelve minutes. Just time for her to pour her coffee into its large reusable cup and stick on her shoes.

Thirteen minutes later, she was sitting in the back of Mike's car, the artificial leather seat covers chafing her thighs. The air inside was thick with an overpowering vanilla air freshener and way too much cheap aftershave, presumably emanating from Mike himself – a burly white guy in his 40s with a scraggly beard and dark greasy hair that fell past his ears. The combination was faintly nauseating. She badly wanted to lower the window, but the rain had gotten much heavier outside. She'd keep her head down, she decided, and try to focus on her phone.

"Awful weather for July, isn't it?" Mike said, staring at her in the rearview mirror.

Jo glanced up and met his eye. "Yeah, it's pretty miserable. Hopefully it won't last too long." She looked back at her phone, hoping the gesture would bring any chit-chat he might've had in mind to an end. She wasn't rude, exactly; she just hated small talk.

"Oh, do I hear an accent?" he asked, oblivious. "American?"

"Irish," she replied, flatly.

"Irish! Oh, I love Irish accents. Very sexy. What brings you over to England, then?"

Because England is where my ex-girlfriend lives, you nosy bastard, Jo thought. She'd moved over from Ireland in a love-fuelled haze – then, six months later, they'd broken up, and Jo had stayed because she'd gotten a good job and, honestly, had nowhere better to be.

But she wasn't about to tell that to *this* guy. "My partner is here. And my job."

"I hear it now, the accent! You *are* Irish!"

Yes, she thought, *I fucking know. I don't need you to confirm it for me.* She replied instead with a small, tight-lipped smile.

"So, you fell in love with an English lad?" he continued. "There's plenty of us about." He winked at her in the mirror, and her stomach sank.

How did you respond to that? She wasn't about to come out to a stranger in a taxi on her way to work.

"You do seem to be everywhere," she mumbled, willing him to sense her disinterest and let the conversation drop.

But no – he pressed on. "You work at the hospital, then? Or are you visiting someone?"

Did it have to be one or the other? "I work there," she said. "I'm a consultant."

Mike's eyes widened in mock surprise. "A consultant? Very impressive. Bet you make a ton of money. What is it you consult on?"

"I'm an anaesthetist." She glanced down at her watch. The journey seemed to be taking forever. She looked out of the window, and realised, with a shiver of anxiety, that she didn't recognise the street they were on. Where *were* they? "Why did you go this way?" she asked.

"Short cut, love. Keeps us out of traffic. Don't you worry." She looked again at the mirror, and saw he was still watching her. "So, you put people to sleep for a living?" he added, with a dirty, chesty laugh. "You must be a boring bitch!"

A smoker, Jo thought. She glared back at him. What sort of idiot said *that* to a stranger?

"Just a joke love," he said, when she didn't reply. "No need to get all serious." The smile had slipped from his face, she noticed; replaced with a hint of anger.

A man who needed to get his own way, then. And whose moods could change at the drop of a hat.

When, moments later, the outline of the hospital appeared in the windscreen, she felt nothing but relief. "Anywhere here, main entrance is fine," she heard herself say.

"Look after yourself, Jo" he told her, as she undid her seatbelt and opened the door. She gave him one last look in the rearview mirror. "You too, Mike."

———

The morning had been busy, as all her Mondays tended to be. She'd been in back-to-back surgeries; they didn't operate at weekends, not unless it was an emergency. It was past two o'clock when she finally got to eat – standing in the canteen, shovelling microwaved noodles into her mouth with a wooden fork. Nearby, two nurses were taking a break of their own: exchanging horror stories as they sipped their tea.

"It's the most vicious thing I've ever seen, and I'm fifteen years doing this," one of them said – a short blonde Jo *thought* was called Samantha, though she couldn't be sure. She wasn't great at socialising – not at work, and not outside of it.

"Poor girl," the other replied – Dee, maybe? "No idea what was happening to her, and for it to leave her like that…"

Curiosity piqued, Jo ambled over to them, noodles in hand. "Who's this?" she asked.

"That young girl in bed eight," probably-Dee said, squeezing Jo's forearm in a way Jo didn't care for. "Sam and I were just with her. It's horrible, just horrible."

There'd been no time since she'd arrived to read through the weekend admissions, and Jo was at a loss. "Who's in bed eight?"

"Seventeen-year-old female," Samantha said. "Five foot two. Came in Sunday morning with tachycardia and severe blunt force trauma to the head. Girl was in and out of consciousness all last night."

"That's not even the worst part," probably-Dee added. "She was raped, and it was…brutal."

"Brutal how?" Jo asked before she could stop herself.

"He branded her. Inside of her right thigh."

Disgust rose, hot and acrid, in Jo's throat. *"Branded* her? Jesus Christ. What did it say?"

Samantha looked away, down into her tea, and Jo got the impression she didn't want to say the word out loud. "Just one thing. Whore."

———

It was good to be home. The afternoon had kept her busy, but the conversation with the nurses in the break room had left Jo uneasy, discomfort clinging to her for the remainder of the day like a fine mist. Between that and the morning's creepy taxi driver, it was fair to say she'd be happy to see the day gone.

She opened a bottle of Merlot, poured herself a glass and left it to breathe on the counter while she cooked. Lasagne tonight, she'd decided; she loved Italian, and while it wasn't always easy cooking for one, it was sometimes worth the effort.

When the doorbell rang, she almost didn't answer it – reluctant to let anything else encroach on her, draw her out of the happy place she was trying to establish.

Then it rang again.

Disgruntled, she answered the door. To be greeted by a smiling young man holding a bright bouquet of flowers with a note attached.

"Dr Higgins?" "Yes?"

"These are for you." He passed the flowers to her across the threshold and held up his phone in anticipation of a signature.

She took in the note; the bizarre message it contained.

I hope everyone you put to sleep today woke up – M.

M? Did she know any *M*s?

Unless… it couldn't be, could it? Couldn't be *M* for Mike – the fucking taxi driver?

"I don't want these," she said, thrusting them back at him over the threshold. "Can you take them back?"

"Take them back?" the delivery man replied, sounding mildly irritated. "There's nothing wrong with them – those buds that are closed should open in a few days…"

"It's not that. I just… I don't want them. I want to… return to sender, or whatever. I don't want them."

"Fine." He *was* irritated now, struggling to grip the bouquet with one hand while holding up his phone with the other. "But you'll still have to sign to say you've rejected them."

With no effort to disguise her own irritation, she ran a fingertip over the display in a looping facsimile of a signature. "But I'm keeping the card," she added, and closed the door – locking and deadbolting it behind her.

She was aware, suddenly, of the smell of smoke emanating from the kitchen. Still holding the card, she raced back to the burning lasagne, turned off the oven and flung open the window above the sink. Then grabbed her mobile, muted the podcast she was listening to, and dialled a familiar number.

"Hello, you're through to Tom's Taxis…"

"I want to make a complaint," she said, before the man on the other end of the line could finish. "Can you put me through to the right area?"

"Oh, I'm sorry to hear that. I can help you, though. What's the issue?" He was young, English – probably no older than thirty, Jo thought.

"It's about one of your drivers. He sent me flowers."

"Aww, that's nice. But you didn't want them?"

"*Awww*"? Did he think it was *cute* that a stranger had sent her flowers? Had sent flowers *to her home address*?

"Of course I didn't," she said, the anger seeping into her voice. "It's massively unprofessional. And, frankly, a little stalky."

She could hear the man typing in the background. "I see," he said eventually. "And did he show up in person to deliver them?" He paused. "What was his name by the way? The driver?"

"Well, no." She felt suddenly wrong-footed. "They were delivered by courier." Collecting herself, she switched to speaker and opened the taxi app on her phone, scrolling back to the record of her last journey. "His name's Mike Hainsley. Black Toyota Prius. You need the reg?"

"Oh, I know Mike!" The response was warm, enthusiastic even. "He's a great guy. I'm sure it was just a misunderstanding. Was it your birthday or something? I can see he took you to the hospital. Maybe he meant it as a get-well gift? Or…"

"No." She cut him off before he could put forward any other scenarios that might absolve Mike of responsibility. "It was nothing like that, I work there. And look – I don't care how nice a guy *you* think he is. He knows where I live, where I work, and he sent me flowers I didn't ask for. So I'd like someone at your end to speak with him and explain why that isn't okay. It's made me really uncomfortable.

More typing. "Got it. *Flowers made her uncomfortable.* "Is there anything else you want to add to your complaint?"

"What?" she said, deflated. *Was it her problem? Was she making too big a deal out of this?* "No. No, I guess not."

She ended the call and reached for her wine glass.

––––––

She couldn't explain even to herself why she did it. There was no reason for her to be on that ward, on that *floor*, but there she was anyway, standing by the patient's bed, looking down at her. Natasha Morgan – Tasha to everyone who knew her. Up close, she looked even younger than seventeen: her face cleansed of make-up and hair flattened down, all bravado gone, just the scared child underneath it all remaining. There was a slash on her right cheek – superficial, and Jo was fairly confident it wouldn't scar, but still, yet more evidence of the attack that had put her there in that bed.

Jo scanned the cubicle for… something. Some sign, some hint of Tasha Morgan's personality, of who the kid actually was beyond her injuries. The girl's belongings were in the locker next to the bed, she knew. The nurses had bagged up her clothes, but the police hadn't bothered to come and pick them up or swab for forensics. Who was she to them? Just another girl out on the town, who'd drunk too much and got herself into trouble. Some people thought *girls like that* had attacks like this coming to them – and, as Jo knew all too well, some of *those* people were police.

A rustling came from just behind her; the sound of over-starched sheets coming free of a mattress.

She turned, and found Tasha staring at her from the bed.

"Who are you?" The girl's voice was a low croak, barely audible.

"I'm Dr Higgins," Jo said quickly. "I was just checking in on you, seeing how you're feeling today."

"You're not my doctor," Tasha answered, eyeing her suspiciously. A smart kid, Jo thought; inquisitive, in spite of the heavy meds she was on.

"No, I'm not. But I heard about your attack, and I wanted to check in on you and see if…"

"When do you think I can leave?" The question came abruptly.

Jo walked to the foot of the bed and picked up Tasha's chart. "Well," she said, studying it, "your head injury is the main concern. We're going to need to keep you for at least another few days, on that basis alone. And your thigh, it's been quite badly…damaged. So we'll need to make sure it doesn't get infected."

"You don't need to dance around it." The girl looked directly at Jo as she spoke. "I've already seen it. The burn, the…brand."

Jo plastered on an attempt at a professional, placatory smile. "They can do wonderful things with skin grafts now."

"Is my phone in that bag?" Tasha nodded to the open locker.

"I'm… not sure," Jo said, thrown off-balance again by the kid's line of questioning. "Maybe. It's evidence now, though, so we can't… touch it."

But Tasha was insistent. "He didn't even see my phone. It was in my bag the whole time. Please, can you get it for me? I need to talk to my friends."

"Where are your parents?" She was speaking to a minor, Jo realised. Probably more appropriate for Tasha to be with *them* now, instead of her mates.

"They were on holiday, but they're on their way back." Tasha smiled for the first time. "Please, can I have my phone?"

Jo knew she was being manipulated – but how was she supposed to say no to someone in that situation? She glanced at her watch, at the door, and then finally back at Tasha.

"Okay," she relented. "I'll bring you the little bag with your phone in it. It's separate from everything else anyway. But if anyone asks, I wasn't here."

She went over to the locker and pushed aside the bag full of clothes, reaching behind it to get to the phone. Unexpectedly heavy, the bag fell, landing on the floor with a soft thud. She picked it up, placed it back on the shelf… and caught the scent of something familiar.

Something sweet but sickly artificial. Perfume, cheap perfume. No; not perfume. Cologne.

It hit, all at once – what it was, and where she'd smelled it before. The day before, inside Mike's car.

Tasha's clothes smelled like Mike.

———

Days passed – and, though Tasha had been released into her parents' care, Jo couldn't stop thinking about Mike. Was he the guy? Could he have done that?

Sure, he was a prick – that was the impression he'd left Jo with, anyway – and he had issues with appropriate boundaries, if the bouquet was any indication. But was he really capable of that kind of attack?

She had no concrete evidence to prove that he was, after all. Just the smell of him on Tasha's clothes, and what her own gut was telling her.

She had no evidence. Though maybe… maybe she could get some.

A plan began to form, at the back of her mind. It was risky; stupid, even. But she needed to know for sure – to have her suspicions either confirmed or definitively denied.

And if he *was* just a regular guy about town… well then, maybe, she could get him out of her head.

———

She didn't know where he lived. But she knew his car, and the general area he worked in; could guess at some of the routes he might drive. And so, the Saturday after Tasha was discharged, she set out on her bike to look for him: cycling round and round the town centre in the hope of spotting his car. Whenever she stopped to think about what she was doing, she told herself it was ridiculous, probably point-less. But then, another voice in her head would counter, so what if it was? Worst case scenario, she'd get a bit of exercise and enjoy some good weather. And if she saw Mike…

Well, she'd cross that bridge when she came to it. *If* she came to it.

A few hours in, she began to lose hope – the odds of actually seeing him seeming slimmer and slimmer with every minute that passed. What were the chances of her bumping into him, really? He might only work nights, picking Jo up early in the morning to take her to work at the end of a long shift. Or he could have gone somewhere else for the day – taken a fare to another city, or to the airport. The possibilities were endless, weren't they?

She'd go home, she thought. Go home and try to forget about it all.

She was freewheeling down Briar Hill when she spotted him – or rather, his car. There was an service station at the bottom of the hill, promising the cheapest fuel and tastiest burgers in town. The car – black Prius, right registration – was parked off to one side, away from the pumps. Which meant, she reasoned, that he must be inside – grabbing food before his shift, maybe?

She pulled into the car park and peered into the service station diner through the side window. And there was Mike: sitting inside in one of the booths, tucking into what looked a greasy fry-up. Judging by the speed of his eating, he'd soon be finished… which meant she didn't have much time to act.

She looked over at the Prius, and weighed up her options – considering, not for the first time that day, what kind of clues it might yield. Slowly, deliberately, she approached it, and reached for the handle of nearest back door. To her surprise, it opened; he'd left it unlocked. Complacent prick. She slid inside and closed the door behind her, staying flat on her stomach, throwing glances back at the diner window. He was still there: the blue sleeve of his shirt moving rhythmically up and down as he continued to shovel food into his mouth.

Time to focus.

The driver's seat was the logical first place to explore. She squeezed between the two front seats and opened the glovebox - noting tissues, car documents, business cards…and nothing else. Frustrated, she slammed it shut, checked the diner window again, and heaved herself back through the passenger seats, checking the side compartment on both doors and inventorying their contents. Water, two bottles; air-fresheners, vanilla and as sickly-sweet as she remembered; everything unusually clean.

She returned her attention to the driver's side. Everything *looked* normal: cloth shoved in the door, most likely for wiping down the windscreen; hand sanitiser, which she hadn't expected, given her initial assessment of Mike's personal hygiene. In a last-ditch attempt to find something, *anything*, she stuck a hand under the driver's seat – and felt a bag at her fingertips. Canvas; smallish. She tried to pull it up, but it was caught on something; with more effort, she pulled the release lever and rolled back the seat, revealing more of the footwell.

Now she was able to pull up the bag – and saw it was brown, zipped, barely larger than a toiletry bag. She unzipped it, and looked up again to check the diner window for Mike's arm… but it was gone. *He'd* gone; was no longer in his booth.

Shit. Where is he?

In her panic, she dropped the bag, and it fell to the floor of the car, spilling out its contents. She scrambled to gather the fallen items and shove them back in the bag. Gloves, torch… a smooth black object, shaped a little like a bike pump. She explored it with her fingers: it was cold, some sort of metal?

And it hit her: what it was, what she was holding. A branding iron. An electric branding iron.

It's him. He's the guy.

She felt something tacky on her fingertips – sticky, like drying paint. Instinctively, she knew it was blood; had been in enough operating theatres to recognise what she was feeling, seeing, *smelling*. Looking closer, she noted a few strands of something long and matted stuck to the clots of blood.

Hair.

Severe blunt force trauma, the nurses had said. *He branded her, on her right thigh.*

The iron had served two purposes, then: knocking Tasha unconscious, and burning her. Marking her.

Through the window, she saw Mike reappear in view – now standing by his table, shrugging on a jacket. Getting ready to leave.

She had to get out of the car. Now…

She replaced the canvas bag under the hold and readjusted the seat to its original position, then eased open the passenger door and back slid out on her stomach – crawling along the tarmac, the other parked vehicles keeping her out of sight, until she was far enough away from the Prius to jump back onto her bike and cycle away.

————

She'd go to the police. It was the right thing to do, the *only* thing to do. She'd just have to figure out how to explain why she'd broken into his car. Although… technically it was open already, wasn't it? So was going inside it even a crime?

But then…what if backfired? What if *she* got into trouble? She could lose her job. Get struck off by the GMC.

Her whole life could fall apart.

She was still weighing up the decision at work the next day; going back and forth between bad and worse options, and catastrophising scenarios.

She'd been in barely half an hour when the first emergency rolled in; heard the commotion in the hall, and the call to prep for surgery.

"She's young," the paramedic announced, as Jo looked over the patient. "I don't know – 15 to 18, maybe? Severe head injury, massive bleeding."

"She can be much over 110 pounds," Jo heard herself say, already weighing up how much sedative would be needed.

To say the girl had a head wound was a hell of an understatement. The back of her skull was half-gone; caved in, so badly crushed that the brain tissue was visible.

The nurses cut her free of her clothes. And Jo saw it: Mike's calling card.

"Trauma to the inside of the upper right thigh," one of the nurses said, unnecessarily. "Looks like a burn."

Jo, of course, knew exactly what it was, what it meant. Mike liked to tag his victims.

To mark them, so they'd never forget. As if they ever could.

When the girl died, just hours later, Jo's decision was made.

———

She knew where he liked to eat. And she knew she didn't have much time. He was escalating now. He'd do it again, probably soon.

So, she went to him.

"Mike, hi!" she said, jumping off her bike and walking towards him as he left the diner. "Fancy meeting you here."

He looked her up and down. Finally, recognition settled in his eyes. "Doctor girl."

"Are you free?" she asked him. "Save me using my app thingy."

"Where are you going?"

"Just home." She pointed over to her bike. "I got a flat. Need to go get my patch kit."

He squinted at the bike. Suspicious. "Yeah? Looks okay from here."

"No, it's a slow puncture. I won't make it home." She felt her heart rate increase, fear and adrenaline pulsing through her. She tried to sound calm. To smile. "You'd really be helping me out."

His eyes stayed on her: tracing her legs, lingering around her shorts, and then stopping to focus on her inner thigh. "Jump in," he said after a moment. There was a huskiness to his voice as he spoke. Anticipation, she thought.

She wasn't safe. *It* wasn't safe. And her fear only increased as she slid into the car and heard the locking mechanism seal her in.

"You never can be too safe," he said, watching her through the rear-view mirror. "Young ones try to open the doors at traffic lights, and all sorts."

"Terrible," she said, almost to herself, panic rising in her. She'd made a mistake. *This* was a mistake. What had possessed her to go through with it, to get into this car with this man she *knew* was danger-ous? What use was the half-baked plan she'd formed in the face of an actual murderer?

"Roadworks along here. I'll have to take the upper road." He didn't wait for her to respond. Just pulled off the dual carriageway and onto the long, winding, mostly empty stretch that led up to the forest line.

"Are you okay?" he added – possibly in response to the fear she was struggling to suppress, that was almost certainly playing out on her face.

He was still staring at her. He didn't actually care what she was feeling, she knew. No, he wanted to know what she was *thinking*.

The forest was on their right, now. Still miles to go before the nearest village. Before they were likely to encounter other people.

"I'm fine," she said, with as little inflection as possible.

So completely preoccupied was she with looking and sounding calm, she barely registered the car slowing, then pulling in off the road until they were actually parked.

"Why are we stopping? "she asked, her voice immediately betraying her.

"It's a nice area, this, up by the forest." He seemed… relaxed. Calm, even.

"Yeah, it is. Look, though, I need to be getting back, I have to…"

"What? What is it you have to get back to? You don't even have a cat. I heard you didn't like my flowers. And there I was trying to be friendly." He chuckled, that same horrible chesty laugh as before.

It died in his throat when he saw what she was holding. The knife in her hand.

He twisted in his seat, mirror forgotten as he swivelled around to face her. "You want to be careful. That's dangerous – you could hurt yourself. Hand it over to me."

"I don't think so, Mike." *She* was calm now. Because yes, this was a dangerous situation – but she knew, all at once, that she'd made the right call. That he was the guy.

She should probably tell him to drive, she thought. Threaten him with the knife and have him take them both straight to the police station. But then what? How long would he get, if he was even convicted? A few years in prison, less? The CPS might decline to charge. He could walk free.

No. She wouldn't be taking that chance. She'd taken an oath to do no harm – but fuck it, everyone deserved a day off.

She reached into her pocket just as he reached for his seatbelt. She couldn't miss; he was coming for her now. He was still yanking at his belt when she lunged at him, ramming the syringe into his neck and emptying the Propofol into his system.

He slapped at himself, like he'd been stung.

"What the fuck did you do?" he said, already slurring. "You fucking bitch…"

Jo smiled at him as, still trapped by the seatbelt, he slumped down in his seat. And that was that.

———

He wasn't as heavy as she'd expected. But he was a dead weight. She'd pulled him out of the car easily enough – gravity had assisted. It was the dragging him into the trees that was the real pain. She had to stop a few times: hands on her hips, head up to the sky. But now they were settled in the forest, away from the road, and she had him propped upright against a tree.

She wanted him to be able to see everything.

Now came the difficult part – waking up his mind, but not his body. She pulled another two needles and a scalpel from her pocket, unsheathed the little blade and set them all down on the forest floor. Such an odd sight: the pristine, sterile operating tools of her work life, nestled in the leaves and dirt.

Time to get started.

A small, lazy noise rose from Mike's his throat, and his eyes slowly opened. Just as Jo was removing the needle from his arm.

"Welcome back," she said.

His eyes darted back and forth: at her, and then down at his own useless body. She got the impression he was trying to move his hand. Most likely willing it to lift and strike her.

It stayed motionless, though – as did the rest of him.

"Odd feeling, right?" she told him. "Trapped in your body. Aware but helpless. Although that's kind of your thing, isn't it, Mike? Trapped, helpless. But not such a turn on now, I bet."

Jo bent over him and undid his belt. His eyes were frantic now: pleading, welling up with water.

She undid the buttons of his jeans, and with a bit of tugging, brought his trousers and underwear down to his ankles.

Then she reached down and picked up the scalpel.

"I promise," she whispered, leaning in, "you won't feel a thing."

mandragora

. . .

TC Parker

YOU MIGHT NOT IMAGINE them a married couple, these fiftysomething white women struggling to drag their cases from the train onto the platform of an empty station – one of them ash-blonde and matronly stern of countenance, the other dark-haired and voluptuous, her expression cynically amused, and the two together reminiscent (to an observer of a certain age and disposition) of the actors Joan Sims and Hattie Jacques, those doyennes of the Carry On Cinematic Universe. But a couple they are: conjugated, as the dark-haired and more loquacious half observed to the baffled student unlucky enough to be seated opposite them for the duration of their journey, "since Hammurabi took the throne."

(The student – a scholar of kinesiology and exercise science but not, alas, of the ancients – interpreted this as *a very long time,* and privately resolved never to board a train again without the protection of a set of headphones).

"Do you think there's a cafe around here?" the ash-blonde woman says, yanking the suitcase free, finally, of the train's now-closing doors. "I'm famished."

The dark-haired woman makes a show of surveying the platform and the uninhabited stretch of station beyond, its aesthetic more rural bus shelter than bustling urban transit zone. "Does this *look* like the sort of place to have a Costa by the ticket office?" she replies, wrestling her own, hard shell suitcase onto its wheels as the train pulls away. "We'll be lucky if there's a taxi rank."

The ash-blonde digs a phone from her jacket pocket and thumbs at the screen, with no small amount of urgency. "How far did you say we were from the hotel?"

"It's a *pub*, Bel. Not a hotel. A pub, with rooms. So please don't go expecting the Dorchester." The dark-haired woman sighs. "And it's about a mile away, give or take."

"We'd better bloody hope there's a taxi rank, then. I'm not walking a mile with this case. Not on an empty stomach."

Again, the dark-haired woman sighs; releases her grip on the suitcase, and gestures around at the open skies and oak-spattered moorlands that encircle the station. "We're in the Pennines. Do you know how many people come here *just* to go walking? People with more cumbersome baggage than ours, I might add. I'm sure you can manage a mile."

The ash-blonde, Bel, mumbles something unintelligible - but unmistakably dissenting - in response. Though has at least the good grace not to look her partner in the eye as she does so.

There is, fortunately, a taxi rank at the station entrance – albeit with only one taxi to be had. The car is neither a black cab nor a compact hybrid of the Uber variety, but a grey Volkswagen estate, such as might more usually be occupied by (for example) a family of four and their St. Bernard. Were it not for the illuminated For Hire sign mounted on the roof, the women might not believe it a taxi at all.

Spotting them, the driver waves and, a beat later, vaults from the vehicle to greet them, his emergence marked by the simultaneous popping-open of the Volkswagen's boot.

"Where can I take you, ladies?" he asks, lifting their cases from the pavement. He's South Asian, sixty or more, faintly ratty about the teeth and nose; bald, but yet to come to terms with it, as evidenced by the sparseness of his combover. Garrulousness radiates from his every pore – this is a man, one senses, who will soon enough be treating his passengers to a well-rehearsed run of reactionary political opinions and anecdotes gleaned from his tenure at the University of Life.

"Lawton," replies the dark-haired woman, whose name is Mo. "The Buchan Inn, if you know it?"

A shadow passes over the taxi driver's face at the name of the town, or the pub, or both.

"You're stopping at the Buchan?" he says – still holding the cases, one in each fist.

"Just for the night," says Mo, retrieving her own case from his unprotesting hand and laying it flat inside the open boot, then doing the same for Bel's. "We've heard wonderful things about the seafood tasting menu. Wanted to come up and give it a whirl."

Bel rolls her eyes. "Absolutely worth four hours on a train first thing on a Saturday morning, I'm sure. With changes."

"It *will be* worth it." There is steel in Mo's voice.

The taxi driver, however, has other things than tuna steaks and wild turbot on his mind. "And they let you book in?" he says – slowly, disbelieving. "I thought they were... closed. Today and tomorrow."

"Wide open, as far as we're aware," Mo tells him, hopping into the back of the cab and gesturing for Bel to join her.

The driver stands for a moment by the Volkswagen, as if debating whether or not to get back inside. Then, with a shake of his head, he returns to the driving seat and starts the ignition.

It's eight minutes in total from station to pub. He says not a word for any of them. Outside the Buchan Inn, his engine snarling like a tiger caged, he takes the ten pound note Mo offers him without so much as a thank you.

They get their own cases out of the boot.

"Well," Bel observes as he drives away, "that was unusual."

Mo adjusts her skirt and waterproof jacket, both bunched and wrinkled from the hours of travel. "I'll never understand people. Still, he got us here in one piece, just about. And look at that view."

Bel does as she's bidden. She takes in the high birch and lower cherry blossoms that line the potholed country road beside which the Buchan Inn rests; the dip of valley immediately behind the pub, and the cresting hill that follows from it, all the way to Rossendale; the bruised Lancashire sky above it all that might as well go on forever.

Lawton, if this portion of it is any indication, is more sparsely populated than Mo's Michelin guide had indicated. Bel spies only three other buildings along this particular stretch of road: squat stone cottages all, peeking timidly out from the trees like frightened Victorian children half-hidden by a nanny's petticoats.

And no lampposts, Bel sees. No telegraph poles or overhead power lines.

"It's like going back in time," she says.

In unison, the women check their phones. There is, to the surprise of neither, no signal to be had.

Bel purses her lips, her expression intelligible even to those unfamiliar with the shared unspoken language of the long-term cohabiting as *there'd better be a hell of a sea bass carpaccio waiting for me after this.*

"Shall we go in?" says Mo, with the brittle brightness of a scout camp leader pitching a tent even as storm clouds gather on the horizon.

From the windows of the cottages, a dozen eyes watch them, unseen.

————

The Buchan Inn similarly suggests an earlier era, specifically the 1970s: a time of burnt orange carpets, fruit machines and indoor smoking, though perhaps not indoor *plumbing*. There are no menus; no maître d' greets them at the door. There seem, in fact, to be no other people in the place at all – neither patrons at the dining tables, nor serving staff behind the bar.

There is taxidermy, however. Row upon row of stiff-furred deer and hare and badger heads, mounted along the brown-papered walls.

"And it won a Michelin star, you say?" Bel whispers, of necessity. Where ambient music, in another venue, might have masked her words, in the Buchan there is only silence.

"Is one of you Moira O'Dell?"

The girl appears before them with Jack-in-the-box alacrity from an alcove beside the door – almost, Bel thinks, as if she were waiting for them to arrive.

"That's me," Mo says, unperturbed.

"Right. Okay." The girl glances down at her feet: uncertain, it seems, of the next steps in their interaction. She's very young, lank-haired and porcelain-white, waif-like in t-shirt and billowing jeans. A landlord's daughter or a weekend glass-collector, not a hotel manager or a barmaid.

"We have a reservation?" Mo prompts her. "Double room, one night?"

"I know." The girl directs her answer to the carpet, rather than her guests. "I've been waiting for you to get here."

"That's... kind of you," says Bel, haltingly.

"I've got your key." The girl reaches into the back pocket of her voluminous jeans and pulls out a key – a heavy brass thing attached to a thick rectangle of wood into which two digits have been carved. "Room 11," she adds. "Through there, and right to the end of the corridor." She gestures behind her, to another door marked *Guest Rooms*.

"Thank you," Mo says, taking the key. "And while you're here, are you able to let us know when...?"

The girl doesn't let her finish the sentence. Only shakes her head, mournfully, and - with not another word more - turns and walks away.

———

"Are you going to tell me *that* wasn't unusual?" says Bel, decanting the contents of her suitcase onto the bedspread.

The room itself, both women were pleased to note upon turning the enormous key in the lock and stepping inside, is a marked departure from the Buchan proper – as clean, modern and spacious as any chain hotel suite. The California king bed is vast and soft, its sheets freshly laundered; the television is wide, flat-screen, devoid of dust and insect carcass.

There is not a trace, not a *hair* of taxidermied animal to be seen therein.

"Just a touch of nerves," Mo says, folding her underwear into the uppermost drawer of the dresser. "She's probably the Saturday girl, doesn't know what to do with herself in front of customers. Poor kid. Really shouldn't have been left to man the decks alone at her age."

"And where were the other guests? The other *diners*? I'm beginning to wonder if the taxi man was right about the place being closed for the weekend."

Mo removes a long silk nightdress from her own case, unfolds it, and arranges it on a coat-hanger. "They let *us* in, didn't they? And they were obviously expecting us."

"So? Perhaps whoever took the booking forgot they were supposed to be closed and didn't want to walk it back after they'd taken the deposit. These things happen."

"In screwball comedies. Not in the world." The coat-hangered dress draped across her arm, Mo flings open the wardrobe door. And freezes.

"Darling?" she says eventually. "Could you come and look at this, please?"

Cautiously, brows furrowed, Bel places the bra she's been unpacking onto the bed and crosses the room to the wardrobe.

Inside, propped up against a corner of the wooden interior like a sleeping child, is a doll. A skeletal doll: a foot in length and eight inches or so in diameter, its body drowning in a black smock more than big enough for a toddler.

Its head is a skull: jaw elongated as a beak, crown topped with a wig of matted grass and mud. Its legs and arms are only bone. Or rather, *bones*: tiny, delicate, yellow-ivory bones, glued - or otherwise held - together to form four limb-like assemblages, complete with brittle fingers and sharp, thin toes.

The fingers clutch at something – a long, twisted, plant-like some-thing. A blanched carrot sprouting green and purple leaves, dry earth still clinging to its crevices.

"It's a mandrake root," says Mo, instinctively attuned to the question that's yet to leave Bel's mouth. "What it's holding. A mandrake root, *Mandragora*. I've seen them at the allotment."

Bel leans in, the better to study the root. "Is that the one that screams when you pull it out of the ground?"

"Old wives' tale. You know better than that."

Both women consider the doll.

"What... are they, do you think?" Bel says, indicating the bones, the skull. "Animal?"

"Fox, possibly? Your guess is as good as mine. There are teeth in its head, though. So not a bird." Mo squats on her haunches, and prods at the skull with the tip of one finger. "*Feels* real. Solid."

Bel winces. "Could do without it being in our room. It's like a little plague doctor."

"Someone must have left it behind. The guests before us, I presume."

The very thought strikes Bel as ludicrous. She lowers herself to the floor beside her wife, knees creaking at the imposition. "My love," she tells Mo gently, caressing the small of her back with a thumb, "that is not a thing you pack with the antiperspirant and the sun cream when you take a holiday. It was *put* there, deliberately. What you ought to be asking is: was it put there for *us*?"

———

They cover the bone-doll with a towel from the bathroom, close the wardrobe doors and head back into the bar, in search of someone to alert to the thing's existence.

The bar is empty. Even the Saturday girl has taken flight.

"That's lunch out the window, then," says Bel. "Last time I let you talk me out of a hot sausage roll from the buffet cart."

The complaint falls on ears that are, if not deaf, then tuned to an entirely different frequency. "This *is* unusual," Mo says, under her breath. "They ought to be serving now. Drinks, if not food."

"They ought to *be* here, is what they ought to be. You can't have a pub with no staff, let alone a hotel. All of this... it's like the Marie Celeste. A formaldehyde-scented Marie Celeste."

She glares, pointedly, at a stuffed muntjac deer head on the wall above them. It stares back at her, glassy-eyed and mournful.

"Why don't we go into town and see if we can find a place to eat?" says Mo, sounding as distracted as Bel has ever heard her. "There'll be somewhere, I'm sure. Then we can have a little wander 'round and still be back for dinner."

"If there's any dinner to be had."

Mo casts a glance of her own at the muntjac head, then over at the unmanned bar counter. "Whatever's going on, they'll have ironed it out by supper time, I'm sure. And it'll be nice to see a bit of countryside, won't it?"

Bel swears she sees the muntjac roll a polymer eye at the suggestion.

With neither map nor GPS to guide them, they take a right on leaving the Buchan: away from the road leading back to the train station, and towards - they hope - the heart of Lawton.

They follow the single, rutted pavement as it curves uphill, past the same handful of tree-hidden cottages they'd spied on their arrival at the pub and on, into a larger concentration of buildings made of that same dark stone. Only a few are commercial, municipal: a bakery, *Closed* sign plastered to its glass-front door; a newsagent-meets-post office, equally shuttered; what might be a gift shop, slabs of plastic-wrapped fudge on display in its window. Most, they take to be housing – though the parked cars, pedal bikes and motorcycles one might expect to encounter outside such dwellings are conspicuously absent. How *do* people get about in Lawton, Bel wonders, without recourse to wheels? There are no bus stops, that she can see. No obvious signs of public transport. Surely not everyone here is prepared to trek a mile on foot to catch a train whenever they want to leave?

And where, more to the point, are all the *people*?

"Bit quiet for a Saturday," she says.

"Hmm." Mo's attention is, again, elsewhere. "You don't see *that* every day, do you?"

Bel follows the trajectory of her wife's pointing finger across the road, to a rectangle of grass perhaps thirty feet deep and twice as wide, walled on all sides by a waist-high crop of yellow-white mineral that looks like but cannot possibly be bone. It's rock, she decides; decorative rock, carved and dyed for whatever reason into an ossuary motif and salted about the outside of the... village green? Town square?

Wooden benches dot the grass at its edges: half a dozen of them, at Bel's count. Perfectly standard, for a such a patch of common land. Or would be, were it not for the way they're positioned.

For these benches face not inwards towards the green, to give those seated the benefit of whatever memorial ceremony or impromptu children's cricket match might be happening on any given afternoon, but *outwards,* towards the wall – necessitating that one look *away* from the central point of the rectangle and stare instead into the bone-like rock looped around its perimeter.

"I think one night here will be quite enough for us," she says, with certainty.

Mo hums again: that same, noncommittal exhalation of sound that doesn't quite amount to words. "Are you still hungry?" she asks, when a few leaden moments have passed. "I thought I saw a cafe opposite the post office. No idea if it's open, but we could chance our arm."

It's past 2pm and, in spite of Lawton and its oddity, Bel is as ravenous now as she was on disembarking the train. They adjourn, therefore, to the cafe: a tiny tea-room, just four tables and a serving counter stacked with custard tarts and millionaire's shortbread preserved under glass.

It too is empty, but for the elderly pinafore'd woman behind the till, who seems positively startled by their appearance in her domain.

"May we sit?" Mo says, when no greeting - indeed, no speech of any kind - is forthcoming.

The elderly woman's mouth tightens in response. She gestures, wordlessly, to a table by the window.

"Thank you!" Bel calls to her, as they take their seats. The table's proximity to the counter makes such hollering wholly unnecessary - the proprietor would surely hear her, even if she were to lower her voice to a whisper - but there's something self-soothing nonetheless about the process of doing so. There is a social script to adhere to upon entering a new establishment in search of nourishment and libation, a set of behavioural norms to follow – and Bel will follow them, damn it, even if their host refuses to play ball.

"The polenta cake looks nice," Mo says, surveying the laminated menu. "Not too heavy either. Shouldn't fill us up overmuch before dinner."

"Are you *still* clinging to the hope of a seven-course supper? Let it go, my love. Lower those expectations. I'll be content with reheated lasagne at this stage."

A soft pad of orthopaedic shoe-sole on linoleum, and the elderly woman is hovering over them, whey-faced and brandishing a plate in each hand.

"On the house," she says, equally softly, setting both plates down on the table.

Each plate holds a generous slice of polenta cake, moist and citrus-smelling and lavishly sprinkled with poppy seeds.

Beside each slice of cake, coiled in spasmodic contortions but arranged as carefully as haute cuisine garnish, is what looks to Bel like a mandrake root.

————

Stomachs growling, they eat the cake despite their reservations – neither commenting on the mandrake roots even as they dance around them with their forks.

The elderly proprietor, reinstalled behind her counter, says not another word after her burst of largesse. Nor does she respond to the half-wave and nervous *thank you* Mo gives her as they leave.

"We will *not* be coming back here after tomorrow," Bel says, closing the door behind her and stepping back onto the pavement. "I don't know what the people of this town think they're playing at here, with all this... Hammer horror ghoulishness, but I've half a mind to ring a taxi now to take us back to the station, bags or no bags."

"How, exactly?" Mo holds up her phone - her useless, signal-less phone - to emphasise the point.

"Then I shall walk. As you said: it's only a mile."

"You'll do nothing of the sort. We're here one night – you can manage that, I know you can. Then train back tomorrow, and home in time for an episode of MasterChef before bed. And it's nearly dark already, look."

It's barely 3.30, but yes – it's growing dark, deep shadows accruing around the buildings, the outer thickets of trees and bushes casting a menacing shade about the footpath. Bel is suddenly, acutely recognisant of the absence of streetlights, of bulbs unlit in Lawton's seemingly lifeless residences.

"Back to the pub, then?" she asks.

Mo nods, and slowly - wary of potholes, of loose and displaced paving stones, of tree-roots poking up through underfoot soil - they retrace their steps to the Buchan. Full dark descends, improbably, before they're even halfway there. It blinds them; leaves them clinging tight to one another's arms, each half-foot forward not a foregone conclusion but a decision to be made.

And then the sound: a fading cascade of notes, light and tinkling, carried to them on the pitch air like dying birdsong.

"Is that... wind chimes?" Mo says, no longer walking but standing stock-still below what Bel deduces through the darkness to be an overhanging birch. She reaches out a hand, the better to verify the hypothesis; feels the flat gloss of leaves and the spikes of branches, as per her prediction, but behind them something harder and more solid. Smooth stone: a wall, of the kind that might separate the front garden of a cottage from a country road.

With her other hand, she squeezes Mo's tensed biceps, and listens.

Yes, she thinks – yes, that sound *is* wind chimes, and coming from somewhere close by.

Close by, and overhead.

"Give me your phone," she tells Mo – *her* phone, she knows, is deep in her shoulder bag, buried out of immediate reach. Mo complies. Bel inputs a password she remembers as well as her own, and activates the phone's torch, tilting her wrist to shine the brightest light the device can muster above their heads. Into the tree, from which a wind chime hangs by a tangle of string.

The wind chime is carved, like the doll in the wardrobe, from delicate yellow bone.

———

The torch-beam lights the rest of their way to the Buchan, Mo's phone squeezed in Bel's fist like a Van Helsing crucifix.

To their unspoken relief, the Buchan is well-lit – and though still devoid of paying customers, now boasts a pallid young barman by the optics, as well as an older and more portly gentleman stationed by the door. The landlord, Bel presumes.

"Welcome back, ladies," he greets them, as if he's known them all his life. "Table for two tonight, was it?"

Mo's relief bursts forth from her every pore. "Oh, wonderful! Yes, please. We were hoping to try the tasting menu, once we've freshened up a bit?"

The landlord's face falls – though there is, to Bel's mind, something disingenuous about the expression. Something *practiced*. "Oh, gosh. I'm so sorry, I'm afraid the chef's not in this weekend. Down with a tummy bug. It's just me and Tommy there on the kitchens tonight, so we're working to a bit of a reduced menu, I'm afraid."

"A reduced menu." Mo's anger rises. Bel is well-versed in the signs, subtle though they are: the tensing of the shoulders, the crisscross reddening of the cheeks.

"Not *completely* reduced." The landlord's appeasing smile is so patently insincere, Bel easily imagines a future in which Mo slaps him, and with such vigour that his fillings rattle. "We can still whip you up a bite to eat, don't you worry. Fish and chips, gammon and pineapple, lasagne and garlic bread..."

"Lasagne?" Mo is now, unmistakably, aggrieved. "Did you just say *lasagne*?"

"It comes with salad," offers the boy, Tommy, from behind the bar.

"I should bloody hope it does," Bel says.

Mo however has eyes only for the landlord. "We came here," she tells him, with dangerous slowness, "for the tasting menu. The tasting menu, prepared by a Michelin-star chef. Not for gammon and chips from the air fryer."

"I can only apologise again," the landlord says. "We'll cover the cost of your meals, of course."

Bel scowls back at him. "You should cover the cost of the *room*. We only booked here for the menu. And between this food situation and that bag of bones in our wardrobe..."

"Bag of bones?" Tommy drops the cola-filed tumbler he's been holding onto the bar top, the noise of glass-on-wood thunderous in the empty pub. "What bag of bones?"

"In our room," Mo replies – gentler with him than with the land-lord. "Someone left us a little... well, doll, I suppose. In the back of the wardrobe. A tiny thing, made out of bones. Animal bones, we thought."

"Sinister as all get-out," Bel adds. "Really *not* one to leave out for your guests, just FYI."

The landlord shoots the boy a look Bel can't quite parse, his ruddy pink face curdled to sour cream. "We'll get rid of that for you now, with your permission. Sort it out, Tommy?"

"There's no need to..." Mo begins, but the boy is already on his way to their room: head bowed, skeleton keys jangling from his belt.

"You know what it is?" Bel asks him. "That... doll-thing?"

At this, the landlord looks almost queasy. "Sounds like a Goodfellow."

"A Goodfellow?"

"It's a sort of..." The man swallows, evidently uncomfortable. "Figu-rine. Like one of those Russian dolls. Or a... what do you call that fertility statue thing? A Sheela na gig. But made of bone."

"I see," says Mo.

"It's not *bad*," he adds hurriedly. "Not like, I don't know... voodoo dolls, or what have you. They're more like... protection. People 'round here like to keep them in the house, for safety. If they believe in that sort of thing."

Bel has to restrain herself from snorting. "You put it in there to *protect* us? To deliver us from evil?"

"*I* didn't put anything anywhere." He rubs his jaw; if Bel were a poker player, she'd consider it a nervous twitch, a tell. "It was my daughter, most likely. Katie. She helps out here at weekends, turning down the rooms. She's the one who gave you your keys earlier. And she can get a bit... superstitious."

It's the first genuine sentiment he's expressed since they walked back into the pub, as far as Bel can tell.

"Anyway," he says, "Tommy'll take it away for you, no bother, so you won't have to look at it again. And to your point about the cost of the room... I'm sure we can sort something out there too, so you're no more inconvenienced than you have been already.

"Now... how about we get those dinner orders sorted, and we can have them ready for you for tonight?"

———

Their subsidised meals are perfectly adequate, though neither woman opts for the lasagne. They retire to their room even before Tommy has time to clear the plates from their table; by 9pm, they're in bed, side-by-side and bolt upright in the California king.

"Did you hear what he called it?" Bel says, turning to her wife. "A *Goodfellow*. Haven't heard *that* word in a long, long while."

Mo's focus remains on the open book that rests between her knees: Benjamin Turner's *Anthology of Northern English Folk Tales*. "I was there when he said it, darling."

"Alright, smart arse. Tell me, then: why the bones, and why the mandrake? What are *they* supposed to signify? And what has either of them got to do with a Goodfellow?"

"Local superstition, as he said. A bit of regional folklore. I shouldn't think too much about it. The origins of these things are always some-what... murky, aren't they? There's never just *one* reason they evolve as they do."

"Do you think it might be...?"

Mo stops her, mid-sentence, with the lightest of kisses to the tip of her nose. "I think it's nothing for us to worry about. And I think this time tomorrow we'll be back in our own bed, full of Merlot and a very good Cajun jambalaya, which I shall have prepared for us with my own two hands. Yes?"

"Will you use that chorizo from the deli?"

"Whatever you like, my love. Whatever you like."

———

It would be wildly optimistic, Bel feels, to expect a cooked breakfast. She's delighted, therefore, to discover one waiting for them in the restaurant at 8.30 the following morning: plates loaded with bacon and sausage, eggs and mushrooms, poached tomatoes and buttered toast lurking on the bar-top below a heat lamp.

The landlord, beaming at them from behind the bar, is ebullient by the standards of the previous day.

"I'm so sorry again for the problems with the menu," he tells them, handing them their cloth-wrapped cutlery. "Good news, though. I've had a chat with the wife, and we're happy to cover the cost of your stay this weekend. And of all this, of course," he adds, indicating the breakfast platters. "Seemed the least we could do."

"Thank you," Mo says. "We appreciate it."

"I'd offer to sort the taxi to the station for you, too – but I've got a feeling you might struggle getting one through. There's roadworks on today, all the way to the square. Bloody diversions everywhere. If you didn't have the bags with you, I'd say you'd be better going on foot, but..." He tails off, a new thought apparently occurring to him. "Maybe *I* could drop you, in the people carrier? Might take a bit longer than usual, and we might have to take a couple of back roads, but better than leaving you stranded, eh?"

"Our train isn't until 11," Mo replies, sounding to Bel's ears decidedly uncomfortable.

"Not a worry. You just let me know when you're ready to go, and we'll get our skates on. Tommy can see to the bar. I shouldn't wait too long, though. Can't guarantee how long it'll take us, with everywhere shut off."

The women exchange brief but meaningful glances.

Are we sure that's a good idea? Bel communicates with a rise of the eyebrow. *We don't know this man. And he doesn't seem terribly trustworthy, frankly.*

Do you have an alternative option? Mo replies, nostrils flaring. *And didn't you want to be away from here sooner, rather than later?*

Fair point, Bel concedes.

"Thank you," she says aloud. "That would be lovely."

They take their breakfasts and the accompanying coffees at a leisurely pace, neither anxious to venture back into Lawton before they depart. Bel strongly suspects they've already caught the town's highlights, such as they are.

At 9.15, filled to bursting with pig, bread and fungus, they retire to their room to pack; by 9.30, nightclothes and underwear returned to their cases, they re-enter the bar, where the landlord now hovers by the door in anticipation of their exit.

Their heavy brass room key returned to its hook, they follow him outside to the people carrier – now parked directly in front of the Buchan, its engine running. And yes, Bel sees, scanning left and right, up and down the street: he was right about the roadworks, seemingly erected by unseen workers while she and Mo slept. The path leading back to the station is blocked by impassable red and white barriers; a yellow *No Entry - Use Diversion* sign explicitly prohibits any attempt to circumvent them. The same stark notice, she assumes, admonishes any traveller unwise enough to try to do so from *outside* Lawton.

The landlord slings the cases into the van, and - with a flourish of traditionalist chivalry that doesn't surprise Bel in the slightest - holds open the back door until both women are safely inside.

They slip away from the barriers and on, crawling at a steady 10mph along whatever circuitous route he has planned. Past the dark stone cottages and their tree-branch cover; past the bakery and post office.

To the bone-walled village green, where the van falters, then stops.

There are people there now, Bel observes through the tint of the back seat windows. A *lot* of people: two or three dozen, milling across the grass like bees in a tightly packed hive.

Streaming, like bees, towards the van.

"Why have we stopped?" Mo asks the landlord – sounding, to her credit, more irked than perturbed.

The landlord neglects to reply. Even as those outside begin to swarm the van, banging on the roof and pressing their bodies against the glass.

There's something wrong with their faces, Bel sees. Or... perhaps not wrong but *altered*.

Masks. They're wearing masks. Regular clothes, jeans and sweaters and branded trainers, but masks on their faces – constructed, insofar as she can tell through the window, of the same delicate animal-bone as the doll in the wardrobe. Masks that contort them: that transform their features from forehead to neck into the same hook-beaked, plague doctor visage.

"Perhaps we ought to..." she begins. And is interrupted, long before her wife can respond, by the electronic click-and-whirr of the van's locks unbolting. By the passenger doors opening, and hands - so many hands - reaching in to grasp her by the arms, by the legs and waist and shoulders, and pull her out onto the pavement.

She hears Mo protesting somewhere behind her as she's dragged along the road to the green; smells the perfumes and deodorants of the bodies behind the masks, the sweat of their underarms and the stale-sweetness of their breath.

They're just people, she thinks. *Only people.*

There is nothing to fear.

The crowd of mask-wearers parts as they drag her onto the green, revealing a newly installed centrepiece: two six-foot stakes driven into the soil, each stake a bundle of long, yellow bone held together with twine. Femur, or humerus; possibly human, doubtless mammalian.

Several of the mask-wearers - big men, beneath their osseous disguises - hoist her up onto one of the stakes, tying her to the upper- and lowermost parts of the bone-bundle by her ankles and wrists. The rope they use is soft, braided; its consistency so wetly organic that it makes her think of flowers, of rose petals and stalks.

She looks right, and sees that Mo has been likewise captured, likewise bound. Then looks further, out into the crowd of masked onlookers. They're so small, some of them; so obviously young.

The residents of Lawton - for who else could they be? - have brought their children out to watch.

Whatever this is, it's a family affair.

"Any thoughts on next steps, my love?" she shouts across to her wife, who only shakes her head, tight-lipped and - as is blindingly obvious, at least to Bel - enraged beyond description.

Another mask-wearer, bulky and round-bellied, reaches up to tighten her restraints.

"Sorry about this," he says, and she recognises immediately the voice, the man behind the mask. It's the Buchan's landlord: the very bastard who brought them here, to be tied to the stake likes Joans of Arc. "I feel terrible about it, just terrible. But it was such a golden opportunity, you two booking in for when you did. We normally shut up shop for the Showing, everyone 'round here does, but when you rang up wanting to come and stay... It's normally two of ours up there where you are, you see. And it's us who has to choose them." He shudders – and this time, Bel thinks, it isn't a performance for their benefit. "No-one wants to do it. Why would they? So having people from outside served up - serving *themselves* up - on a platter, at just the right time... how were any of us supposed to say no?"

"I see." She tastes the fury in Mo's every syllable. "And might you elaborate on what this *Showing* entails?"

He doesn't answer her. Doesn't even look at her directly. "I really do feel terrible," he continues instead. "We all do. Why'd you think Katie put that Goodfellow in your room? She got it in her head it might protect you, somehow. God alone knows how." He drags a hairy forearm across his scalp, where beads of perspiration have already begun to form – though from exertion, Bel wagers, rather than guilt.

"The Goodfellow." Mo's words come slowly, carefully. "Of course, the Goodfellow. And tell me: is it this Goodfellow we're to be *shown* to today?"

The landlord gives the rope one final twist and steps back, vanishing into the throng. If they're to receive any answer, it won't be from him.

Around them, the crowd begins to shift and undulate in such a way that Bel is reminded not of bees but of royal subjects in a medieval courtyard, making way for the arrival of the king's procession. The hive of them disperses, then reforms into a rough circle that pens them in on all sides.

Together, the circle begins to chant – a high-pitched ululation that's more scream than melody. It assails Bel's ears, inducing her back teeth to grind together, the tip of her tongue to press hard against her incisors.

Only when she's built a modicum of resilience in the face of the assault does she look closer and realise – it isn't the *crowd* that's chanting. The cacophony comes instead from what each adult and child now cradles between their hands: *mandragora*, the mandrake root, the mouth-like slit that bisects its vegetable trunk wide open and screeching to the heavens.

"An old wives' tale, you say?" she shouts to Mo over the din.

"Really," Mo shouts back at her impatiently, "does now *feel* like the time for *I told you sos*?"

As suddenly they began, the plants fall silent. A masked woman, thin and slight, steps into the centre of the circle, her back to Bel and Mo and the bone-stakes that tether them.

"Turn away," she says, projecting out into the air with a town crier's bombast, "for the Showing is upon us."

Heeding her command, the crowd turns as one to face the wall – the older and more physically fragile among them lowering themselves to the benches for support.

"Though we see not his face," the masked woman continues, "we feel him among us. Rise up, then, Robin Goodfellow. Rise up and take what's owed you."

Another sound, smaller but familiar, keens out from the woman's midsection. It's her mandrake, Bel deduces – the song it sings, while still a caterwaul, now bearing a trace of hymnal musicality.

A crack appears in the grass and soil of the green, just inches from the patch of ground on which she and Mo are fettered. Steam billows upwards from the fissure as it opens and widens – splitting and growing, until it's the length and breadth of a man.

Then a hand, gnarled and grey-brown as an ancient oak, shoots up from the earth to grasp at the soil.

"I see," says Mo, again.

An arm follows after the hand, then legs, then a body, and finally a head. And there, standing before them in all his terrible glory, is Robin Goodfellow: hair wild, brown teeth bared, skin knotted with ridges and sprouting with leaves.

———

It's been Nellie Wright's pleasure to serve as the Goodfellow's steward these past twenty years. For twenty years, she's ushered in the Showing, and the Feasting after; for twenty years, she's helped the Goodfellow watch over Lawton and its people.

No Showing, in those twenty years, has ever gone quite like this one.

"What *do* you think you're playing at?" she hears one of the sacrifices call out from their palisade of bone.

There comes a tearing, and the heavy thud of foot on grass – much as might be made, Nellie thinks, by a body freeing itself from its cattail shackles and jumping down to the ground. Still, she dares not turn around.

"Hold your tongue, woman," the Goodfellow answers, his voice light and mellifluous as air. "No creature shall defy the Lord of the Forest."

Another round of tearing; another of those worrying footstep thumps.

"Your mum said you'd taken up here the last few decades, Jack Green," Nellie hears the other sacrifice say. "We wondered whether we might run into you when we booked to come away. But seeing you try to pass yourself off to this lot as a Goodfellow, a bloody *hobgoblin*...

what do you think she'd have to say about *that*? Let alone all this business with *roots* and *bones* and who knows *what* else."

Nellie shouldn't look. She *mustn't*.

But she's weak. She can't stop herself.

She turns. She looks.

She sees the Goodfellow – his claws unsheathed, his bark-teeth bared.

And she sees... something that shouldn't be there, where the sacrifices ought to be. Where the sacrifices *were*.

They've torn off their ropes – she can see as much from the tattered bits of cattail in the dirt beside the palisades. But where they - the sacrifices, the *women* - ought to be stand instead two monstrous things, each one taller and broader than the Goodfellow. They have the *shape* of women, Nellie can't deny it. Two legs, two arms, a head. But their skin is bark, not flesh, and rougher - more mottled and marbled and sinewed - than the Goodfellow's own. Green and yellow leaf mound crawls, like Medusa's serpents, from their scalps; their fingers curl to needle-sharp twigs and club-like branches.

Their vertical snake-eyes are the butterscotch amber of November foliage.

Before them, the Goodfellow - the *Goodfellow* - falls to his knees.

"Forgive me, Elder Mothers," he says – no longer Lord but supplicant. "I... had no knowledge of your presence in these valleys."

"Oh, get *up*, would you?" replies one monster. One *Mother*. "And you can drop that way of speaking, while you're at it. This isn't the bloody *Faerie Queene*."

"Let the boy speak, my love," says the other, laying those knotted, curling fingers on the first Mother's arm with what Nellie would swear blind was tenderness. "I'm sure this is all just some dreadful misunderstanding. Even if Jack here *has* been deceiving the locals into... supplementing his diet."

"It is! I promise, that's all it is – a misunderstanding," the Goodfellow tells them, and Nellie will be damned if she doesn't hear a pleading, wheedling note there that reminds her of the way her youngest, Daniel, used to talk to her, those times he'd get caught trying to buy a pint in the Buchan when he should've been at school. "I never would've... *they* never would've if I'd known it was you."

"And yet," the Mother's voice, in turn, makes Nellie think of the way *she'd* talk back to Daniel, right before giving him a hiding, "you'd happily do this to others, is that it? Grind them to ruin after making them worship you like some sort of god? Promising them who *knows* what, if only they keep you in bone and gristle and what have you. Honestly, Jack Green." The Mother sighs, world-wearily. "Your mum raised you better than that."

"Sorry, Mother," says the Goodfellow, with just the barest hint of insolence.

"Let's just... put a stop to this now, shall we?" says the other Mother – who is, Nellie would put money it, the more forgiving of the pair. "Get out of this place and take young Jack here with us. We can nip across to Sherwood and drop him off at his mum's on our way home – that should keep him out of any more mischief."

"What was that?" Nellie hears something else in the Goodfellow's voice now – something, impossibly, like fear.

"Sounds like a wonderful idea," the first Mother - the sharp-tongued one - agrees. "Mo, darling... how would you feel about us driving that godforsaken people carrier back, instead of taking the train? We could listen to the radio."

Nellie is sure she sees the more forgiving Mother's dry mouth rearranging itself into a smile. The kind of smile Nellie's own Julius used to give her before he passed. "Whatever you want, my love. Whatever you want."

She can only watch as the Mothers stride out of the green to the van they arrived in, the Goodfellow between them like an errant child brought to heel. As they open the doors, shove the Goodfellow in the back and drive away with a finality that leaves Nellie Wright in no doubt at all that there'll be no Showing this year in Lawton, no Feasting.

And that it'll be her – will *have* to be her – who explains it all to the waiting crowd.

about the authors

Sonora Taylor is the award-winning author of several books and short stories, including Little Paranoias: Stories, Seeing Things, and Without Condition. She also co-edited Diet Riot: A Fatterpunk Anthology with Nico Bell. Her work has been published by Rooster Republic Press, Raw Dog Screaming Press, Cemetery Gates Media, PseudoPod, Ghost Orchid Press, and others. In 2024, her nonfiction essay, "Anything But Cooking, Please," was a Top 15 finalist in Roxane Gay's Audacious Book Club essay contest. She co-manages Fright Girl Summer, an online book festival highlighting marginalized authors, with author V. Castro. Her latest novella, *Errant Roots*, is out now from Raw Dog Screaming Press. She lives in Arlington, Virginia, with her husband and a rescue dog.

MJ Mars is a geek, ghoul, and horror enthusiast living in Lancaster, UK. Her debut novel, The Suffering, was published by Wicked House in 2023. When she isn't writing, you'll find MJ playing pool, trying to skateboard (badly), or listening to rock music. She owes every success to her mis-spent youth. Her short story collection, We've Already Gone Too Far, is out now. Coming in 2025: The Fovea Experiments, a second novel to be published by Wicked House. MJ is currently working on a sequel to The Suffering. Join her on Twitter @MJMars, Instagram /mjmarsauthor, her Facebook page, MJ Mars Author, and visit her website: mjmarsauthor.com

Anna Orridge lives in London and works in the field of education and sustainability. Her short fiction has appeared in Mslexia, the Gothic Nature Journal and the anthologies Rock Band and Rewired, published by Ghost Orchid Press. Her essay *Bihexuality in The Craft* is published in the Off Limits Press anthology Divergent Terror. Phengaris, her debut novella, came out in 2025 with Nefarious Bat Press. Find out more at annaorridge.com or visit @anna-orridge.bsky.social if you really do want to witness a very bizarre stream of consciousness.

TC Parker is a writer and researcher based in Leicestershire, where she lives with her partner and family. The author of Tradwife, the El Gardener crime trilogy (The Debt, The Push and The Remembrance, recently reissued as The Long Con omnibus) and the horror novels Saltblood, A Press of Feathers, Salvation Spring, Hummingbird and the Hummingbird Murder Mysteries, she's been a copywriter, a lecturer and, very briefly, an academic. Now she runs a semiotics and cultural insight agency by day and dreams up stories at night, when the kids are asleep.

Hailey Piper is the Bram Stoker Award-winning author of Queen of Teeth, A Game in Yellow, A Light Most Hateful, and other books of horror. She is also the author of over 100 short stories appearing in Weird Tales, Pseudopod, and many more publications. Find her at www.haileypiper.com.

S.H. Cooper is a Florida based author of horror and fantasy. She is an exceedingly boring human being, which she tries to make up for by being a decent writer. You can find her online at www.authorshcooper.com or on most social media platforms as Pippinacious or S.H. Cooper.

R. J. Joseph is an award winning, Shirley Jackson and Stoker Award™ nominated Texas based writer/speaker/editor. Her creative and academic work examines the intersections of race, gender, and class in the horror genre and popular culture. She occasionally peeks out on various social media platforms from behind @rjacksonjoseph or at www.rhondajacksonjoseph.com

Elizabeth J. Brown was born in Kent, England. This probably explains her obsession with tea and cake. She currently writes the Brimstone Chorus series - dark fantasy horror featuring demons, witches and a whole host of things that go bump in the night. Her debut novel, The Laughing Policeman, takes place in 1980s England and features detectives, dark supernatural forces and dry humour. When she isn't in front of her laptop or spending time with her family, Elizabeth is usually absorbed in a book, film or anything that involves the strange, fantastical or supernatural. Get your FREE Brimstone Chorus starter story at elizabethjbrown.com

Sarah Jules is an indie horror author from Yorkshire. She is a self-professed accidental hipster (who refuses to apologise for this). She is also the owner of Sarah Jules Writing Services, a job that allows her to work in her pyjamas, which she is immensely grateful for. She has written four novels - YOU INVITED IT IN, YOU NEED TO LEAVE, DON'T LIE & FOUND YOU - and edited BLOODY HELL: An Anthology of UK Indie Horror. If Sarah isn't working (or writing), you can find her with her nose stuck in a book, travelling the UK with her partner, and her rescue pup, or sweating it out in the gym. She is a mental health advocate, coffee-addict, and loves all things spooky and/or creepy.

Candace Nola is a multiple award-winning author, editor, and publisher. She writes poetry, horror, dark fantasy, and extreme horror content. Books include Breach, Beyond the Breach, Hank Flynn, Bishop, Unmasked, The Vet, Desperate Wishes, Transformation, Shadow Manor and many more. She is the creator of Uncomfortably Dark Horror, which focuses primarily on publishing and promoting indie horror authors with weekly book reviews, interviews, and special features. Uncomfortably Dark Horror stands behind its mission to "bring you the best in horror, one uncomfortably dark page at a time."

Ai Jiang is a Chinese-Canadian writer, Ignyte, Bram Stoker, and Nebula Award winner, and Hugo, Astounding, Locus, Aurora, and BFSA Award finalist from Changle, Fujian currently residing in

Toronto, Ontario. She is the recipient of Odyssey Workshop's 2022 Fresh Voices Scholarship and the author of *A Palace Near the Wind*, *Linghun*, and *I AM AI*. Find her at www.aijiang.ca

Leigh Kenny was born and raised in the garden county of Wicklow, Ireland. She lives by the Irish Sea with the love of her life, two wonderful boys, a black Labrador, and a three-legged cat that hates people. She has released two books independently and has appeared in a multitude of anthologies. You can find out more about Leigh's work here: https://linktr.ee/leighkenny

Lisa Hutchinson is a born and bred native of the rolling hills and endless countryside of County Durham, England, where she enjoys the quiet life with her fiancé James and two sons. With a love of horror that began in childhood, she has always been drawn to all things morbid and spooky, and is an avid collector of oddities. If it's dead, she just has to have it. Lisa began co-writing in 2020 then went on to release solo pieces from 2024, and can often be found furiously cursing at her laptop.

Emerald O'Brien is a Canadian author. She was born and raised just east of Toronto, Ontario, and graduated from her Television Broadcasting and Communications Media program at Mohawk College in Hamilton, Ontario. She began her career as an author in 2014, but Emerald has been a lifelong reader and writer. As a bestselling author of over 25 unpredictable stories packed with suspense, Emerald hopes to give her readers some of what her favourite stories have given her, including subverted expectations, a thrill ride while you root for the characters you love, and a way to confront some of our worst fears, and face them together as an audience who can discuss and connect afterwards. To find out more and subscribe for your free ebook, visit Emerald on her website: emeraldobrien.com

Megan Stockton is an indie author who lives in rural Middle Tennessee with her husband and two children. She primarily writes dystopian, horror, thriller, and science fiction/fantasy novels that are character-driven and immersive. She is known for delivering works that are raw, thought-provoking, brutal, and cinematic.

RUTH ANNA EVANS is a book cover designer who loves all things horror. She began designing for her own books in 2022 and then just for fun. Once she sold her first book cover, she hasn't looked back. She has a wide range in her style, from polished cinematic covers to modern retro. Her work can be found at www.ruthannaevans.com and in the Facebook group Ruth Anna Evans Cover Design.

SHAUNA MC ELENEY is the Managing Director of Nefarious Bat Press. The author of the novels Awake in the Night and Where the Bluebells Lie (forthcoming), she hails from County Donegal in the Republic of Ireland.

about nefarious bat press

Nefarious Bat Press is a women-owned independent publisher specialising in queer and inclusive, intersectional feminist horror, crime and dark fiction.

Find them online at www.nefariousbatpress.com

about sisters uncut

100% of the profits from this anthology will be donated to Sisters Uncut, a charity supporting women and gender-variant people at risk of domestic violence.

So you can rest assured: your anger will be put to good use.

"We are Sisters Uncut. As women and gender-variant people who live under the threat of domestic violence, we fight alongside all those who experience domestic, sexual, gendered, and state violence in their daily lives. We are fighting for our right to live in safety. We are fighting for our lives."

Visit Sisters Uncut at https://www.sistersuncut.org/